Only now that the children were safe could Johanna move.

But where? How? She could make a run for it, but already she saw her soaked shoes sliding, twisting; saw herself falling, felt the bullet strike her body. She drew in an enormous, trembling breath and slowly let it out. Words were weapons; with words she might have a chance. So—so now she would begin to stroll toward the villa, as casually as though—

The falsetto voice spoke from behind the tree: "And now, *peccato*, there will be a second drowning. An accident."

Also by Harriet La Barre:

STRANGER IN VIENNA

THE FLORENTINE WIN

Harriet La Barre

IVY BOOKS • NEW YORK

To Ruth and Harold

Ivy Books
Published by Ballantine Books
Copyright © 1988 by Harriet La Barre

Library of Congress Catalog Card Number: 87-25362

ISBN-0-8041-0408-5

This edition published by arrangement with Walker and Company.

All the characters and events portrayed in this story are fictitious.

Manufactured in the United States of America

First Ballantine Books Edition: April 1989

❖ 1 ❖

LAST NIGHT, LYING IN THE UNFAMILIAR BED IN THE PENsione Boldini, she had shivered with delight. An intoxicating mixture of gasoline fumes wafted up from cars speeding past on the Lugarno below the little balcony and mingled with the rank odor of the sluggishly moving Arno. In the dark, she had reached out and made sure that the alarm on the bedside clock had been pulled out; she had set it for 6:00 A.M. Here she was at last. She could hardly believe it. At last in Florence.

And now, just ten hours later, how bitter! At nine o'clock in the sunny pensione breakfast room, she stared miserably down at the white tablecloth where the waitress was setting in front of her the plate with the hard roll, the dish of butter with the little square of cheese, and the pot of coffee. God, she must not let herself cry! Not here, shamefully, among the chattering guests. If only she had dark glasses. She tipped her head down, aware that a couple of sweatered young men, Italians, had paused in their breakfast several tables away and were looking at her, unabashedly taking inventory of her short, curly brown hair, her triangular face, and the thick, dark-gold eyebrows that shadowed her very blue eyes. She was twenty-four and she had become so accustomed to being noticed that she herself was no longer aware of it. Except in situations like this. *Do not cry.* With a shaky hand she lifted the heavy pot and poured coffee.

"Signorina March?" Frederico, the white-jacketed captain in charge of the dining room, was bowing over her; at his elbow stood a slight man in a dark suit. "The pensione is very crowded this week, Signorina March," Frederico said in English. "You do not mind that another guest shares your table?"

She shook her head, managed a polite "*Prego*," and the slight man sat down. Flicking out his napkin, looking a little shy, he murmured his name, which she did not catch, and added that he was from Bologna. He ordered eggs and pancétta, which she knew cost two thousand lire extra.

Sipping her coffee, keeping her eyes down and managing to blink away tears, she saw that he wore a beautiful braided gold and platinum wedding ring. His dark suit was so well cut that she found herself thinking it odd that he was stopping at this second-rate little pensione rather than one of Florence's deluxe hotels, like the Excelsior; perhaps he was unfamiliar with Florence? But no, the plump little waitress who had taken his order had addressed him by name, saying she was happy to see him again at the Pensione Boldini, and adding, "The pancétta was well done, Signor Botto, the way you like it . . . and the two extra pieces."

Still, something about Signor Botto's stopping at the Pensione Boldini did not fit. Later, she would say to Jeff Thornton with terrible regret and chagrin, "I did not pay enough attention, I was too upset." And there would be little more she would be able to tell the police.

But at the moment, once again lifting the heavy pot of coffee in a trembling hand, she overturned the cup. The brown stain spread slowly across the tablecloth. "Oh, damn it! *Damn* it! It is too *much*!" She spoke in Italian, her voice shaking; she bit her lips to keep from crying.

"Signorina! Nothing! It is nothing, Signorina!" Signor Botto, roused from frowning over his inward thoughts, folded his napkin in half and spread it across the stain. He righted Johanna's cup and refilled it. He waved a hand as though he had performed a magic act. *"Ecco!"* He smiled comfortingly at her. She murmured a weak thanks and looked at him for the first time.

She saw a man in his thirties, with brown eyes in a thin, sensitive-looking face and with tightly curling fair hair receding at the temples. But what struck her was the drawn expression about his mouth and the two deep lines between his eyes. Even smiling at her, he seemed tense. He said, with what was clearly an effort at lightness, " 'Too much!' you say. As you Americans say, 'The ultimate straw.' " He had a cultured Rome accent.

" 'The last straw,' " she corrected him mechanically, trying unsuccessfully to smile back.

"There is always another one." His tone carried an undercurrent of such startling grimness that momentarily it drew her out of herself to stare at him. He quickly added, "On the other hand, you Americans say that—that it is always dark night before the day arrives?"

" 'Darkest before the dawn.' "

"*Si!* 'Darkest before the dawn.' " Signor Botto was frowning as he ate pancétta and eggs. "At school in Rome, when I was a boy, I had American friends. All boys, a boys' school—sons of diplomats, educators, businessmen. Most of my English I learned from them, not from my proper classes. What I learned was hardly proverbs!" A sudden smile lightened Signor Botto's tense face.

"Oh?" Johanna said inattentively. She was thinking how dark things seemed to her, and that she could see no sign of dawn. She only saw herself at seven o'clock this beautiful September morning walking across the Ponte Vecchio, innocent and eager; reaching the other side of the Arno, walking up Via Guicciardini past the Pitti Palace, making the left turns according to her penciled map, then a right onto the cobbled, narrow street. Number Eleven had a black iron grilled gate and an electric bell; beyond was a courtyard with flowering trees and a fountain. From an open window came the sound of piano music. She'd been thrilled, full of anticipation and pleasure at being in Florence. She had pressed the bell. A buzzer answered her.

Johanna went through the gate, past the fountain and up the stone steps; it had been just as Signora Patrizia Sagoni had told her, yet even more marvelous. The first door on the left, yes; and the door was open, the room dazzlingly white, immaculate, with brilliantly colored aerobic exercise photographs on the walls. And seated at the free-form plastic desk, Patrizia Sagoni, grey-haired and chic in a navy busi-

ness suit. She had regarded Johanna tragically, black smudges
of mascara damp with tears beneath her eyes. Patrizia gestured at the yellow cablegram on her desk and announced
that seventy-year-old Giuseppe Correnti, president of Boston's *Health News*, had dropped dead of a heart attack while
playing tennis in ninety-eight-degree heat at his Cambridge
tennis club.

"Dio mio! Dio mio!" Signora Patrizia Sagoni lifted her
hands in an empty gesture and gazed helplessly at Johanna.
"It is all my fault, Johanna, your wasted trip! I haven't even
enough money for your flight home!"

Home. In her mind's eye, Johanna, standing there in the
dazzlingly white room listening to Patrizia Sagoni's voice,
had thought of "home" and seen a gauzy curtain billowing
at the window of a room in an empty house; outside, blowing
seagrass and dunes and Massachusetts Bay. Home no longer
existed.

Signor Botto, buttering a roll, said more to himself than
to her, "I had one special friend, an American boy. But
unfortunately—even among one's own people it is hard to
understand each other. And with foreigners—different cul-
tures, different mores. There was much truth in the Tower of
Babel. *Mah!* A misunderstanding. Unfortunately, being
young, I was fiercely idealistic, saturated with ideas of
'honor.' "

She had no idea what he was talking about; besides, she
was not listening. She closed her eyes and a feeling of such
desolation swept over her that she shuddered.

"You are cold, Signorina! *Cameriera!*" Signor Botto sig-
naled the plump waitress to close the window.

"Grazie." Johanna thanked Signor Botto, hardly aware
of him. She was hearing Signora Sagoni's unhappy revelation
that Giuseppe Correnti had left nothing in writing about his
promised backing of the Sagoni School of Aerobics opening
in Florence, Italy.

"Not a penny! Not a cent of the one hundred and eight
thousand dollars he promised!" Signora Sagoni had theatri-
cally seized a pile of bills on the free-form desk and held
them up in despair. "Nothing paid for! This desk, even! And

you, Johanna, I promised—but I even owe you for your flight from Boston!''

Yes, the money Johanna had scraped together with such difficulty. Not to mention the promised first month's salary in advance—money she had counted on for living expenses here in Florence, this jewel of a city that she loved so, had looked forward to so much, and that now she would have to leave.

Signor Botto was saying something in a polite voice. She caught the last words: ''. . . September cool in Florence, one needs a sweater. . . . This is your first visit?''

''Yes. I arrived last night.''

By way of Pisa had been the cheapest, the charter to Pisa, the San Guisto airport, then the train to Florence.

Signora Patrizia Sagoni, dabbing at her smudged mascara, had wept openly, declaring that she had expected the first twenty thousand dollars from Giuseppe Correnti to be deposited in the Banco Americana in Florence today. She herself was returning to Boston, she said, a noon flight; by telephone she had salvaged her own job as an aerobics instructor there. ''But I will try again to finance a school in Florence. Fanatical, no? Maybe yes! Anyway, I shall. But you, Johanna, I led you into this because you're the best aerobics instructor I ever saw—and now I can't give you a cent! Even my ring isn't a real diamond.''

''I'll be fine,'' Johanna had lied, ''I have enough money.'' Even as she spoke, she wondered how she would pay the bill at the Pensione Boldini; and the same moment she resolved with sudden, fierce stubbornness that somehow or other she would manage to stay in Italy. And she knew why: Since early childhood, in some inner eye she had carried a vision— strangely, piercingly sweet—of a longed-for place, and that place had been Italy. Why Italy, she had no idea. But there it had always been—and surely it was why, entranced, she had studied Italian through the years. And now that at last she was here, she could not give it up.

''Buon giorno! Buon giorno!'' The white-jacketed Frederico was bowing goodbyes to the guests who were straggling out of the Boldini breakfast room, through the arched door

of the little sitting room with its shabby, hard sofas, and into the front lobby.

Signor Botto put down his napkin, started to rise, then sat back, abruptly exclaiming, "Ideals!" His voice was bitter and the lines about his mouth deepened. "Ideals! Barzini—you know the writer, Barzini? Barzini says that the solitary Italian is actually born on the day that he realizes that things are seldom what they seem."

What did he mean? Johanna stared at Signor Botto pulling at his tie as though it had suddenly become too tight, as if it were choking him. " 'On that day, he understands he will surely come to grief if he carelessly tries to live according to the rules he has been taught, like a blind man groping his way in a room in which the furniture is not where he expects it to be.' "

A muscle twitched in Signor Botto's narrow jaw; such pain and fury showed in his face that Johanna, with a sudden feeling of delicacy, shifted her gaze past him toward the arched door.

A thickset, bearded man was standing just on the other side of the doorway, stone still, half-hidden in the shadow of the dark green portiere, staring at Signor Botto. Johanna realized she had been vaguely conscious of the man's figure there for some minutes; but now, as she looked directly at him, he shifted his gaze to her. An instant later the solid figure drew back and was gone.

Almost simultaneously, Frederico appeared at Signor Botto's elbow. "*Mi dispiace*, Signor Botto! I sent Maria for *La Nazione* a half hour ago, but she stopped first at the laundry, the stupid girl, and Luigi's was sold out! But perhaps the newsstand near the Piazza della Signoria. . . ." And he bowed, looking exasperated, and distressed.

Johanna said impulsively, "I have this morning's *La Nazione*, Signor Botto—you can have it, I've already finished it." She had read it on her little balcony, spreading it out on the gritty glass-and-iron table, inching over the want ads in despair, hoping that at least a language school needed a fluent-in-Italian language teacher. Perhaps with her temporary work permit . . .

"Grazie . . . Grazie, tanto."
"I'll get it," she said.

Signor Botto waited on the pensione's narrow third-floor landing, while in her room Johanna crossed to the door to the balcony where she'd left *La Nazione*. She turned the knob and pulled, but the balcony door was stuck. She pulled harder. Hopeless. Perhaps Signor Botto could open it. She hardly hesitated before going out to the hall to call him; she had sensed somehow that he was trustworthy. "Signor Botto!" she called.

"Si?" He came up the stairs from the landing, and when she explained, he crossed the bedroom and obligingly put a shoulder to the door and pushed; it burst open and the force of Signor Botto's thrust carried him onto the balcony, where he fell on one knee.

"Dio mio!" He rose, dusted the knee of his trousers, and looked around. *La Nazione* lay on the balcony floor, its pages in disarray. Johanna picked it up.

"No, no, Signorina, let me!" Signor Botto took the paper from her and straightened the pages himself, then folded the paper open to the sports page. "It is the *calcio*—the soccer—that interests me. I am a *tifoso*—a fan." He glanced around the balcony and nodded appreciatively. "I, too, have a little balcony, but on the side street." He had to shout over the noise of the morning traffic below. He stepped to the balustrade and looked out. The balcony faced the Lungarno, the street that ran parallel to the Arno. Across the river rose the hills of Florence and the lush greenery of the Boboli Gardens. *"Bello!"*

Johanna nodded, rather than trying to make herself heard above the racket of cars and buses without mufflers, the roar of workers' and students' motorcycles zipping through traffic. Signor Botto rested the newspaper on the balustrade and scanned the sports page, seemingly unable to resist immediately devouring the soccer news.

Amused, Johanna moved to the balustrade and glanced down.

Below, in the lines of vehicles held up by the traffic light at the next bridge, a man in a white Mercedes convertible smote the steering wheel with a closed fist of exasperation, a gesture so futile that Johanna laughed. Almost as though he heard her, the man glanced up.

Grinning, Johanna thought how she and Signor Botto must look to the man in the white Mercedes, like a vacationing tourist couple idly sunning themselves on a balcony over the gently flowing river.

The traffic light changed, but the white Mercedes did not move. Its driver, a tanned, dark-haired man, still gazed upward at the balcony as though mesmerized.

"Avanti! Avanti!" A bus driver shouted, riders on motorbikes cursed, a man in a Fiat shook a fist. The white Mercedes shot forward.

Johanna noticed that as the convertible moved on, the driver adjusted the rearview mirror to reflect the balcony receding behind him.

SHE DID NOT SEE LUCIANO BOTTO AT DINNER THAT NIGHT. She dined alone at the little table, the plump waitress serving first green lasagna, then veal with roast potatoes, followed by ice cream cake and espresso. She drank sparingly one glass of wine, a San Gimignano Vernaccio that the white-jacketed Frederico recommended; he then put the bottle on the sideboard with her name on it, against the following evenings' dinners. She was exhausted, her eyelids felt grainy and heavy, discouragement nagged at her. It had been a dreary, rainy day, piercingly cold and with sudden gusts of wind. Wearing her raincoat and carrying an umbrella that was useless against the wind, she had walked miles on uneven stone-paved streets, feet wet and aching, but she had persisted, doggedly visiting four language schools. She had been met at each one with a discomfiting blend of pity and antagonism. It was made cruelly plain to her that Florence was infested with American would-be teachers who thought they were fluent in Italian; and while Signorina March's Italian was indeed exceptional, indeed classical and as pure as Dante himself could have desired, despite being learned in the United States—and so on. No, there was nothing they could suggest . . . all positions for the season had been filled long ago. *"Peccato!"* they said. "Too bad!" And they smiled with cold eyes, threatened by this American girl.

On her way to breakfast the next morning, she glimpsed Signor Botto descending in the glass-and-gilt elevator cage. *"Buon giorno!"* she called. In response, because it was again a dark, rainy day, Signor Botto lifted his umbrella and shook his fair head, making a comic face of resignation. Johanna watched the little elevator sink from sight.

An hour later, she herself left the pensione on her wretchedly humiliating round of job hunting. She left at precisely ten o'clock, as she was to tell Captain Grippo not so many hours later. Wet and uncomfortable, she plodded persistently on despite the rain. At the third school a florid-faced, balding director with little pig eyes reprimanded her: "Signorina! You should have made an appointment! We are not available to everyone who sticks his nose in the door!"

"Thanks for your courtesy, *Signore!*" She walked out, slamming the director's door behind her. Downstairs in the school canteen crowded with foreign students, she ate stale peanut butter crackers out of a machine and drank a can of Coke. The hell with it! She threw the empty can into the canteen trash basket.

Outside, she wastefully took a taxi back to the Pensione Boldini. It had stopped raining, the sun shone, and the air was dry and clear. She washed, put on fresh make-up, and changed into slacks and her best silk shirt. Then, with an angry, happy feeling of rebellion against the ugly fates that plagued her, she went out into the streets of Florence. She window-shopped along the fashionable Via Tornabuoni, then sat in the sun at the Caffè Rivoire on the Piazza della Signoria, drinking cappuccino and gazing across the piazza at the Palazzo Vecchio and the statues under the arches of the fourteenth-century Loggia della Signoria—*The Rape of the Sabines, The Rape of Polyxena*, and Cellini's bronze masterpiece, *Ajax with Body of Patroclus*. But on the Piazza in the sunlight, violence was somehow unreal. Everyone seemed to her carefree and enviable—the gaggles of Italian girls in T-shirts and jeans strolling by, eating ice cream; the chic women in suede pants, costly earrings, and stunning Missoni sweaters, seated at the cafes, chatting; the businessmen with expensive-looking briefcases going briskly past or stopping to talk with friends. Children ran around, shouting. Men and boys assessingly eyed the girls and women.

She paid, finally, and left to mingle with the crowds on narrow streets. It was a weekday; the shops were open from three-thirty until seven-thirty. Besides, it was Friday, and the streets were jammed with shoppers—*too* jammed, she thought. So she walked across the Santa Trinità Bridge to the less crowded side of the Arno. There she hesitated, then shrugged and turned north. What did it matter? She walked slowly, drinking in everything, even studying menus in restaurant windows, sniffing the air. She bought a ripe peach at a fruit stand and ate it as she walked, smiling at children, blinking at the insinuating, hopeful whisper of an adolescent boy who thought *she* was the ripe peach that might by luck fall into his hands . . . something to boast about later to his friends? Yet, in her pleasure, she even smiled at him.

A bell tower bonged seven rich strokes that shuddered through the air. Seven o'clock; the afternoon of escape had been a catharsis. Now she'd head back to the Pensione Boldini. She looked around. A street sign painted on the side of a stone building said Via Dei Bardi. She took out her street map and studied it, realizing as she did so that the skies had darkened so much that she had difficulty reading it. But she saw that if she continued ahead and turned west, she could cross the Alle Grazie Bridge and be back at the pensione in a half hour, maybe less.

Lightning flashed. She looked up. The sky was black with

clouds; an instant later, thunder crashed, a wind swept up the street, and huge raindrops spattered the ground. Damn, not again! She ran, made a turn, then another. Ahead, across the cobbled street, was a shop. Its windows blazed with light. She fled across cobblestones and darted inside.

Milky, frosted chandeliers shone down on gold-legged tables bearing elegant stationery and on glass cases displaying a rich variety of a stationer's craftsmanship.

"Posso aiuter La? Can I help you?" A young clerk in a vested suit bowed to her from behind a counter. She shook her head. "The rain," she began—and at the same instant she saw Signor Botto. He was standing with his back to her, speaking to an older, sandy-haired clerk with eyeglasses. "Yes," he was saying, sounding pleased, "that shade of blue exactly! But without the lines. It must be ready Thursday afternoon. I'll pick it up. Be sure it is gift-wrapped."

A crash of thunder; the glass door rattled, Signor Botto turned. "Signorina March!" His narrow face appeared more drawn than she remembered; yet he looked, even if momentarily, almost lighthearted. "So, Signorina March! You're in Florence hardly a minute and you discover the best shops!"

"The rain swept me in." She gestured at the darkness outside.

"Ah? If that's all—" And he approached, smiling, took her arm and turned her toward the door. "Then a cup of cappuccino, hot and strong, is an even better escape! I know of a cafe not three minutes from here—if you don't mind, Signorina, that we run between the raindrops?" As the glass door closed behind them, she had the absurd notion that Signor Botto was almost dragging her away from the shop.

The cafe was at the river's edge. Its lights reflected on the wet stones of the street that ran along the Arno. Beyond the waist-high parapet, lights across the river glimmered.

The rain-soaked canopy of the cafe flapped in the wind like a giant bird's wings as they ducked inside. The place was shabby, badly lit, and crowded with customers sleeking rain from their hair and shaking dripping umbrellas onto the floor. "Over here." Signor Botto, a light hand under Johanna's elbow, led the way and settled them at a little round black marble table.

The cappuccino, when it came, was delicious. Johanna sipped, blissfully savoring the nutmeg and whipped cream atop the steamed milk and espresso. Signor Botto ordered a plateful of almond-flavored rusks, and Johanna loved them from her first bite. She wrote down the name in her little notebook, Signor Botto spelling it out for her.

"An Italian specialty," he told her. He took out his wallet to pay the bill, and Johanna noticed a buff-colored bit of paper slip from his pocket and flutter to the floor. She picked it up and handed it to him. "You dropped this."

"*Dio mio!* My Totocalcio ticket! If I had lost that!" Seeing Johanna's blank look, he said, "The soccer pool." He bet every week, he explained, on "the weekly pool, the Soccer League games." He'd played soccer himself, he went on, and he carefully studied the teams—their strengths, their weaknesses. "I'm good at figuring which teams will tie, which are likely to win, that sort of thing. You mark it all on your Totocalcio ticket. One of these days, I'll win the thirteen."

"The thirteen?"

"Yes. You watch the last game on TV on Sunday, that's always the last of the top thirteen games, the 'wrap-up.' I'm already close."

She saw, with curiosity, that the fair-haired Italian's face had brightened, and his drawn, grim look had disappeared.

"Who knows?" He slapped the buff-colored ticket in his palm. "Who knows! With this ticket, I could win a million! Not a million *lire*, Signorina March—a million *dollars*." He paid the bill and turned back to her. "But if I'd lost my ticket, *nothing* if I won. Nothing! I'd be out of luck because the bettor's name isn't on the ticket. But thanks to you, Signorina March, I didn't lose it. If I win, Signorina, I'll give you a good share." He smiled at her, his face still bright. "I promise it!"

A deafening clap of thunder nearly drowned out his last words. A child screamed in fright, a wine glass slipped from a startled woman's fingers and broke with a sharp sound.

Then everyone laughed. Signor Botto came back to himself, his smile disappeared, his face grew tense again, and the two vertical lines between his brows deepened. He looked at his watch, then toward the windows that were being lashed by the downpour.

"I'll try for a taxi, Signorina. Wait inside the door, perhaps the taxi driver will have an umbrella."

She saw him stand up, saw him turn up the collar of his jacket, saw him move past the bar and out the door. Why she did not wait, she never afterward could say. She swept her notebook and pencil into her purse, stood up, and followed him. Was it some fragmentary remembrance of the bearded watcher behind the portiere? she wondered afterward; but that had been too fleeting a thought—a thought? an apprehension?—even to mention later to the police. *Just outside the breakfast room at the pensione, near the portiere* . . . No, impossible. More sensibly, logically, she was eager for the dry taxi back to the Pensione Boldini.

Outside, a gust of rain slapped across her face, making her gasp and smudging her vision. The stone-paved street was empty, there was only the darkness and the rain-blurred street lights edging the river . . . and yes, there near the parapet was Signor Botto's slight figure, hands gripping his collar against the strong winds.

And there came a heavier, dark figure moving swiftly up behind him, and the dark figure's uplifted arm, and the arm terribly smashing downward—and Signor Botto's broken-off cry, and his body falling.

"*Aiuto!* Help!" A gust of wind tore her screams from her mouth and sent them toward the heavy, dark figure; the man's head turned toward her. A flash of lightning lit the street, but the bearded face was concealed by a brimmed hat unlike her own, which must for an instant have shown up clearly. Thunder rumbled.

Then the dark figure bent over the fallen man, reached out, picked him up, and heaved him over the parapet into the river.

❖ 3 ❖

VOICES, FLASHING LIGHTS, POLICE BOATS ON THE RIVER.
She sat shivering and wet in a police car; the police radio
was squawking in Italian, but it was as though she had forgotten the language. For a while she had forgotten everything
that had happened before and after she had run screaming
back inside the cafe and the aproned owner had called the
police. The police car was crawling along beside the Arno.
It had been inching along, stopping and starting, for an interminable hour, windshield wipers clicking. Johanna sat between the driver and another police officer, a captain. On the
river, the roving searchlights of the police boats and fire
boats were beginning to focus in at a spot further along the
river bank. The police radio squawked again, something
about the street beside the river, the Borgo San Jacopo, then
something else about this side of the Ponte Santa Trinità,
then something incomprehensible about the river current.
"Good!" the driver said. "Lucky!" And he speeded up.
The radio squawked again with the news that "it" had
lodged offshore on rocks, then swirled free again.
She knew the "it." She sat sunk in the seat, feeling heavy
as a sack of potatoes. Minutes later, the police car stopped.
The two policemen jumped out and disappeared. She could
hear voices from the river bank calling directions, com-
mands; she knew numbly that they must be snaring the body
with . . . hooks? . . . then hauling the bundle of the body,
streaming with water, into a police boat and bringing it to
shore. She sat staring at the raindrops sliding down the windshield.
The police car door opened. The police captain who had

14

been in the car with her politely asked her to get out. They wanted her to identify the body.

She got out. At the river's edge, she stood among the glaring police searchlights and forced herself to look at the body, at Signor Botto. Half closing her eyes did no good. She nodded. She could not deny the dripping ugliness she saw.

She managed to whisper, "Yes."

They drove her back to the pensione. The captain accompanied her inside; in the elevator cage they stood wordlessly until they reached the tiny lobby, where the captain shed his plastic raincoat and announced he would wait while the Signorina March changed into dry clothes. "*Mi dispiace, Signorina*, I am sorry, but I must ask you a few questions." Numb, wet, in a nightmare that she knew was reality, she nodded and left him in the empty little lobby with its polished desk, bronze wall lights, and the little settee and damask-covered chairs. Upstairs, she changed fumblingly, mindlessly, leaving her wet clothes on the bathroom floor; only after she left the room did she notice that she had forgotten even to change her shoes. Out of all proportion, that seemed to add to the horror.

Downstairs again, seated on the hard little settee, she mechanically answered the captain's questions. Captain Grippo was a burly man in his fifties with a stern, heavy, mustached face and keen eyes that were reddened with strain; he had unbuttoned his jacket and his belly bulged over his belt. He stood beside the reception desk and wrote down everything in a spiral notebook, meticulously, with a red ballpoint pen. When had she first met Signor Botto? Had Signor Botto said anything to indicate he was in danger? Exactly why had Signorina March followed so swiftly on Signor Botto's heels when he left the cafe? Precisely, Signorina March, what . . . Precisely when . . . On and on.

Finally, just when she thought she couldn't bear it another minute—

"*Grazie*, Signorina March." The captain tapped his notebook in a final way. "If necessary, we will call you, but that is unlikely." He half turned and impatiently smacked the bell on the reception desk. "Where is the desk clerk? Or the *padrone*? Someone! Idiotic to leave the desk unattended, and in these times! People complain of robberies, what can they expect when—ah!" He broke off and glared angrily at the black-clothed, elderly woman who appeared from the passageway. It was Signora Carpino, the *padrona*, owner of the pensione; she was a widow in her seventies, with sloping shoulders and a gentle face. She looked with alarm at the police captain, then at Johanna's pale face.

"*Che c'è?* What is it? What has happened? Something in the pensione?" Signora Carpino glanced quickly at the wooden board with the guests' keys. "*Dio mio!* Ettore, the desk clerk, took sick, I had to leave the desk, a problem in the garden—the rain heavy on my tomato plants—" She clasped her hands in agitation. "*Che c'è?*"

The captain told her.

"Signor Botto? Not *our* Signor Botto!" Signora Carpino pressed a hand to her bony chest, eyes dazed with horror. "No!" A pitiful, hopeless denial of that death, then a burst of outrage: "Muggers! Murderers! They're not content with robbing you! They also have to kill you! With knives—or throw you into the river! Terrible!"

"Terrible," Captain Grippo agreed. He clicked open his red ballpoint pen and, notebook again in hand, began firing rapid questions at the *padrona*. Johanna listened to Signora Carpino's answers intently despite her exhaustion, as though some clue, some key to the brutal murder, might surface.

"Luciano Botto came to Florence every few months," Signora Carpino was saying. "He always stayed three or four days . . . Yes, for the last several years." His business? Signora Carpino spread her hands. "*Mi dispiace*, I'm sorry, I do not know—Signor Botto was a very private person, I could not—I refrained . . ." The *padrona* shrugged. "So kind, so polite! But unless he cared to say, one could hardly . . ." Married? "Oh, undoubtedly! He wore a wedding ring . . . though he never spoke of his wife or children. As I said, a very private person. He did not speak of himself either."

The captain hissed out a sigh. "Habits?"

"Signor Botto smoked sparingly . . . and drank the best quality wines, but barely tasted them."

"Finances?"

"He did not seem to lack for money. Not extravagant, mind you! Except . . ." Signora Carpino hesitated.

"Except?"

"He always ordered a taxi, when he went out. And arrived back here by taxi. An idiosyncrasy . . . or perhaps a foot ailment . . ." She shrugged. "So, money. Generous, a generous man. He tipped well, so Maria and Frederico were always bowing, running, smiling like a pair of—"

"His bank, credit cards?"

"Signor Botto always paid his bill in cash. He also paid the pensione rate which included dinner. But he dined out. Not that he had anything against our excellent dinners, he assured me of that! But it was necessary for him to dine at fine restaurants in Florence with business associates, it was important—he explained that to me. Of course I—"

"His interests?"

"Mah! A *tifoso*, a soccer fan, of course! Like everybody! He would look at the soccer results on television—we have a television set in the lounge, there is even a piano, books, newspapers, a chess set, cards—"

"*Si . . . Si . . . Grazie.*" The captain clicked back his ballpoint and closed the notebook.

When he had gone, Johanna still sat unmoving on the settee. She was thinking about what Signora Carpino had said about muggers not content with robbing you, a mugger who would throw your body . . . She frowned, concentrating her weary mind on the mugger. Because she, Johanna, had seen the attack and screamed, the mugger had had no time to rob Signor Botto. And the mugger had approached his victim from behind, so Signor Botto had not seen him and would never have been able to identify him. So *why*? Why then had the attacker thrown Signor Botto into the river to drown?

"Signorina March, you should go to bed." Signora Carpino's anxious, gentle voice seemed far away.

Because of course it wasn't a mugger. It was someone who

wanted Signor Botto dead. The attacker had wanted it to look as though Signor Botto were the victim of a mugging, a victim robbed and unfortunately killed by the mugger's injudicious blows. But she, Johanna, had interrupted the plan. The attacker had responded by throwing Signor Botto into the Arno. So, no, it wasn't a mugger. She had known that all along.

"Signorina! You are still in wet shoes. You could catch a cold. I will send Maria up with an extra blanket."

And the polite, chubby Captain Grippo, clicking back his mechanical **pen,** knew very well it was intended murder. It was his business. It was *their* business. Not hers. She was out of it.

Out of it. It had nothing to do with her, had it? A flash of lightning, the murderer turning to look toward her, his face concealed by a brimmed hat. But it had been only for an instant! And the driving rain had been a gray veil between them.

So for her it was over. Except that frustration and rage burned within her over the murder of Signor Botto.

But what could she do about it? As far as she could see—nothing.

❖ 4 ❖

THE NEXT DAY, SATURDAY, HER BREAKFAST AND DINNER AT the pensione were torture. Guests coming in or leaving stopped at her table to exclaim over "The Botto Murder." The drowning had been a small item in *La Nazione.* The guests at the pensione badgered Johanna for more details. They recounted grotesque scenarios of murders that had occurred in their own towns or cities. Their greed for the macabre surpassed their sympathy and horror. They stood over Johanna's table arguing among themselves over conflicting impressions of Signor Luciano Botto. They disagreed over his job, how many children he probably had, whether he was friendly or unfriendly. They took sides over the color of the tie he was wearing that fateful day. A couple of guests eyed Johanna and asked prying questions, hinting that she and Signor Botto were more than acquaintances.

Sunday night was worse, the two sweatered Italians hung over her table, talking right through the appetizer and the entrée. One of them poured her wine, the other one touched her wrist lingeringly to make a point concerning the physical aspects of drowning. In desperation, forgoing dessert and coffee, she escaped up to her room.

The phone was ringing as she unlocked the door. It was the Questura, the Polizia Criminale. Captain Grippo came on the line. Something had come up concerning Signor Botto. The police wished to ask her more questions. The Signorina was to come to the Questura at ten o'clock tomorrow morning.

"Ten o'clock. *Certo*, certainly." She took down the address and hung up. She hoped the Questura was on a bus route or else that it was not too far to walk. A taxi would eat up lire like a hungry puppy devouring a biscuit. And she had so few lire left. During these last two days—the whole weekend, Saturday and Sunday—she had been sick at heart and unable to plan, unable to pursue her own life. She had lain supine in the sun on the balcony in an old canvas lounge chair, or she had sat at cafe tables on obscure little piazzas. She felt unable to separate her life from Luciano Botto's death.

She still could not think what to do. She knew only that now that she was in Italy at last, she could not give up. She would persist, doggedly, stubbornly. She would find some sort of job—clerk in a shop, waitress, receptionist; and she would get whatever work permit the job demanded, if that was allowed. Was it?

In any case, she would have to pawn her father's gold watch, the stickpin with the diamond, and his Phi Beta Kappa key. The gold alone, at the current exchange, would get her enough money to keep her at the Pensione Boldini for at least another week. And then?

Again in her mind's eye she saw the lost home, the gauzy curtain billowing at the window, and outside, the blowing seagrass and the dunes. She saw herself getting up weekdays at 5:00 A.M. on dark, frosty mornings all the past winter, making her father comfortable and then driving in the jeep, the old, khaki-colored jeep, to Boston to teach aerobics. She would drive fast through the dawn, her red woolen scarf wound around her neck against the wind, her father's ravaged face always before her. And each night she drove back to care for him. Neither of them wanted anyone else there. She didn't think caring for him herself was a sacrifice. She had wanted to be with him, this still-young-looking small town newspaper editor, a man who, outrageously, was dying in his fifties.

"Bad luck," he had said wryly to her, "and your mother, too." And he had grimaced at the long-ago loss of Johanna's Danish mother, Erika, whom Andrew March had loved, married, and adored. But at least Johanna had had a few childhood years of that soft-bosomed, brilliant-cheeked mother, before the tragic death on the highway, the sun blinding the truck driver.

Johanna, aged eight when it happened, had been cared for afterward by a succession of housekeepers, several of whom had aimed to marry Andrew March. But for him, it had been Erika, only Erika. And, after a while, occasional weekend trips to Boston or New London from which he returned haggard, rumpled, and self-despising.

The newspaper had died along with Andrew March. It had been her father's personality, his style, his opinionated editorials that had kept it alive and vigorous. Johanna was left with medical bills like endless laundry lists—bills for drugs, therapy, cobalt treatments, nurses' extra duty, surgery, operating room costs. The bills for those last heartbreaking weeks had gulped down Andrew March's insurance, like a minnow swallowed by a whale. Johanna had had to sell the house, the sixteen acres, the station wagon, her father's small collection of rare books, his piano.

Then, a week after the funeral, while Johanna was teaching an afternoon class at the Boston Aerobics Center, Signora Patrizia Sagoni had walked into the classroom.

And now . . .

Tomorrow, after the visit to the Questura, she would pawn the watch.

"So you see, Signorina March," and Captain Grippo hunched forward over his desk, "there is no Luciano Botto from Bologna."

"But . . ." She faltered, incredulous. She looked from the captain to his two fellow officers seated nearby in varnished chairs and saw the confirmation in their faces. She looked back at Captain Grippo, who now picked up an identification card with a photograph on its face. "Here, Signorina March, is the anagraph 'Signor Botto' carried."

"Anagraph?"

"Si, Signorina March. Every Italian at the age of sixteen is registered at the borough hall of his city or town, which has the family archives. Two witnesses must sign the identification card. The anagraph is renewed every ten years with new photographs." The captain dropped the identification card on his desk and tapped it with a forefinger. "False," he said. "Remarkably well done. It must have cost . . ." He raised his eyes to heaven. "And this anagraph, this identification card, is not new. 'Signor Botto' must have been using it for some time. Years."

"Then who was he?—Signor Botto?" She leaned forward in her chair, bewildered, perplexed. How was she to know— and later she could not tell even Jeff Thornton because she dared not tell anyone—how was she to know that an hour after she left the Questura in Florence, never to see Captain Grippo and his fellow police officers again, that *Who was Signor Botto?* was the one question whose answer she would desperately *not want ever to know?*

The captain said shortly, "Not traceable. No identification. No police record of his fingerprints in Italy or abroad."

He nodded to one of the two officers. The man leaned forward and depressed the button on a recording machine on the desk. "Now, Signorina March, again, exactly, your relationship to Signor Botto. And once again, precisely what you saw when you came out of the cafe."

She began to tell it again. She could see now how strongly the police were hoping for a tenuous link, a link that involved *her*—sexual or illegal business, maybe political, the Red Brigade for instance, or perhaps drugs. The two police officers sat with fingers laced, listening with intently frowning faces. In the midst of her recital, a young policeman brought in a sheaf of papers and placed them on Captain Grippo's desk. The captain glanced at them, picked them up, and leafed rapidly through them. Then, with an exclamation of impatience, he abruptly reached over and switched off the recording machine.

"Thank you, Signorina March." He saw her surprise. He tapped the sheaf of papers. "A computer printout, Signorina. Information from, ah, abroad. We are sorry to have wasted your time." He cleared his throat. "It is unfortunate about the Sagoni School, life plays unkind tricks. We hope, however, that you will enjoy Italy—the museums, the fountains, the"—he floundered—"the ice cream."

He accompanied her to the door. "Whatever this 'Signor Botto's' activities in Florence, they were undoubtedly illegal. The killing likely was a falling out among criminals, one ring against a rival ring, an execution. The blow on the man's head was not lethal, the killer threw 'Signor Botto' into the river to drown him. To make sure."

"I see," She felt unaccountably depressed at the thought, as though Signor Botto, if he were a criminal, had in some sense betrayed the elderly Signora Carpino, bringer of warm blankets and worrier over wet feet.

"Wild beasts," Captain Grippo said. "They are wild beasts, those criminals. Let them tear out each other's throats."

They shook hands. She walked back toward the bus stop. She didn't believe it. Signor Botto, whoever he was, was not a wild beast or a criminal. He would never have torn out anyone's throat. Of that much she was sure.

She got off the bus at Piazza San Lorenzo; nearby would be several pawnshops. She had written down their names from the *Pagine Gialle*, the telephone yellow pages that Signora Carpino kept on the shelf under the reception desk. But first . . .

She sank down at one of the little tables of an outdoor cafe and ordered a mozzarella in carozza and tea. She had skipped breakfast at the pensione, unable to face more familiarity from the sweatered Italians.

She ate hungrily but slowly, drawing it out; she was resisting the inevitability of parting with her father's watch. But finally, the last crumb gone, she paid the waiter from her depleted wallet. Then, reluctantly, she took her little notebook from her purse. On one page was the list of pawnshops she had penciled in. On the opposite page was the name of the almond-flavored rusks that Signor Botto had spelled out for her in the cafe. And protruding from the notebook was the corner of a buff-colored slip.

She drew out the slip.

It was Signor Botto's Totocalcio ticket.

Impossible. She stared down at the ticket, bewildered. Impossible that she had it. She had seen Signor Botto put it back in his wallet, surely she had seen—but no. No. He'd laid it down to break one of the almond rusks in two and dip it into his cappuccino . . . and then the sudden clap of thunder, the wine glass breaking, a child crying out; and on the heels of everyone's laughter, Signor Botto looking at his watch and rising, tense again . . . and an instant later she, Johanna, getting up to follow him, sweeping her things from the table into her purse, and with them, unnoticed, the Totocalcio ticket.

She held the ticket in both hands.

Absurd, absurd even to look. A chance in how many millions to be one of the winners? Yet she reached to the next table and picked up a newspaper someone had left behind.

Absurd. Nonsensical hopes and fantasies. She turned the

pages. Hopelessly confusing figures. The results of the Soccer League's major games could have been written in Chinese. But try, *try*. Try, at least as a commemorative act to Signor Botto.

Twenty minutes later she still sat, alternately staring at the newspaper with its results of the Soccer League's thirteen major games of the preceding week and the buff-colored Totocalcio ticket. Her heart was thudding.

Impossible. Or was it?

"Pretty hair," Carlo reached out and touched a tendril near her ear.

"Thank you." She smiled at him. The younger of the two sweatered Italians, he was dark-haired, in his twenties, with a fledgling mustache. Enrico, the older one, was putting the checkers away in the box. They all three sat at the game table in the television room. It was an hour before dinner. The two Italians had been happily surprised when she had come up and joined them as they were finishing their game.

"And pretty shirt." Bolder now, Carlo lingeringly touched the collar at Johanna's throat. She kept the smile, but this time she jerked back. "No—come on now! About the Totocalcio."

"Stupid to buy a ticket unless you know the game," Enrico said. "Don't waste your money! If you're not an expert you'll never win."

"I can learn, can't I?"

Both men laughed. Carlo said, "Your pretty hair would be gray a thousand times over by the time you learned enough to bet like an expert."

"When someone wins," she said tentatively, "—their life must become insufferable—people tying to sell them houses, cars, jewelry. Asking for contributions to charities—"

"Exactly!" Enrico closed the box of checkers. "So a lot of winners won't go themselves to collect their money. If you want to be anonymous you go to a lawyer. Or a notary. Preferably a notary. In Italy, a notary is an official, if you want to make a deal for buying a house, or other deals, it's a notary."

"So you go to a notary?"

"You give the notary your winning ticket. The notary goes to a local bank and gives them the ticket. The bank then goes to the Totocalcio office, collects the check, and banks it for you."

"In your name?"

"In your name. You keep it all, no taxes. The government has already taken its share. So has the National Sports Authority—they're the ones who sponsor events."

Johanna made circles with a fingertip on the checkerboard. "How much can a person win?"

Enrico shrugged. "If a lot of people have made the same thirteen selections, there are a lot of winners. In that case, you might get two hundred and seventy thousand lire—about twenty thousand dollars. Other times you could get five times that, even ten or twenty times more. It has even happened that a man once got twenty-seven million lire! Two million dollars!"

Carlo fidgeted, smoothed his hair, touched his fledgling mustache. He put an arm across the back of Johanna's chair; his fingertips grazed her bare shoulder. "Would you like a Campari before dinner?"

"I'd love it." She smiled at him.

"The red Alfa Romeo," she said to the custom-tailored salesman in French cuffs who stepped forward, eyebrows raised. It was a brilliant morning, three days later, early—nine-thirty. The sun shone through the glass walls of the showroom onto the jewel-like cars.

"The red Alfa Romeo," the salesman repeated. He looked startled. Johanna enjoyed that. She was wearing her old jeans, a white sweater left over from university days and gold hoop earrings. In her shoulder bag was her international driver's license. The two necessary passport-size photos had cost her another ten dollars. She had hoped that in Florence she might be able to afford to rent a used car on some weekends.

But now! Now in her shoulder bag was a new Banco Americana bankbook in her name and a checkbook with a dozen blank checks, ready for use; also a credit card with which she could obtain sizeable amounts of cash or credit. In a new suede wallet in her purse was two hundred dollars in lire for spending money.

The notary she had gone to was a discreet, fussy, honest, and efficient little man who over the years had handled various affairs for Signora Carpino. He had charged her a surprisingly modest fee, particularly in view of her winnings. Figured in dollars, of the ten million dollars bet nationally that week, half had gone to the government and the National Sports Authority. As mandated by the rules, the five million left was divided equally in two amounts: Half of it—two and a half million dollars—went to those people who had come close to guessing the results of the thirteen major games, to be split among them. The other two and a half million went to the happy few who had guessed all thirteen major games.

Only two people had guessed all thirteen; Signor Botto had been one of them.

Johanna's share was one million two hundred and fifty thousand dollars.

The custom-tailored car salesman stood at her shoulder, trembling slightly while she sat at the waxed eighteenth-century table making out the check. She filled in the date, September eleventh, then sat staring down at it. Signor Botto had been murdered only six days ago. Yesterday, the newspapers had carried a small item saying that the body of the drowned man was, after all, unidentified. For the bare breadth of an instant, Johanna saw Luciano Botto's drawn, shy face. She shivered; then quickly she signed her name.

"I'll pick up the car later today, at seven o'clock. Please see that the gas tank is full."

"But—!"

"Today," she said firmly.

"*Certo*, Signorina! Certainly!"

When she left, she could see the reflection of the clerk in the showroom window; he was already at the telephone, check in hand, undoubtedly calling the Banco Americana.

She shopped. Ferragamo shoes and crinkly leather boots; a cobwebby silk-knitted Missoni coat-sweater, feather-soft.

In exclusive little shops on Via Tornabuoni and Via della Vigna Nuova, she slid satin chemises through her hands, choosing the peach, the pale blue, and one with a latticework bodice of satin ribbon in lavender and silver. She bought dresses with narrow skirts and dresses with skirts that fanned out beautifully when she twirled around. She bought a butter-soft suede jacket that was pale pink lined with pink-and-yellow checked silk. She bought two Fendi purses, ridiculously big and expensive and beautiful. She chose to carry nothing. "Please have it sent," she told the clerks. She could tell that the salespeople in these exclusive shops had never heard of the Pensione Boldini.

She stopped for lunch in a crowded trattoria on Via delle Belle Donne. She sat over an espresso, thrusting away an insidious, uneasy feeling, and doggedly made plans: As an American citizen, she was subject to worldwide taxes. "You must add your Totocalcio winnings to your taxable income," the scrupulous little notary had told her. Now for the first time she was glad that her taxable income was nil—all she had was debts. She would pay the rest of her father's medical bills, get rid of that burden first. Then the big thing.

The big thing would be the March-Sagoni Aerobics School. She, Johanna, would be the angel who had been Giuseppe Correnti, who for all she knew was now a *real* angel. Johanna March, President; Patrizia Sagoni, Vice President. She would build up the school—a branch in Florence, a branch in Boston or New York. With it, she'd have an international life-style—she'd spend half the year in Italy, half in the United States. She'd meet people in business and the arts, she'd fall in love with a man who loved and admired her. It would be a sensational life, a rich life, a . . .

She got up abruptly. Downstairs at the phone next to the toilette, she dropped in a *gettone*, called the Questura and asked for Captain Grippo. Luckily, he was in. She found her voice: Was there any further news about Signor Luciano Botto?"

"Yes Signorina March, further news. The further news is that our inquiries, in all areas, whether involved with political crimes or other—ah, nefarious activities—have yielded nothing." He sounded harassed, uninterested; he had newer crimes, fresher bodies to worry about. "One visitor only to the Medico-Legal Institute to view the body—a man thinking Signor Botto might be his missing cousin. But he was not. That is all, Signorina. The page remains blank."

She thanked him and hung up. Relief made her feel as though a weight were sliding off her shoulders. So relieved! But . . .

Unfinished. Like an undercurrent, a whisper . . . a whisper. A whisper that all day she had heard and resisted, trying not to listen to it, trying to push it away. She had heard it while buying the Ferragamo boots, the Missoni coat-sweater, the lovely chemises. She had heard it while writing the check for the red Alfa Romeo.

She dropped her head and rested her forehead against the glass side of the phone booth, the cool glass. She stood there for some minutes, eyes closed.

The whisper. She could hear it now, sounding in her conscience. It was not as though she had a choice. She knew she had not. She had resisted it, that whisper; but she knew, knowing herself, that she really had no choice.

She could not ignore it.

The back of the taxi driver's neck was sweating. "Signorina! The address!" he begged again. His voice sounded ready to break with exasperation. She ignored his tone. "Make a right here." She was sitting forward, looking left and right so as not to miss any street signs; if she saw the right one, she would recognize it, but she had no map. They had crossed the Santa Trinità Bridge and driven north, then slowly crisscrossed a dozen streets. Twice they had ended up stuck in traffic at the Piazza Pitti, where they had almost been asphyxiated by the carbon monoxide from the rows of tourist buses parked with their motors running while tourists trooped in and out of the Palace.

The taxi reached a corner. "Here!" She glimpsed the street sign for the *Via dei Bardi*. "Stop!" The taxi screeched to a halt and she jumped out, the fare and an extra-big tip already in her hand; she thrust it at the driver. "Thanks!"

She slipped into a stone doorway to avoid the dazzlingly brilliant sun. A moment later another taxi rounded the corner, jumped the light that had just turned red, and sped close on the heels of the first taxi. For a flashing instant, she saw the figure of a man hunched forward, close to the driver's shoulder like a jockey at a horse's neck, and she was left with the vague impression of a bearded man.

In the doorway she concentrated, trying hard to recreate a darkening sky, thunder, rain that became torrential, herself running in the rain. Eyes narrowed, she stepped out into the sunlight and began walking. A turn here, then there . . . a cobbled street, a shop. She stopped. *There.*

She crossed the street. Then stopped, hesitating. What exactly had she reported to the police? To Captain Grippo? Only that she had been window-shopping, that it had started to rain, that she had encountered Signor Botto, whom she knew from the pensione, and that caught in the sudden torrential downpour they had ducked into the cafe on the Arno.

Nothing about this elegant stationery shop.

The whisper was in her ear again, Signor Botto's voice to the sandy-haired clerk: *On Thursday afternoon I will pick it up. Be sure it is gift-wrapped.*

She was rich, she had a million dollars. But someone had murdered Signor Botto.

The strange thing was that the shop owners here surely would have read about Signor Botto's death in the newspapers. Surely they would have called the Questura. But Captain Grippo had told her in a "case closed" voice only an hour ago that there was nothing. No lead at all.

Nothing.

On Thursday afternoon, I will pick it up . . .

Today was Thursday.

She opened the shop door and went in.

The sandy-haired clerk was alone in the shop. He was an artistic-looking man in his forties with brown eyes, reddish sideburns, and a thin, high-bridged nose. He turned from arranging a display of stationery on a table. He recognized her at once.

"Ah, Signorina! *Buon giorno!* Beautiful weather today, yes? Not like that other evening—a regular tempest!" He shook his head. "How can I help you today?"

What had she expected to learn? She did not know. But *something*. She said helplessly, in confusion: "My friend mentioned some note paper, some attractive—"

"Signor Cardarelli? A gentleman of excellent taste!" And the clerk bowed and led her toward the back of the shop where he went behind a glass case of notepaper and envelopes. "This is the kind of thing he chooses. Admittedly expensive. But if you have an eye, you cannot settle for the mediocre. *Non è vero?* Isn't that true? Signor Cardarelli has an eye."

She followed slowly. She looked at the paper and envelopes. They could have been loaves of bread, for all she saw. She was seeing a drowned body. Signor Botto, Signor Cardarelli. Was there even a Signor Cardarelli?

She chose some stationery, drawing out her choice, selecting carefully a rich, creamy paper with hand-torn edges. And while the sandy-haired clerk was wrapping it—"Oh, I almost forgot! Signor Cardarelli had an appointment, he cannot come for the—the gift he ordered. He asked me as a favor to pick it up and deliver it. We are good friends, he would do the same for me."

"Certainly."

The clerk disappeared into a back room and a moment later brought her the gift-wrapped package. "Beautiful, no?" It was a flat package, wrapped in a bright green shiny paper splashed with sunbursts of color; the paper had been so ingeniously folded that no tape or ribbon had been necessary. A little envelope had been tucked securely into a fold. "Yes, beautiful."

There was fourteen thousand *lire*, about ten dollars, due on the order. "Would you rather a check or cash?" she asked.

The clerk bowed. "Signor Cardarelli always pays in cash. But a credit card or personal check is of course always acceptable."

Signor Cardarelli always paid in cash. Of course. She had

known that. *Signor Botto always paid his pensione bill in cash*, Signora Carpino had said.

She paid cash. She picked up the package and her own purchase. *"Buon giorno, buon giorno."* But at the door she turned back with a vexed little laugh.

"Mah! Signor Cardarelli forgot to tell me *where* to deliver the package! To whom!"

The clerk laughed with her. Then he looked blank. "But I don't know where!" He spread his hands. "Signor Cardarelli always picks up the present and delivers it himself." He frowned. "But you can telephone him from here, Signorina, for the address."

She shook her head. "He's . . . at his appointment, I don't know where." She held the package. At least she had tried. At least that! She had tried hard to make the whisper go away, tried by acting out this whole little scenario with the artistic clerk. She had done what she could. She turned away.

"Ah!" the clerk said suddenly, *"Momento*, Signorina! One time he could not come, we had to send a boy—a moment please, Signorina."

He left her. At the back of the shop he went into a glassed-in enclosure two steps up. She could hear him whistling under his breath and the rustling sound of pages turning. She stood holding the present; an ache of tension gripped the back of her head, like a giant hand squeezing.

The clerk came out. "Success!" And he handed her a slip with the address.

❖ 5 ❖

THE SHINY GREEN PAPER WAS DAMP FROM HER NERVOUSLY
sweating hand by the time her taxi had crossed back to the
other side of the Arno and neared the Duomo.

"Seventeen Via Niccolo Nero," she repeated to the driver.

"*Si! Si!* I know it! My brother has a butcher shop on the
corner. Otherwise you could look forever—a pin in a hay-
field." The taxi inched ahead in the frustrating traffic that
was almost a solid belt of cars, four abreast, surrounding the
magnificent cathedral and the bell tower; the encircling
streets were crowded with people, souvenir peddlers, cafes,
ice cream shops, jewelry and leather shops. The driver circumvented a troop of uniformed school children, swerved
down a street away from the Duomo, and with one hand on
the wheel, steered the taxi swiftly down narrow streets past
fruit stalls and small shops and around time-stained stone
fountains in little piazzas.

"*Ecco!* Umberto's Butcher Shop!" The taxi stopped. "Via
Niccolo Nero, in there." The driver gestured toward a hand-
hewn stone arch that lead into a courtyard.

The taxi gone, Johanna walked through the arch and found
herself in a cobbled cul-de-sac lined with old buildings. The
end was blocked off by a squat church with dusty stained-
glass windows. Children played and shouted on the sun-
splashed church steps.

Seventeen Via Niccolo Nero. A four-story tenement. A
sign in a first-floor window read *Sarta* (dressmaker) and in
smaller letters, T. Mantello. The name with the address in
Johanna's hand was T. Mantello.

She stepped into the hallway, found the name Mantello, and pressed the bell. In response, a buzzer sounded.

"Buon giorno, buon giorno." The woman, her back turned, was tacking pins at the shoulder of a jacket on a dressmaker's dummy; she had a low, husky voice. She added, apologetically, "I'm sorry, it is not ready—I would have telephoned you but—" She turned. "Oh!"

She was in her thirties. She had tried with make-up unsuccessfully, to conceal her swollen eyelids and a ravaged look. She had dark hair in a bun and wore a navy cotton dress and a black apron. She was small and slender, with a pale, oval face, and she looked as though she were holding herself together by some iron force of will.

"I'm sorry, I was expecting Signora—another customer." She brushed the dark wings of her eyebrows distractedly with her fingertips, clearly making an effort at composure. She managed a smile. "I am Signora Mantello, Teresa Mantello. Please, sit down. What do you have in mind, Signora?"

Johanna looked from the woman to the sewing machine near the window and the ironing board and the heavy, professional iron next to it. "I'm sorry, I'm not a customer. I—" She held out the beautifully wrapped present. "I am delivering this from the Dardanno Shop. It was ordered by Signor Cardarelli."

"Ahhh!" The expression on the woman's face made Johanna gasp; she had never seen such a look of devastation, of heartbreak. "Ahhh!" the woman repeated. She stood motionless, making no move to take the package.

The door banged open. "Mama! I got the candles for the cake. Green ones!" A small boy rushed in, then stopped short at sight of Johanna. *"Scusi, signora."* He was about seven, with dark eyes in a narrow face. He wore short black pants and a white shirt. His gaze fell on the package in Johanna's hand and his eyes widened with delight. "My present! My birthday present from Signor Cardarelli! Where is he? Why didn't he bring it himself? He *always* brings it himself." His mother did not answer.

Johanna held out the package. The boy took it, placed it

on the ironing board, and began to open it as carefully as though he were handling a fragile bird's egg, managing not to tear the paper. "Look, Mama! The way they wrapped it this time!" The present was a sketchbook. On the cover was the name *Francesco*. "Look, Mama! He knew! He knew this was the paper I wanted!"

The boy cast a shy smile at Johanna. There was something familiar about him, she could not think what. Was it something in the narrow jaw or the dark eyes? He was talking on, talking to her, Johanna, pointing to three little watercolors on the wall beside the window—"I made those!"—and pointing then to a terra cotta Della Robbia angel on a low table in a corner. "My Granny made that, she works in a pottery workshop in Impruneta. When she comes home from work, I'll show her my sketchbook."

"Francesco, enough." Signora Mantello had pulled herself together. She smoothed her dark hair with an unsteady hand.

But the boy still had something on his mind:

"Signor Cardarelli is coming, isn't he, Mama? He *always* comes on my birthday." Turning again to Johanna, with careful social grace, he explained so as not to leave her out: "Signor Cardarelli is our good friend, Mama's and mine. My father is dead. Granny says he died *before I was born*. Can you imagine that?"

"Yes," said Johanna.

"Francesco!" said Signora Mantello. *"Enough!* We'll talk later about Signor Cardarelli. Go set the table." Her voice sounded strangled. "The cake is in the kitchen."

The boy gone, Teresa Mantello said formally, "Your shop makes such beautiful stationery. Thank you for delivering the present, Signora—" she paused.

Johanna hesitated. In her old jeans and white sweater, she was a delivery girl. But she was on a trail, a trail compounded of guilt and outrage. An exasperating sense of decency had brought her here, and stubbornly she would not give up. *In for a penny, in for a pound.* For the blink of an eye, she wondered if that were an American proverb Signor Luciano Botto had known.

"March," she said, "Johanna March," and she saw a slow, horrifying comprehension in Teresa Mantello's eyes: Johanna March, the American girl who had figured so largely in the newspaper item about the drowning of Signor Luciano Botto.

"No." Teresa Mantello whispered; and she turned her head from side to side, pleading into space, "Please God—*no*." She took a step and sank into the chair at the sewing machine.

She knows, Johanna thought. Botto too is a name significant to her. Link upon link: She knows Signor Cardarelli is the murdered Luciano Botto. She looked at Teresa Mantello there in the chair and thought she had never really seen such a frightened person, someone so terrified. And that in itself was frightening to look at—the affrighted look in the woman's dark eyes, the fist unconsciously clutched to her breast.

"The police do not yet know who he is, Signora," she said gently. "And I—I, too, want to trace him, this man who called himself Botto and sometimes Cardarelli." But the awful, mocking irony was that she did not really want to trace the murdered man, she did not want to find his family and dependents. *I only want to prove that he is untraceable and that the million dollars is mine. MINE. I am not a thief. I cannot bear—*

"How did you find me?" Teresa Mantello's voice was barely a whisper.

Johanna told her.

"You weren't followed?"

"Followed?" She recalled standing in the shadowed doorway on the Via Dei Bardi, seeing a taxi flash by, the bearded passenger like a jockey whipping on the driver. "No," she said slowly, "No one followed me *here*." She looked at Signora Mantello's pale face with its despairing look of vulnerability. "Who *was* Signor Cardarelli?"

Teresa Mantello pulled the collar of her navy dress close around her neck, as though a chill wind had crept into the room. "There was no Signor Cardarelli. Just as there was no Signor Luciano Botto." She drew her collar closer with both hands. Then abruptly she looked fully at Johanna. "He was my lover, I loved him. The false names—he had a reason."

Johanna stared. She said incredulously, "But—but some-one murdered him! Your lover! Yet you didn't go to the police when you read—"

"I couldn't!" Signora Mantello's slender hands still tortured her collar. "Because I can't—I can *never* tell them! And, worse—" Her dark, tear-swollen eyes were wide with fear. "Signorina March, if you tell the police about me, the murderer will follow the trail to me!—to Francesco and me! As it is, I can only hope the killer *does not know I exist.*"

Teresa Montello's despairing words lingered in the silence; they seemed to spread and encompass the sewing machine the ironing board, the watercolors on the wall, even the little table with the terra cotta angel. *The killer does not know I exist.*

"Mama! Eight kids, and I can only find seven forks." Francesco was back. Dark eyes, narrow face, a little frown forming two vertical lines between his brows.

"Use the good ones. In the top drawer."

Alone again with Signora Mantello, Johanna stood silent. From the kitchen she could hear the clash of silver, from outside came the sound of children playing, shouting on the church steps. Inside the room, it was dead quiet.

"Signorina! I beg of you!" Teresa Mantello's low, husky voice was despairing. She stood up; she looked so small, so slender, so defenseless, her hands unconsciously outstretched.

Fighting for time, yet already knowing her answer—because how could it be otherwise, with pity swelling in her throat—Johanna pulled her white sweater around her hips, then bloused it up; down again, then up. She found her voice: "Signora, I promise you. I won't tell the police."

She was at the door when behind her she heard Teresa Mantello say something indistinguishable.

She turned. "What? I'm sorry."

Teresa Mantello repeated it: "Be careful."

When she returned to the pensione she found a message from the Alfa Romeo salesman. As she had requested, the car would be ready for her to pick up at seven o'clock, gas tank full; but would the Signorina March please ring the side bell, as the showroom closed for the day at six. *Grazie tanto*, and *complimenti*.

"And packages, many packages came," Signora Carpino at the desk told her. "I had Maria put them in your room. From Giotti, from Celine, from Beltrami." She looked at Johanna with astonished eyes, at this American girl in the old white sweater and worn jeans.

"Fine. Thank you." Upstairs, she stood for a moment looking at the piled-up, shiny white boxes. Then she sank down at the dressing table and gazed unseeingly into the mirror.

Teresa Mantello.

Swollen eyelids and heartbreak on Via Niccolo Nero. And fear. What kind of nightmare must Signora Mantello be seeing in her mind's eye, while she bent her dark head over her sewing machine? Did she suspect, did she *know* who had murdered her lover? Yet fear kept Teresa helpless; she was as helpless as though she lay trussed and gagged at the bottom of a well. She was obdurate, a rock wall. She would never divulge her lover's real name. So that particular door leading to "Signor Botto's" identity was forever closed.

At the dressing table, Johanna sighed. She was thinking that she knew two things.

One, that Teresa Mantello and her son Francesco would be safe only if she, Johanna, never saw them again.

And second, that they had loved each other deeply, Teresa Mantello and the murdered man—Luciano Botto or whoever he was. If "Luciano Botto" had remained alive, a sizeable amount of his Totocalcio winnings would have gone toward making Teresa's and Francesco's lives comfortable.

"I *know* it!" Johanna said aloud. She knew then that, willingly or not, she was going to give Teresa Mantello a share of the Totocalcio money.

She felt a sudden lift of spirits, a kind of exhilaration. It puzzled her; then she realized she'd never before had the pleasure of generosity. She laughed. She now had the power to affect someone's life as hers had been affected. She thought of how, shopping today, the secure knowledge of her riches had given her a sense of ease and enjoyment. For the first time in her life, she had experienced the pleasure of buying a sweater or dress without her skin tightening with anxiety at the expenditure. And, ah, the pleasure of buying a pretty watch because it pleased her—never mind that she already had a watch! Teresa Mantello would soon have that same pleasure.

But now the baffling problem of how to give Teresa money without some explanation of where it came from. Instinctively Johanna thought, the Totocalcio source of the money must remain my secret. But she couldn't just *give* the money to Teresa—to Teresa she, Johanna, was a far-from-rich American girl in sweater and old jeans who stayed at an inexpensive pensione. A gift of a large sum of money from Johanna would be too puzzling to Teresa, too mysterious—it might even frighten her. Well, then, an anonymous gift? But that would be even more mysterious, *more* frightening! No, the money would have to come from a reassuring source. From where?

Back downstairs in the little lobby, she found Signora Carpino behind the desk. The telephone, Signorina? *Certo*, right behind her, the glass door, she could make a telephone call and pay afterward; and Signora Carpino took out the accounts book.

Johanna closed the glass door behind her. On the phone, she reached the fussy, honest little notary who'd handled her Totocalcio winnings. Yes, he told her, what she asked could be arranged: a transfer of funds from her new account at the Banco Americana to a trust fund opened by a Signor Cardarelli, supposedly some years ago, in the name of Teresa Mantello, Seventeen Via Niccolo Nero, with instructions for it to be turned over to Signora Mantello.

"When, Signorina?"

Johanna named the current year and added, "Make Mr. Cardarelli's designated date within the next few weeks, if that's possible."

"Certo, Signorina." He would have papers for her to sign in a few days. "And the amount, Signorina?"

"The amount in lire, equivalent to four hundred thousand dollars."

"Certo, Signorina." Was there a touch of awed surprise in the little notary's voice? She found herself smiling.

Upstairs, she showered and made up. Then she pulled expensive tissue-wrapped clothes from boxes. She put on an ivory-colored satin chemise. She dressed with exquisite pleasure in high-heeled shoes, a copper-colored knit-silk skirt, a salmon-colored silk shirt, and dangling jet earrings. She left her neck bare but slipped a Florentine gold bracelet over her wrist. She dabbed perfume at the base of her throat.

She stepped out onto the balcony and stood at the balustrade, resting her hands on the rough stone. She was still rich, even though not quite as rich as she had been before tracking down Teresa Mantello. She would drive in the Alfa Romeo into the lovely countryside above Florence, perhaps toward Fiesole for dinner. Her personal celebration. At about eleven o'clock, she would telephone Signora Patrizia Sagoni in Boston, and she would tell her about her plans for the school. She would lie about where the money came from. Signora Sagoni would be delirious with joy.

A breeze ruffled the flatly gleaming surface of the Arno. Just here, she had stood with Signor Botto, he studying the sports page of *La Nazione*, she glancing down at the traffic on the Lungarno. She looked down now, past the balustrade, tipping her head, feeling the jet earrings swing against her cheeks. A white convertible, a Mercedes, was parked just below. A policeman was standing beside it, writing out a ticket.

". . . have no one here registered by that name? Ah, I'm too late, then! May I inquire when he checked out?"

The man's back was to Johanna. He stood at the reception desk in the lobby talking to Signora Carpino. She would have to pass him on her way out.

"But no, Signore! We have had no guest named Signor

Faziolini staying at the pensione!'' Signora Carpino looked perplexed.

The man was an American. Johanna could tell by his accent, his clothes, even the casual way he stood. He said patiently in atrocious Italian, ''But Signora, surely you are mistaken? I saw him myself only last week, he was on that balcony above—the third floor, a balcony—''

''But no, Signore! Unless—'' Past the American's shoulder, Signora Carpino's eyes met Johanna's. ''Unless he was perhaps a visitor, someone visiting another guest.'' And Signora Carpino looked down, courteous but ungiving.

Johanna stopped. *Keep on walking*, she told herself. *Go out the door, do not look back.* A fragment of poetry by Robert Frost slid into her mind: *Two roads diverged in a yellow wood . . .* Which was she to take? She had the Totocalcio riches, she would be a fool, a fool!—to jeopardize . . . Moral obligation be damned, she was not a saint! The money was *hers*! No, she must not jeopardize—

She heaved an enormous sigh. ''Signore?''

It was magnificently all right. They stood on the Lungarno next to the white Mercedes, talking: ''So you see . . .'' and ''Terrible, a terrible experience for you, Miss March . . .'' and ''I read about it—this Signor Botto—robbed and drowned, wasn't that it? Lord!'' And the American said also, ''You know how it is—when you have someone strongly on your mind, people you glimpse often look to you like that person. So when I saw the man on your balcony, I thought, My God! There's Alessandro! But of course it's been years, I knew him in Rome . . . Yes, ridiculous.''

The American's name was Thornton. Jeff Thornton. He was in his thirties, dark-haired, with a tanned ugly, attractive face. He wore casual pants, a jacket and white shirt, no tie. ''Look,'' he said, ''can I drop you somewhere?'' And he smiled at her, right from the top of her head to the toes of her high heels, though he never took his eyes from hers.

But he didn't drop her. Instead, he parked and came right into the Alfa Romeo showroom with her. He raised his eyebrows when he saw the gleaming little jewel of a car. He looked at the bowing salesman and he looked at the bright new keys the salesman handed her. He watched Johanna look through her expensive suede purse for her international driver's license. He grinned when he heard her curse roundly in English when she remembered she'd left the license at the pensione when she'd changed purses. "My, my," he said. And he took her by the elbow, nodded to the salesman, and said, "She'll pick up the car tomorrow."

In the white Mercedes again, he made a stab at running her life and she didn't object. "I'm taking you to dinner outside Florence," he told her, "to compensate for the lack of the new car." He drove across the Santa Trinità Bridge in the violet dusk and up winding roads through a village high in the hills. Finally, above the village he stopped at a restaurant called Strettoio, a rambling stone building that he told her was once the Tuscany home of a lesser de Medici. The view overlooked the city of Florence and the surrounding hills. "The word for it is 'breathtaking,' " Jeff Thornton told her, "but for God's sake, pretend I didn't say it."

Inside, in a room with a high arched ceiling and a fireplace, there was an Empire sofa, soft chairs, and less than a dozen tables. It was early, so there were still only a few guests. "I've brought a friend," Jeff Thornton told the owner who came smiling up to greet him, "so if you'll have Paolo set another place at my table, Antonio. . . ."

Before dinner, they drank Cinzano and Jeff Thornton told her he was an importer, in Italy on a buying trip. "Expensive housewares—teapots to ice buckets," he explained. In Milan, he had rented the white Mercedes; he had driven down to Florence where he had been for a week, and had been heading out to San Gimignano and nearby towns for several days of business appointments when, at the traffic light on the Lungarno, he had looked up and seen Johanna and Signor Botto on the balcony. "Alessandro Faziolini was strongly on my mind—I'd known him in Rome at the university when I was an exchange student from Columbia." Jeff Thornton paused. "Alessandro—We were close friends, best friends— then, well, we quarreled, a terrible—it ended our friendship. But the quarrel—it was a misunderstanding. A couple of months ago, in California, I learned the truth. I want to clear it up with Alessandro. I owe him an apology. But I can see him when I get to Rome.'' He sipped wine. ''Sounds foolish, but even after all this time, the misunderstanding gnaws at me.''

She, too, Johanna told Thornton, she, too, couldn't bear misunderstandings. She smiled at Jeff Thornton, happy to be here with him, happy and secure again in her riches, the shreds of dark clouds blown away. ''What's he like—Alessandro?'' She didn't really care. She only liked the timbre of Jeff Thornton's voice; it had a depth, a resonance. She wanted him to keep on talking. She wondered if he was married.

Alessandro was the oldest son of the Faziolini family. The Faziolinis, explained Thornton, were one of the richest families in Rome. ''They're the biggest sellers of sports equipment in Italy. At the university, I'd expected Alessandro to be arrogant, like a couple of other rich Italian boys I'd met. Anyway, I had the stupid notion that Italian men were all arrogant and were all male chauvinists and sexual exploiters. I lumped them all—'' Jeff Thornton stopped; he gave an exasperated laugh. ''If I hadn't made that mistake, I wouldn't have accused him of—'' Again he stopped; he looked at Johanna. ''What's he like? Far from arrogant. Unpretentious, earnest, generous. Private, too—and secretive. I used to think that if he were cheated, betrayed, he would be pitiless. Still, although I didn't know it then, he was overwhelmingly a romantic, with more ideals than Don Quixote—and of that variety.''

Johanna sat smiling across the table at Jeff Thornton, liking his absorption and his warmth in describing his friend, liking his earnestness, liking the quirk at the corner of his mouth; she began to try to decide whether his eyes were hazel—or were they gray with little flecks of green?

''Shy, too,'' Thornton remembered, ''and with the damndest love of proverbs, American proverbs particularly. The more hackneyed, the better; but he always managed to screw them up.'' Thornton laughed.

Johanna did not laugh. She sat very still. And she was no longer debating the color of Jeff Thornton's eyes.

They dined on pappardelle—the long, broad noodles mixed with spiced hare, and drank a red wine. Johanna felt feverish. She knew her color was high and her eyes bright and that it was not from the wine—she had barely touched her glass— no, it always happened when she became almost unbearably tense. She told Jeff Thornton little about herself, saying only that she was an aerobics instructor on vacation, and he said, "Indeed?" as his glance wandered to the Florentine gold bracelet on her bare wrist. But he did not pry, he talked amusingly about Italian culture: how it was now, goodbye to the years when Italian food meant spaghetti and meatballs to the uninitiated; how pasta had now become chic; how these days Italian meant the Venice Festival, Milan, and Torino fashions, and personalities like Pavarotti. He talked more soberly about the dark side of Italy: the Red Brigade, the kidnapping and murder of Aldo Moro, the foothold of the Mafia. Mostly, though, he just looked at Johanna. He had a listening look, as though trying to detect a sound just barely out of range.

They were waiting for dessert when Johanna put the back of a hand to her flushed cheek and said abruptly, "He's probably forgotten all about it—your friend, Alessandro, I mean— the misunderstanding. After all, it's been what? Nine, ten years?"

"He'll remember."

Johanna said, "I bet not." She smiled across the table at Jeff Thornton, eyes bright, challenge in her voice.

"Do you, Johanna March?" Thornton looked curiously at her, at her very bright eyes. His own eyes narrowed. "What are you putting up? The Alfa Romeo? One night of love?"

"This." She pulled off the Florentine bracelet and dropped it beside his wine glass. "And my guess against your surety."

Jeff Thornton looked at the gold bracelet with its Florentine *satinato* luster. He smiled at Johanna. "You're making me curious myself." He got up.

Alone at the table, she sat tensely waiting, staring into the flame of one of the pair of candles burning on the table. If, when Jeff Thornton returned, he had spoken to his friend

Alessandro on the phone, it would mean that Alessandro was not the unidentified Luciano Botto—and she would still be rich. It could be merely coincidence that Alessandro Faziolini also screwed up American proverbs, couldn't it? Of course, merely coincidence. She stared at the candle—tense, hoping desperately—then suddenly the candles guttered as, close to her shoulder, a draft swept through the door of the terrace behind her. Involuntarily she shielded the candles with her palms and glanced back. The glass door was closing again, but through the crack she glimpsed a man's hand pushing it shut. The man's shadow on the terrace loomed for a moment, then shrank as he moved away. Slowly she withdrew her hands. She heard again Teresa Mantello's low, husky voice saying, *Be careful*. She sat very still, waiting for the answer Jeff Thornton would bring her.

Ten minutes later he was back, pulling out his chair and signaling the waiter for fresh coffee. Relaxed, smiling, watching the dark-gold liquid pour into his cup, he said that he had telephoned Alessandro in Rome. A maid had answered and told him that Alessandro and his wife were, as usual in September, at Vittorio Faziolini's hunting villa, La Serena, in the mountains south of Treangoli, a little village between Siena and Rome. "Vittorio is Alessandro's father," Thornton added, "head of the family." He was taking his time, looking at Johanna.

"So?" She gazed back at him, hiding her impatience. She clasped her hands tightly; the bracelet lay beside them on the table.

"So the maid gave me the telephone number of La Serena. And I called." Thornton paused. He reached over and toyed with the bracelet. She watched his hand; a tanned, strong hand. "Well?" Her lips were dry, she felt breathless. "You reached Alessandro? You—talked to him?"

He was the cat, she the mouse. But something in her face made him relent. "I spoke to his mother, Sabina. She remembers me well, she was delighted—Alessandro had never told her of our quarrel. He's on a Faziolini sales trip, he's expected at La Serena tomorrow night by dinnertime, if he's not delayed overnight in Milan. Sabina Faziolini insisted that this old chum of Alessandro's come to La Serena for the weekend, or better yet, for the week. La Serena is big, rambling, with plenty of rooms, there's pheasant hunting, wine from the Faziolini's own vineyards, a good cook.. 'You remember old Serafina?' Sabina Faziolini asked me. 'She still makes her own pasta, but now with eggs. And the rabbit sauce you love—she'll make that for you again.'

"I accepted with pleasure. I'll stop at La Serena at least overnight on my way to Rome, see Alessandro, perhaps spend the weekend there." Thornton glanced down at Johanna's bracelet on the table. "So our bet is on hold."

"Then—you didn't speak to him," Johanna said, "to Alessandro? For all you know—" She picked up the bracelet, then sat holding it as though she hadn't the strength to slip it over her wrist. All the brightness had gone from her face.

"Know what?"

"Nothing."

The road down was as dangerously narrow and curving as a toboggan run, but with stone walls broken occasionally by a doorway or an open field; at intervals a street light shed a yellow pool on the road. The Mercedes' headlight slashed at the stone walls as the car swung around tight curves. The city lay somewhere below. Jeff Thornton drove as nonchalantly as though he were taking a stroll.

"Then you're leaving tomorrow?" Johanna said. She hung onto the door as the car rounded a curve.

"Around noon. After La Serena, I have business in Rome, then two or three days in the south. Then"—Thornton glanced at her—"I owe myself a vacation. So why not take it in Florence? I asked myself at dinner tonight somewhere between the hare and the espresso. Why not return to this medieval city where Johanna March is staying?" He slowed the car, made another curve; the headlights swept across a couple walking—teenagers, arms around each other. They flattened themselves against the stone wall and blinked, smiling toward the headlights that an instant later left them in darkness. Jeff Thornton said, "Did I mention I'm not married? I was. But no more."

The road straightened, widened. The city glittered below; the Arno was a silver snake. Johanna said, "I, too, am going to Rome tomorrow—some things I want to buy. I'll be driving the Alfa Romeo. I'm thinking—I've never driven a stick shift before. And on the Autostrada, I don't know—it's a little scary. The Italians drive like bandits!" She gave a little laugh. "What I was thinking—if I had someone with me, at least for the first part of the way . . ."

"Yes?"

"For moral support . . ."

When a half hour later they parted in front of the Pensione Boldini, it was settled: Jeff Thornton would turn in his rented Mercedes. Johanna, driving the Alfa Romeo, would drop him at the Faziolini's country place near Treangoli and continue on to Rome. After Thornton's visit to La Serena, he'd go on to Rome with one of the Faziolinis, who were always back and forth; there he'd rent a car and drive south to Naples and Bari to finish his business. "When I get back to Florence," Thornton said in parting, shaking his head at Johanna, "be prepared to spend a lot of time with me, Johanna March—I don't do favors like this for nothing." And off he drove down the Lungarno.

So that was the plan.

Or so, Johanna thought, as five minutes later in her room she twisted the gold bracelet off her wrist and dropped it on the bureau, that's what Jeff Thornton innocently supposed was the plan. She ought to feel guilty, lying to Jeff Thornton about never having driven a stick shift before—she, who'd been driving that old Jeep in Massachusetts since she was eighteen! But she'd had to lie. She was determined to get to La Serena at once and stay until Alessandro Faziolini turned up, to assure herself that he was alive. She couldn't bear suspense, she'd never been able to. But how to arrange it? She couldn't expect the Faziolini family to invite her, a stranger, to stay at La Serena.

Frowning, she walked around the room, biting a fingernail. She must, she *must* think of something, some way, no matter how silly, how ridiculous, how farfetched.

She stopped at the bureau, picked up her map of Italy,

spread it out, and studied it. *La Serena, south of Treangoli*, Jeff Thornton had said. A village. But Treangoli was not on the map. Still—she looked at her watch. Almost midnight.

Downstairs in the little lobby she found Ettore, Signora Carpino's eighteen-year-old nephew, sitting behind the desk doing a crossword puzzle by the light of the brass lamp. The telephone, she told him, and Ettore took out the accounts book as Johanna went into the little booth and closed the glass door behind her.

The telephone operator was efficient: Treangoli? *Momento*, Signora . . . Si, Signora, Treangoli . . . Two doctors only, one a veterinarian, the other a general practitioner—Rosella, Giorgio. Johanna took down Dr. Rosella's number and called, feeling a fool hearing the phone ring a long time, then Dr. Rosella's *"Pronto!"* sounding a little irritable. But he proved a sentimental man, and chuckled when Johanna explained. In love with the man, eh? An excuse to be with him for the weekend at La Serena where he would be a guest? And the excuse, Signorina? He listened to what she wanted—and again she heard the chuckle of a jolly-sounding man; the good *dottore* was amused.

"Simple enough, Signorina! So, around two o'clock tomorrow, eh? I'll be in my office, everyone in Treangoli knows where it is! My fees for such services are reasonable!" And once again he chuckled.

Back again upstairs, she undressed, sleepily showered, then drew from its tissue paper a Givenchy nightgown of cream-colored satin sprinkled with tiny violets, and slipped it on. She slid between the coarse cotton sheets and turned out the light. Lying there, hearing the traffic beside the darkly flowing river, she thought how quickly she had learned to love the luxury of riches. Yet she had barely touched her fortune, barely tasted its delights.

She felt tempted then to go downstairs, call Dr. Rosella, and tell him she had changed her mind. She rose on one elbow, but staring irresolutely into the dark, she saw again the body taken from the river, and in the glare of a police searchlight, she again looked down at the face of "Signor Botto."

She sank back on the bed, pulled up the covers, closed her eyes, and tried to go to sleep.

❖ 6 ❖

PEPPINO BRACCIA WAS SWINGING THE THIRD CHICKEN UP onto the chopping block when he heard the car stop. The front door of the trattoria would be locked; he didn't open up until one-thirty. Everybody in Treangoli knew that. So—strangers. He rested the squawking chicken on the block, hesitating, gazing toward the mountain pines on the slope above the village. He was in an undershirt and he was sweating, sweating heavily, but not because of the brilliant noontime sun on his head. No, it was a wine sweat. Ordinarily he didn't drink like a pig. But occasionally when he listened to the world news on the radio in his and Luisa's bedroom over the trattoria, or when he looked at the news on the little TV on the bar, what with the murders and the mess of the world, he felt a sense of doom. And he would begin to drink wine. Drinking, he would talk morosely about the state of the world. Villagers who hung over the bar could always count on a few drinks on the house, the price of listening.

So—strangers. Let them go away. Sweating, and with a head like a balloon, he hadn't yet prepared any food, not even fresh pasta; and Luisa had gone yesterday to her sister's in Arcidosso, to the one who wore green nail polish, so it was all up to him.

The wine sweat made his armpits dank, and his arms were beginning to tremble. He shouldn't be handling the hatchet, killing chickens. Better to be hospitable to the strangers than maybe cut off his fingers at the chopping block! He sighed. *"Vengo!"* he shouted. *"Vengo! Vengo!* I'm coming!'' The chicken under his hand was still squawking; he released the bird's legs. "God's eye is on you—lucky bastard, you!" He went in through the kitchen and unlocked the front door.

A man and a young woman. They weren't Italians, he could see that. Americans. The young woman carried a folded map and was tapping her chin with it. The wind had mussed up her short, curly hair, but she was very pretty. She wore city clothes: a yellow dress and a tan coat and high heels. The man, though, was in brown corduroy pants and dark red sweater and no shirt. He was just over medium height, maybe an inch or two taller than Peppino himself. He had a tanned, ugly face that, for some reason, sent a stab of envy through Peppino. That was aside from the fact that these two Americans were certainly people who had never had to worry about money. They had that look.

The young woman was hungry, and when Peppino had seated them she said so, emphatically, in good Italian, smiling at Peppino. "Famished! *Famelica!*" It turned out that she was the one who had insisted on stopping in Treangoli. "*Famelica*," she repeated, and she surveyed the bar, the empty tables, even the windows that overlooked the road.

Peppino brought them what he had: this morning's bread that Rosa's kid had delivered, some tomatoes, yesterday's cold pasta with peas, butter, and cheese. The man drank beer; the girl asked for tea.

They were friendly. They had come from Florence, the man said, driving down through Siena on the regional highway that ran almost parallel to the Autostrada between Florence and Rome. "It is easier driving," the girl broke in. South of Torrenieri, they had left the highway and on country roads had wound through the mountains and hills near the Castiglione d'Orcia, crossed the Orcia River, and driven south through the mountains and hills, passing near Arcidosso. They were heading for a villa near Treangoli.

"La Serena. You know it?" the man asked. He had a resonant voice. "Belongs to a family named Faziolini."

The Faziolinis. Peppino sweated again. Just hearing the name, *Faziolini*, spoken so carelessly by these Americans, was almost enough to drive him back to the wine. The Faziolinis! What they had lived through, that ordeal! Peppino reached around to the pitcher of yesterday's water on the bar, poured a glassful, and gulped it down before answering.

"Yes, La Serena. Not more than a half hour from here. You take the road south, then west." Yes, he added, he knew the family, everyone did. He shut up then, not adding also that he, Peppino, knew them better than most. That was because old Luigi, the Faziolinis' gamekeeper, who did the Faziolinis' slaughtering and made their sausages, had children and grandchildren in Treangoli; and when old Luigi came to Treangoli, he would stop at Peppino's for a glass of wine and bring him some sausages. Luigi would talk about the Faziolini family; he had been with them for twenty-five years, and his wife Serafina was their cook. When the Faziolinis were in Rome, Luigi and his wife were the caretakers at La Serena.

"Pheasant hunting," the American said, "I remember. Is it still good around here?"

"*Mah!* None better! The signore, Vittorio Faziolini, still hunts pheasant. Pheasant hunting! That's his great joy. He hunts nearby. The mountains here—we have violent storms, you could drown in the ravines. The storms sweep hunters into my trattoria." Peppino hesitated, then stopped. Vittorio Faziolini—that handsome, white-mustached, vigorous old man hunted pheasant with young Matteo Del Bosco as his hunting companion. Matteo Del Bosco's father had been Vittorio Faziolini's closest friend; perhaps that was why Signor Faziolini was so kind to Matteo Del Bosco, whom Peppino disliked for no clear reason.

Except for Matteo Del Bosco, the Faziolini family had had no guests at La Serena since that terrible ordeal. It was said that even in Rome, the family had withdrawn into itself. It would take time for them to erase those terrible weeks of agony, of fear. A week ago, old Luigi, one gnarled hand around his wine glass at the bar, had said sadly to Peppino: "Still no one! Not like before—all those parties, the guests, the good times! Serafina cooking for fifteen people, twenty! Nobody invited any more."

But now, these Americans!

Peppino stood beside the table, rolling the strings of the apron he had tied in front, rolling and rolling the strings between thumbs and forefingers, looking at the Americans. In his philosophy, the more you talked and acted, the less time you thought about your troubles and the miserable underbelly of the world; and the fewer wine sweats you had. He was not a gossip. But it was not in him to resist the comment: ''You're the Faziolinis' first guests since it happened.''

They looked at him. The girl's blue eyes, beneath thick, dark-gold brows, were alert. The man said, mystified, ''Since what happened?''

Peppino stared. How could friends of the Faziolinis not know? Impossible! ''You don't know?'' He was bewildered. ''How could you not know!''

But now the man, introducing himself as a Signor Thornton, was explaining that he was an old friend of Alessandro Faziolini's, just arrived in Italy; he had been out of touch, he had spoken only a few words to Alessandro's mother. The young woman, Thornton went on, was a friend of his who was on her way to Rome.

Ah, so that explained it. Peppino drew a breath.

''The kidnapping! In Rome, the Ligouri twins! Eight years old, a boy and girl—they're Signor Vittorio Faziolini's grandchildren! The children of his daughter Elisabetta. Fifty-four million lire, about four million dollars in your money, those kidnappers, those swine, those *banditi* got away with before the Faziolini family got the children back.''

Negotiations. Secrets from the police. Agony. Peppino told the Americans all he knew: how the twins, Felicia and Tomasino, had a bad habit at their school recess of escaping to the park to buy ice cream. They had been caught, scolded, warned. But one day, anyway: ''The man wore a school guard's outfit with visored cap, like that of the guards at their private school, and mirrored sunglasses. He swooped down on them from behind at the ice cream cart and in a high, angry voice ordered them into a car, to take them back to the school; they would be punished. But immediately in the car, while they were still dazed and frightened, he gave them each a piece of chocolate. Doped, of course. When they woke up, they found themselves blindfolded, tied up. They never saw the man again. But two or three times they heard his high voice.'' Peppino compressed his lips. ''The terrible part was that when they came awake, they didn't even know at first that they were still together.''

The girl drew in a sharp breath. The man, Thornton, reached out and touched her wrist, a casual gesture. Peppino guessed they felt as he did: outrage, fury, murderous rage.

''Twenty-six days!'' Peppino said. *''Twenty-six days!''* He hated it that his voice shook; this time it wasn't the wine-sweats, it was that he'd like to wring the kidnappers' necks. Telling this pretty girl and the signore, he tried to calm himself.

''The fifty-four million lire ransom those *rapitóri*, those kidnappers demanded—No one in the family held back, they would have given anything to get back the twins. I think even their lives!'' The Faziolini family was small; Vittorio and his wife Sabina had only their two married children—Alessandro and his sister Elisabetta, who was a widow and the mother of the twins.

But it was a close family. They even all lived in the same huge apartment building in Rome—an old converted palace. ''Vittorio Faziolini took charge, he managed to deal with the kidnappers in secret. Against the police. The family had to lie to the police. You understand? The police wanted to capture the kidnappers—our Italian police are determined to stamp out kidnapping, it has become too big a business, full even of amateurs! So the police wanted—but the Faziolinis wanted only the twins! They were frantic that they shouldn't endanger the children's lives—And to—'' he hated to say it, ''to get them back in—in one piece.'' No tender little forefinger, no waxlike child's ear mailed in a box to the frightened family.

''And the twins are—were not . . . ?'' The young woman's voice faltered.

''Are now enjoying life at La Serena!'' Peppino rolled the apron strings; he gave the young woman a reassuring smile. ''After the Faziolinis paid the ransom, the children were left tied up and still blindfolded in a cabina on the beach at Ostia. Not hurt!'' He kept smiling; but now he also kept his mouth shut. Not hurt, but—how had old Luigi called it? Different, somehow. Always in the woods, always dirty. Last week old Luigi had frowned and muttered uneasily about it, looking down into his wine glass; then he had changed the subject.

''*Scusi*,'' Peppino said now to the Americans. He went back to the kitchen and despairingly sliced and chopped and boiled and fried whatever came to hand; it was almost one-thirty.

By two o'clock there were a couple of customers at the bar, and a few more were eating lunch at the tables and grumbling that there was no decent food today; where was Luisa, and had Peppino's feet turned to lead? Peppino noticed that the young woman with gold eyebrows who'd said she was so *famelica* had eaten almost nothing. But the signore, Thornton, was digging with relish into a second order of cold pasta and peas. And then—

''Good *God*!'' The American girl was suddenly on her feet and halfway to the door. ''I forgot! I'll be right back! The car keys, I left them—'' The flash of a yellow skirt around pretty legs and she was gone.

''Johanna!'' the American called after her, but he was too late.

''Don't worry,'' Peppino reassured him, ''no one steals a car in Treangoli, there is only one road, the whole village would right away see who was the thief. This village is made of eyes!'' The American glanced at him, then dipped a hand into the pocket of the poplin jacket he'd been carrying and that he'd hung over the back of the chair, and Peppino heard a slight jingle. Americans, he reflected, were made of keys, like Treangoli was made of eyes.

A few moments later the American got up and went outside. But before Peppino even had time to serve a couple of espressos at the bar, he was back. Alone. He sat down, picked up his fork, and started in again on the pasta. He ate slowly, even thoughtfully.

''And the signorina?'' Peppino asked, passing with a pile

of dirty plates, knowing it was none of his business but curious anyway.

"Yes . . . the signorina. Chasing butterflies, maybe. At least I caught a glimpse of her disappearing down the end of the road."

"Butterflies?" Peppino laughed. "More likely something from the *tabaccaio*, there's nowhere else to go in Treangoli!"

The girl was gone a long time. Twenty minutes? More. Her companion finished the pasta and peas. Then he ordered the special dessert called Luisa's Baked Ambrosia, which was really a sweet waffle with a slice of ice cream on top. He ate the Baked Ambrosia. And waited. To Peppino, the American's ugly, interesting face revealed nothing more than patience.

Then there she was back again, the American girl. Only a little different: One arm was in a sling. A black sling.

"Careless!" The young woman was scolding herself. She sat opposite Thornton again. Peppino hovered, making sympathetic sounds. The girl, not finding the keys in the car, had turned to come back but had tripped and fallen, painfully hurting her wrist. Villagers had directed her to the doctor's office down the road. A bad sprain, Dr. Rosella had diagnosed. He had bandaged the wrist. He had given the young American woman pills against the pain. He had warned her that the pills would make her drowsy. "So *careless*!" the girl repeated, and she looked from Thornton to Peppino and made a helpless gesture with her left hand. It was the right wrist that was sprained.

"And the keys?" Thornton was sitting back, relaxed, smiling across at the girl. "The car keys?"

"Yes, the keys!" The girl's face was flushed. "When I saw they weren't there, I realized you must have taken them."

"Yes. You left them in the ignition when we got here," Thornton said. "You forgot them when we got out of the car. You didn't hear me say I'd take them?"

The girl cradled her bandaged arm. She looked fully at Thornton. "Did you say that? No, I didn't hear."

"Ah," the American said, still smiling, and he reached

into the pocket of the poplin jacket and took out the car keys. "Shall we be on our way? Or do you want to try Luisa's Baked Ambrosia?"

The girl, her face still flushed, said she did not want dessert.

Peppino took a minute to stand in the doorway to watch them go. The man got into the driver's seat of the Alfa Romeo. Naturally, the girl could not drive, not with that right hand in a sling—the Alfa Romeo had a stick shift.

How then, Peppino wondered, could she drive to Rome?

But abruptly he became too busy to wonder. Dr. Rosella had arrived—white-haired, rosy, cheery, and in an unexpectedly open-handed way buying drinks for his friends at the bar. Two drinks could make Dr. Rosella giddy. Today, the drinks started him winking an eye significantly and giggling as though he possessed laughable secrets. When he took out his snap purse to pay, Peppino saw an astonishingly thick roll of new twenty-thousand-lire notes.

❖ 7 ❖

ELISABETTA LIGOURI SAID FIRMLY, "ONLY AS FAR AS THE woods, now!" And the twins nodded obediently and started off. Elisabetta stood in the sun-gilded field that stretched to the woods behind the villa and watched them go—bare, scratched little legs, blue shorts and jerseys, dark curly heads. From behind, they could be the same sex. Her babies. A constriction of the heart. "Aren't you afraid to let the twins out of your sight?" her friends in Rome had wondered, "after that terrible—after . . . ?"

And yes, yes, she was. Fear had her by the throat. And what did *they*, the twins, fear after their dark experience?

She couldn't guess, and they wouldn't tell. But she was determined not to transfer her own dark fears to the children; she must not imprison them in the cage of her own terrors. The ultimate calamity had happened: Her children had been kidnapped. But now she had them back. She had kept her head—or had she been frozen in shock?—through those anguished days. And finally, the children released, she had gathered their dirty little bodies in stained clothing to her heart and held them close without a tear. After that, she had wept for a week. It was like a catharsis. But the fear remained, like a sliver in her heart. Her brother Alessandro had tried to reassure her, saying that the kidnapping was like an amulet that protected the twins. It had happened. It was over. How had Alessandro put it? Yes, a proverb about lightning never striking the same place twice. And here at La Serena the twins couldn't be safer.

"Signora?" It was Giorgio, old Luigi's grandson, a seventeen-year-old from Treangoli who was helping out at the villa during the autumn. This was when Luigi's work was the heaviest, what with the slaughtering added to the care of the vegetable gardens, the pruning of trees on the estate, and the feeding of the geese, chickens, and hogs in their pens.

"Yes, Giorgio?" Elisabetta smiled at the boy—a handsome, spoiled, good-natured youth in jeans and boots; he was not so different from her own two almost-grown sons, aged eighteen and nineteen, at school in Ferrara.

"The Signor Thornton has arrived. Is it all right that I moved your Masarati around to the front of the stables so I could park his car in the garage? There wasn't a single space left in the garage, I—"

"That's fine, Giorgio."

When he had gone, Elisabetta stood breathing in the crisp air, a motionless, sturdily-built figure in the golden field behind the seventeenth-century villa. She was forty years old, widowed now three years. She had sun-faded, reddish hair pushed carelessly behind her ears, deep-set gray eyes, and a tanned, freckled skin. She wore a faded old red cardigan with deep pockets, culottes, and rough shoes. Here in the country she was comfortably indifferent to her uncared-for looks.

Now she gazed toward the hills that were fenced in for the grazing sheep, goats, and cows; at her right were the outbuildings and the garage. She loved it all.

She swiveled on a heel and turned her affectionate gaze onto the country house itself, with its colonnaded upper loggia. She sighed with contentment. Since the horror of the kidnapping, she could no longer sit chatting at elegant cafe tables in Rome with friends, or study chic Italian fashion magazines for the latest styles. It was as though, with the twins back safe in her arms again, she had awakened in another place, on another planet; a familiar old planet of her childhood vacations, the planet of La Serena. She would sit on a stool in the kitchen near the old brick oven, watching Serafina making the pasta dough, helping to slice mushrooms or grind basil or trim artichokes. She felt at rest, pregnant with a kind of heavy peace.

"Signora?" This time it was Rosa, the "younger" maid. Rosa was in her fifties now, but the Faziolinis still thought of her as the "younger" maid—as opposed to Franca, who was a half-dozen years older than Rosa. Both were from Treangoli, and they had stayed at the Faziolini country villa when needed, since the time Elisabetta was ten years old and Alessandro only four.

"Yes, Rosa?"

Rosa had come to tell her that her mother was expecting her in the upstairs salon. "Signor Thornton and a friend are already there, the fire has been lit, and Franca has brought up the wine. Also the *spuma d'arancia*, that orange custard cake that Signora Faziolini remembered the Signor Thornton was always so greedy for."

"Signor Thornton and—a friend?"

"A young woman, Signora."

"Right away, Rosa, right away."

Thornton. "Jeff Thornton coming to La Serena?" she had exclaimed, startled, when her mother had mentioned it last night. She was surprised. Hadn't Alessandro and Thornton once had a bloody fight at the university? Something about a girl—she'd had that impression, she could not have said why. She remembered the bruise on Alessandro's dead-white face, his swollen nose, his refusal to tell her about it. "Didn't Thornton and Alessandro . . ." she had begun, but at her mother's inquiring look, she had hastily broken off. No need for her mother to know about it . . . probably Thornton and Alessandro had long ago made up . . . though Alessandro had never mentioned it.

Anyway, with Alessandro arriving surely before sunset, the situation between the two men would all become clear.

Elisabetta turned to go inside, then turned back and cast a final glance toward the twins playing at the edge of the woods. Immediately, Tomasino, who was facing her, shot up a hand and waved. Reassured, Elisabetta waved back, smiling. Then she went inside.

VITTORIO FAZIOLINI, STILL IN HIS LACED HUNTING BOOTS but with his white handlebar mustache twisted into perfection, smiled sympathetically at the American girl who stood near the salon fireplace, one arm in a black sling. "*Peccato!* Too bad!"

"The Faziolini," as he was known in Rome, was tall, robust, and impressive, but with melancholy eyes, as though he had secret sorrows. Because of his riches and business interests he belonged to the ruling establishment in Italy. It was a class strongly against the inroads of—socialists? communists?—sometimes Vittorio hardly knew. The truth was, he had never been able to care; he believed implicitly in his own abilities, even if Satan himself were to take over Italy. Besides, politics bored him, put him to sleep. "*Noiosa! Noiosa!* Boring!" he would mutter, hearing the political news. He was, all in all, a family man. It saddened him that

Alessandro's wife, Lucilla—"the pale Lucilla," as Vittorio called her in his mind—would stubbornly never now have children.

"*Peccato*!" he said again to the American girl, Signorina March, and he looked at the black sling and shook his head.

The girl smiled back at him. "My own *fault*," she said. "Hurrying is my worst habit!" She half turned from the crackling fire and looked appreciatively around the comfortable, high-ceilinged salon with its frieze of ancient Tuscan hunting scenes of bear and deer. There were mellow old paintings on the walls, and scattered on the rugs were worn couches and soft chairs and heavy round tables, one of which right now bore cheeses, a round-bellied bottle of brandy, fruit, and cake. The salon was Vittorio's favorite room, especially after hunting—it invited relaxation. He kept the long walnut shutters in the embrasures open to the light and the views. Between two of these embrasures, on a stone pedestal, was a bust of Emperor Augustus, Gaius Octavius, the only Roman emperor that Vittorio admired; on a tall dark chest was Elisabetta's childhood collection of ceramic barnyard animals.

"What a marvelous room!" The American girl's gaze had come to rest on a table that held family photographs.

"Signora?" Franca was at her side with the silver tray.

"*Grazie.*" The girl reached to take a glass of red wine from the tray.

"No wine, Johanna! Better not!" Jeff Thornton said instantly from where he sat on the arm of one of the old couches, eating a piece of *spuma d'arancia*. "Alcohol could interact with the painkilling pills the doctor gave you."

"Of course!" And the girl hastily withdrew her hand and cast Thornton a look. She flushed.

"Franca will bring up some soft drinks," Vittorio said to the girl. She had very blue eyes, and with her face so flushed, they looked even bluer. She had thick eyebrows, dark-gold, and her brown hair was darker than her brows. An astonishingly pretty girl, thought Vittorio; not as pretty as Sabina had been, though—nobody could be. And he looked over at Sabina—his darling, warm-hearted, hospitable wife, with her ample Rubens figure and her fair, gray-streaked hair sliding out of the pinned-up coronet atop her head. Sabina was standing at Jeff Thornton's elbow, watching him devour the orange custard cake like a lioness who has just given a choice morsel to her cub.

The four of them were alone in the salon. Vittorio knew that Lucilla would not appear until dinnertime. As for Elisabetta, she was late as usual. Thornton had just finished explaining the problem of Signorina March's sprained wrist. Now he said, "I'll drive Johanna back to Florence, then return here for the weekend."

"Nonsense, isn't it, Vittorio?" Sabina Faziolini flung out her beringed hands, appealing to her husband. And to Thornton she said, "I won't let you go! Now that you're here, you're my captive—I claim you my captive!" She gave her delightful contralto laugh. "Miss March can also be our guest, we have plenty of room—we could house a battalion—and we sometimes do. Almost, anyway! Besides, Miss March looks as though she doesn't eat much! Not that we won't fatten her up!" And Sabina laughed at herself in delight. "Grilled lamb ribs with rosemary for dinner tonight! That's what we always have when Alessandro gets back from a trip. We grill them outdoors and dine picnic style in the field— muffled to the ears if it's cold—to please Alessandro. You'll love being my captives!"

Vittorio, sipping brandy, knew that Sabina would have her way. He turned to Thornton. "Give in, you might as well," he advised the American, though the advice was superfluous since Signorina March was already warmly thanking Sabina and saying she'd love to stay.

"And I'm so *sleepy*," the American girl added, and she blinked drowsily. "Those painkillers, I guess."

"And shock, too, probably," Sabina said, feelingly. "You'd better have a nap until dinnertime. Come along, I'll . . ."

"Buona sera! Buona sera!" It was Elisabetta, coming in, still in her beloved old culottes and sweater. At least she had just combed her hair with a wet comb—Vittorio could see the dark wet streaks in his daughter's reddish-blond hair—

and she had put on fresh lipstick. He looked at her with a lift of the heart, glad that her fixed, staring look during those terrible days of the kidnapping had finally disappeared.

Elisabetta crossed slowly to Thornton and took both his hands. "Is it really you? I'm glad that you and Alessandro—I mean, I hope—oh, *nothing*!" And she swung his two hands in hers and laughed.

"And this," said Sabina, "is Johanna March. A friend of Jeff's."

Elisabetta turned to the American girl. "*Piacere*—so pleased." Then she stood looking at Signorina March there in her yellow dress and with her arm in the black sling, the tiled fireplace and the crackling fire behind her; and a little frown formed between her brows. "Johanna—March? Surely we've met?"

"I don't think so."

"Your name is so—so familiar. I thought for a minute—in Rome. Playing tennis at the Padulazzis', in Olgiata—I used to play there a lot. And at the Strolas'." She looked perplexed. "No, that's not it, is it?"

"No, I've never—"

"Of *course*!" Elisabetta exclaimed. Her brow cleared; she gazed at Johanna March with interest. "That tragedy in Florence! It was in the papers and on television! You're *that* Johanna March!"

"Yes."

"*Please*, Elisabetta," her mother said forbearingly, "the tragedy in Florence! *What* tragedy in Florence?"

"Mama, we were talking about it last night, remember? The drowned man? Mugged and thrown into the Arno? And how there was an American girl from the same pensione with him? The girl who called the police." She turned back to Johanna:

"Botto! That was his name, wasn't it? Botto. From Bologna. The papers said later that he was unidentified."

"Yes."

"How dreadful! You poor thing!" Sabina Faziolini said; at the same time she abstractedly attempted to push up the gray-streaked hair sliding out of the coronet atop her head.

And to Franca who was coming back into the salon with a newly laden tray she said, "Orange juice, just the thing! Orange juice for Miss March, then a nice nap."

"Yes! How awful for you!" Elisabetta said warmly to Johanna, "I mean, after all—it was murder, wasn't it?"

"That's what the police think."

Vittorio Faziolini, listening, standing on the white bearskin rug near one of the worn couches, saw the girl cast a look of appeal at Jeff Thornton. To Vittorio's surprise, Thornton ungallantly ignored it; he just sat on the edge of the couch, twirling a wine glass in his hand and watching her.

"Do you think," Elisabetta persisted, "that they'll ever find out who did it?"

"There don't seem to be any—any leads." To Vittorio, the American girl's voice sounded nervously exhausted.

"Or even," Elisabetta went on curiously, "that the police will ever discover who he is? The drowned man, I mean. Botto."

Vittorio frowned forbiddingly at his daughter. *"Abbastanza*, Elisabetta—*enough."*

"Yes, Elisabetta!" Sabina said. "Stop badgering Miss March! Anyway, we're going!" She took a glass of orange juice from the tray and shepherded the American girl ahead of her toward the door. "You'll love the southwest corner room, Miss March. It overlooks the hills toward Treangoli, a marvelous view, all gold and violet at sunset. I want to show you—*peccato*! We'll have to draw the curtains so you can sleep. Never mind. Tomorrow, you'll see how enchanting . . ." And together with the American girl, Sabina left the room, still talking.

Vittorio looked after them. Signorina March—Johanna— what a frankly appreciative and interested young woman she was! He glanced over at the table of silver-framed family photographs and its accumulation of unframed snapshots. Even those had caught her eye. Really a charming girl! What was she to Thornton? Friend? Lover?

Vittorio took a sip of brandy and studied Jeff Thornton, who stood talking with Elisabetta. Thornton wasn't the *gio-*

venotto, the candid, uncomplicated young man Vittorio remembered. *This* Thornton, with the strong, ugly face and dark eyes with their quizzical look, had become a man worth measuring. Elisabetta, kneeling with one knee on the couch beside the American and looking up at him as she talked, seemed to have reached the same conclusion. Vittorio touched one end of his perfectly waxed white mustache and raised his brows.

WIDE AWAKE, JOHANNA LAY SUNK INTO THE SOFTNESS OF the chaise lounge in the darkened room, listening to Sabina Faziolini's retreating footsteps. The heavy drapes were drawn; in the faint light the armoire, the overstuffed chairs, and the bed bulked like huge sleeping animals.

When she could no longer hear Sabina's step, she flung off the knitted wool throw, swung her feet to the floor, and turned on the table lamp beside the chaise. She wore only her slip and the Dior satin robe from her weekend bag, which Sabina had had Rosa bring up. The black sling lay on the table.

In the lamp's soft glow, she sat on the edge of the chaise and flexed her bandaged wrist, marveling that it had all worked—her risky little plan! In Treangoli, when she'd deliberately left the keys in the Alfa Romeo's ignition, it was touch-and-go after Thornton took them out, but she'd pretended she hadn't heard him tell her so. In fact, it had worked even better that way: Since he'd taken the keys he'd known the car was safe, so he hadn't come after her. He simply kept filling his apparently bottomless stomach with pasta and peas until she returned.

But if he *had* immediately come after her? What would

she have done? She didn't know. That had been the weak
spot. She'd have had to fake a fall and a sprained wrist suc-
cessfully and let Thornton accompany her to Dr. Rosella's
office, praying that the doctor was a good actor!

As for the Faziolinis—there, at least, she had felt confi-
dent. After all, what gracious family wouldn't offer hospital-
ity to an old friend's friend who was groggy with painkilling
pills and the trauma of a sprained wrist?

She frowned, annoyed. It was only Jeff Thornton who had
lacked sympathy for her, there in the salon, stuffing himself
with orange custard cake and telling the Faziolinis he'd take
her back to Florence! And she'd been longing so for a glass
of red wine! The close way he was watching her—why?—
she hadn't even dared approach the table with the photographs in their silver frames.

Her watch showed a few minutes after five. The picnic
dinner would be about eight. "I'll send Rosa to wake you at
seven-thirty," Sabina Faziolini, departing, had told her. So
three hours from now she hoped politely to be saying "*Piacere*—glad to meet you," to Alessandro Faziolini, and
shaking his hand, a warm-blooded hand, the blood pumped
from the heart, the alive heart, and thereby knowing with
enormous relief that the unidentified drowned man was not
Alessandro Faziolini. She would then feel like Prometheus
freed of the enormous boulder on his shoulders. She sighed,
exasperated. A conscience was a terrible burden. Without it
she might now be in a carefree mood, shopping on the elegant Via Tornabuoni in Florence or planning an expensive
backing of the March-Arpino School in Italy—the precious
Totocalcio fortune still undeniably hers.

But instead here she was. Because the fact was—and she
faced it now clearly, unalterably—that more than the Totocalcio money had brought her to La Serena. Anger and outrage at the brutal murder had brought her here. If the
murdered man were indeed Alessandro Faziolini, she must
immediately telephone Captain Grippo. It would be a step
closer to catching the murderer. As for the Totocalcio money,
that was her secret; she'd worry about it later.

Feeling restless and impatient, she got up, went to a window, and drew aside one of the heavy draperies. The sky was already spectacular in the setting sun. The sky looked like a purple curtain jaggedly torn to reveal turquoise and streaked with brilliant red-gold remnants of clouds. Beneath it the woods were green-and-yellow smudges; a strand of spangled gold, a narrow river wound through the woods.

Dark, chilly-looking outbuildings stretched away from the villa. At the corner of one—stable or garage, Johanna could not tell—two people came into view: a teenage boy in jeans and a long-haired girl in white pants wheeling a bicycle. The girl got on the bicycle saddle, sneakered shoes touching the ground; then, with the back of one hand, she pushed her long brown hair back over her shoulders and turned her head to the boy. The boy moved in close. They kissed, a long kiss, then the girl twisted away her head, shoved at the boy's chest, put her feet on the pedals, and bicycled off. The boy—Johanna recognized him as the handsome, dark-eyed boy who'd taken the Alfa Romeo off to the garage—turned and disappeared around the corner of the outbuilding.

Johanna let the drape fall closed. Then, feeling suddenly exhausted and realizing it was from tension, she lay down on the chaise lounge and tried hard to think of nothing, *nothing at all*.

But she left the lamp on.

And every few minutes she raised her arm and looked at her watch.

IT WAS NOT ROSA THE MAID, BUT ELISABETTA FAZIOLINI who knocked on Johanna's door at seven-thirty. She came in carrying a pair of hiking shoes and a heavy woolen cable-

knit sweater. "You're awake? Good! The field is stony so I
brought you these shoes—they belonged to my eldest boy
when he was ten years old—they should fit you. And the
evening always turns chilly, so here's a sweater—it was his,
too, I made it myself, it was in a trunk in the attic so it smells
of *palline antitarmiche*—mothballs. In this family we never
throw anything away!" Elisabetta laughed and shook out the
sweater. "Later, when they get bigger, Tomasino and Felicia
will wear the sweater."

"Thank you." On the chaise lounge, Johnanna sat up,
faking a yawn. She supported her bandaged wrist carefully
with her left hand while she slipped on the black sling. And
carelessly she asked, "Has your brother arrived?"

"Alessandro? Not yet. But any minute. Does your wrist
hurt?"

Johanna shook her head. "The pills helped." While she
washed in the little bathroom, combed her hair, and put on
fresh lipstick, she listened to Elisabetta, who sat on the edge
of the chaise lounge talking through the open door about
Rome and the current tennis matches and how pleased the
Faziolinis were to see Jeff Thornton again. Elisabetta wore a
long woolen skirt and a gray, cowl-necked sweater. Her faded
red hair was parted in the middle and floated loose over her
ears. She had touched her eyelids with something that gave
them a silvery sheen. To Johanna, coming back into the bedroom, the effect was somehow medieval; it made her think
of early Italian masterpieces or of pictures she'd seen of Tuscany murals painted on old castle walls, paintings so often
of mothers with their young children at their knees.

"The twins," she said impulsively. "Of course I've
heard about the kidnapping. I'm so sorry! And so glad that
finally—" She turned up her palms, helplessly.

Elisabetta said soberly, "Thank you. You'll meet Tomasino and Felicia tomorrow. They're already in bed." She
clasped her hands over one knee and sat staring down at
them. "They'd gotten so *thin*! Skinny as twigs. And in only
twenty-eight days! At bedtime now, I take them up each a
glass of warm milk topped with melted butter. I know that
after I go downstairs they pour it down their bathroom sink—

Rosa told me.'' Elisabetta sighed. ''But I still bring it, I don't care, I bring it to them not just as food, but so that they'll feel safe and loved. And carrying it up the stairs, I think to myself, What can make them feel more secure than milk and a mother's love?''

''Nothing I can think of,'' Johanna said slowly. ''Nothing.'' She was thinking of two impressions mixed together: She was remembering her Danish mother's word for milk, *mjolk*, so long forgotten; she was seeing the little blue stone mug and the creamy whiteness of the milk that filled it and, hazily, her mother's face smiling down at her. And mixed with that memory was a penetrating apprehension that she had liked Elisabetta Faziolini from the moment they'd met in the salon and had liked Sabina and the white-mustached Vittorio as well. But until now she had hoped only for her own selfish reasons that Alessandro Faziolini was not the dead man, the unidentified ''Botto.'' She had hoped that she could keep the Totocalcio money without a single qualm of conscience and at the same time be relieved of any moral obligation to report a connection between the dead man and the Faziolini family to Captain Grippo in Florence—a report that could only draw her back in and involve her with the murder. But now, looking at Elisabetta Faziolini's sad face, she hoped for the Faziolinis' sakes, too, that Alessandro was alive. *Be alive*, she said fiercely to herself. *Damn it, Alessandro, be alive!*

Elisabetta helped her dress, tying the laces of the hiking shoes, working Johanna's right arm through the sleeve of her shirt, careful of the injured wrist, then pulling the sweater over her head—''Careful! Careful!''—and drawing the black sling back over Johanna's arm again.

Downstairs, Elisabetta led the way across the terrace out to the field. It was not yet full dark, and the field smelled heavily, deliciously, of sweet-grass—the same pungent grass that Johanna as a child in Massachusetts used to weave into baskets. Although the grass in the field was still baking upward from the day's sun, the air already had a touch of chill. Elisabetta swung an unlit flashlight in one hand and took deep appreciative breaths as they walked toward the little group that had formed around a stone hearth from which smoke rose.

"*There* you are!" Sabina Faziolini called out as they approached. "*Buona sera*, Signora March—Johanna! You napped *beautifully*, I hope?"

"Yes, thank you—beautifully." Johanna swept a glance over the group; Sabina Faziolini stood next to the hearth; Vittorio Faziolini was helping a gnarled old man in a greasy cap feed wood to the fire. Jeff Thornton sat alone on a rough wooden bench; he met Johanna's glance with a curiously opaque gaze, and a little smile flickered across his mouth— Johanna looked quickly away. To Thornton's left, standing to one side and staring into the fire, was a young woman wrapped in a fringed purple wool shawl. She was thin and angular, with bony wrists, and her fingers clutched the shawl, nervously twisting the fringe.

There was no one else. No Alessandro.

"Elisabetta, you sit over there with Jeff—Johanna, too." Sabina herself sat down on the opposite bench, then turned and looked up anxiously, appealingly, to the shawl-clad young woman. "Lucilla, *cara*, you come sit with me . . . Come now, *cara*, sit down . . . And you haven't met Johanna March, *cara* . . . Come now. Johanna, this is Alessandro's wife, Lucilla."

The young woman turned a reluctant look on Johanna. Her lips moved silently in unsmiling acknowledgement. She was, on second glance, not so young after all; certainly she was in her late thirties. She had thick, frizzy dark hair—an aureole of darkness carelessly cut to below her ears. Her face was angular with protruding brown eyes and a bitter-looking mouth. She could never have been pretty, even in youth; but her neck, from which the shawl fell away, was slender and delicate; it had such a look of vulnerability that to Johanna there seemed to be something poignant and tender, like a child's innocence, about the woman.

"*Cara*, darling," Sabina appealed again. At that, Lucilla Faziolini gave a shrug and a sigh and sat down beside her mother-in-law. She pulled a pack of cigarettes from a pocket, lit a thin, brown cigarette, and began to smoke, gazing moodily into the fire.

"And this is Luigi"—Vittorio Faziolini waved a hand toward the old man in the cap—"the *factotum* at La Serena. He built this unmatchable fire over which I'll now broil his savory little sausages—another of his masterpieces. He won't even tell *us* what herbs he uses in making them." And Vittorio began carefully to place pale, shiny-skinned little sausages on the iron grill.

"What!" Sabina Faziolini exclaimed reproachfully. "We're not waiting for Alessandro?"

"Not a minute more! We could have starved to death a thousand times waiting for him—he knows what time we dine, and he's already a half-hour late!" The sausages sizzled, and a delicious smell of herbs rose from the grill. "Besides, *cara*, it is the roast lamb with rosemary that our Alessandro loves. Meantime, the sausages will soothe our hunger pangs."

They ate the crisp, hot little sausages with hunks of torn, chewy Tuscany bread and a dry white wine from Umbria, eating with their fingers from heavy china plates in their laps, wine glasses beside them on the wooden benches. Johanna found herself sipping wine nervously, her throat a little dry; it had something to do with the odd way Jeff Thornton was looking at her from time to time—it was disconcerting. She would glance his way simply because she was drawn to look at his lean, ugly, attractive face, and she would find him watching her, that half-smile around his mouth. Once or twice, she could swear he looked faintly puzzled. Then, when she raised her wine glass to her lips and realized in surprise that it was again empty, she found that he was already standing beside her, refilling it. The glass trembled in her hand, perhaps because of the chill of the evening; and he put a warm, steadying hand over hers on the stem of the glass. "Careful!" And he added, "You've brought the bracelet?"

"Bracelet?" For a moment she was lost. "The Florentine gold bracelet," Thornton said. "You didn't bring it, Johanna? You're that sure of winning our bet? That Alessandro won't even remember that he and I quarreled at all?'' His voice was low; behind him, Sabina and Elisabetta chatted, Vittorio was talking with Luigi, and Lucilla had walked a little way into the field, where she stood smoking.

"Oh." She had forgotten all about that bet they'd made in the restaurant above Florence; it seemed years ago, not only a day ago. She thought now how Jeff Thornton couldn't possibly guess that the bet had been only a ruse for her to learn if he could get in touch with Alessandro on the telephone in the restaurant, to reassure herself that Alessandro could not possibly be Luciano Botto.

"I brought it." But she wasn't sure she had; anyway, it no longer mattered. She would part with a dozen *satinato* Florentine bracelets, or even a thousand, if only Alessandro would arrive.

"Vittorio!" Sabina said. "How dark it's getting! I'll light the candles." She got up and lit two tall yellow candles on a small wooden side table that held bottles of wine and baskets of bread. Elisabetta began to tell funny stories, looking mostly at Jeff Thornton as she talked. She told about how when she was sixteen she had ambitiously started a cookie business, then a boat chartering business, a crochet-your-own-dress-in-two-hours business, and a chocolate soldiers business. "I offered Perugina the rights to my chocolate soldiers provided they would make me a senior vice president, but they declined." Everybody laughed except Lucilla, who still stood away, smoking.

Then Jeff Thornton talked knowledgeably about the Italian economy with Sabina and Vittorio, and Vittorio talked about wine-growing and the wine they were drinking. It was an Orvieto Secco, 1979, chosen by Sabina, who had been born a Torriero of the famous wine-growing Torriero family in Emilia-Romagna. "By the time Sabina was ten years old, a drop on the tip of her tongue was enough for her to name and date any number of wines."

Johanna didn't speak at all. There was no wind and the candles burned steadily, brightly. Johanna sat facing the villa, where lights in the downstairs windows had gone on. She sat staring past Jeff Thornton's shoulder toward the villa, listening tensely for the sound of a car arriving. But nothing, not even the distant ringing of a telephone—Alessandro perhaps phoning to say he was delayed.

"Damn it, where's Alessandro!" Vittorio broke out suddenly, exasperated. "Luigi, put the lamb on the grill!"

And then, as the old man began to lay the ribs over the coals, Johanna heard it: a car motor. Certainly a car motor! But it was so faint that no one else seemed to notice. Five minutes passed. Then, with an immense feeling of relief, Johanna saw a dark figure cross the terrace and start across the field. "Alessandro!" she exclaimed.

Sabina followed her gaze. "Alessandro! *Finally!*"

"About time," Vittorio said grudgingly, but he sounded pleased. He was bent over the grill, turning the ribs; he did not look up.

At that moment, Johanna saw the dark figure stop. The person, a man, was simply standing there at the edge of the terrace, not calling out a hello, just standing and—and what?—raising something to his shoulder. What was it?

Then she knew. A rifle. For an instant, kaleidoscopically, she saw a bearded figure in a taxi, saw a man half hidden behind the dining room portiere at the Pensione Boldine, saw—

A shot exploded, and immediately another. She felt the wind of the bullets past her cheek. Then both candles went out. They sat in darkness, except for the fire in the grill. Into the stunned silence, Lucilla Faziolini said flatly, "Matteo. It's Matteo."

"*Idiota!* That idiot!" Elisabetta exclaimed angrily. She turned her flashlight on the dark figure that now approached. "Matteo, that was stupid! You could have hurt someone! Your shooting isn't *that* infallible."

"Matteo, darling, you frightened me," Sabina said reproachfully to the solidly-built young man who had now reached them. At that the man laughed, leaned down, and kissed her cheek. "*Tresoro!* My treasure! The fault is Vittorio's! He said I couldn't shoot out the candles at sixty paces."

"*Mah!* I didn't mean while we were dining!" Vittorio smoothed his white mustaches and looked rueful. "But Matteo is right. I'm to blame.'' He turned to Johanna and Thornton. ''This is our Matteo . . . Matteo Del Bosco. I apologize, I did tell him—but *I* didn't take it seriously.''

Matteo Del Bosco bowed to Johanna. ''*Piacere*, so pleased. *Mi dispiace*, I'm sorry, I didn't know the Faziolinis had guests.'' His smile flashed white in the candlelight. He was tanned, black-haired, in his thirties, with a handsome but heavy-jowled face. He wore country clothes—tan pants and a brown turtle-necked sweater, but somehow, to Johanna, he had a look she identified as ''city.'' She was not surprised, minutes later, to gather from the conversation that he was with a brokerage house in Rome. He poured himself a glass of wine and complained that he had only just returned from a wearisome business trip to Naples. ''I've missed a week's good hunting at La Serena.''

''Never mind,'' Sabina said, and she put an affectionate hand on Matteo's shoulder. ''At least you're here now, *caro*, tomorrow you can hunt''—and smiling to Johanna— ''Matteo is our *amico della famiglia*, our 'friend of the family.' Do you know what that is, Johanna? It is common in Italy.''

''Yes,'' Johanna said. And she did know: In all the Italian short stories and plays she had read, that was the character she invariably envied—the *amico della famiglia*. A bachelor or widower friend who practically lived in the family's home, he was always welcome at family meals, he was available for a game of cards in the evening, he was privy to the family's problems with their children. If he was elderly, he had the privilege of falling asleep by the fire or even in the midst of a confidence. As for Matteo Del Bosco, she now learned that he even had his own room at La Serena, and though his work kept him in Rome he spent holidays, vacations, and weekends at the villa when it pleased him. She looked curiously at this *amico della famiglia*, the first in her experience, feeling that same old twinge of envy. She wondered how it had come about that Del Bosco was the Faziolini's privileged friend. And wondered more than that: Why was he so easily forgiven for shooting out the candles?

Jeff Thornton said unexpectedly, drily: "You're a better shot than you used to be, Del Bosco."

"*Che?* What?" Matteo Del Bosco, holding the rifle with the barrel aiming at the ground, stared at Thornton.

"Ten years ago—maybe eleven," Thornton said, "I was at La Serena, we hunted together—you and I and Alessandro. There was—"

"*Certo!* Certainly! I remember! You're Alessandro's university friend. The three of us, we—"

"No," Thornton said. "Four of us. There was someone else with us. A man several years older, a dark, tall—"

"Renzo!" Elisabetta exclaimed. "Renzo Grimini! Our neighbor from the villa La Raccòlta."

"Yes." Thornton nodded. He looked at Elisabetta. "You remember, how when he slipped . . . ?"

"The accident!" Elisabetta cried. "Renzo stumbled, his gun went off! The bullet went right through Alessandro's shoulder. The blood, the awful . . ."

"You know, I'd forgotten!" Sabina exclaimed. "Poor Renzo," She gave her rich contralto laugh. "Afterward, Vittorio had to give him whiskey, he was ready to faint. 'I might have killed him!' he kept saying, 'I might have killed him!' He's never gotten over it. He still never hunts!"

Matteo Del Bosco, too, laughed. Surprisingly, it was a high giggle. "That leaves more game in the woods for us!" He placed the rifle carefully on the ground beneath the table. At the grill, he leaned over and sniffed luxuriously. He rubbed his hands together—strong-looking, stubby hands, one of them streaked with oil from the rifle. "*Ahh*, roast lamb! And I'm in good time!" He looked around. "Where's Alessandro?"

"Not here yet." Vittorio Faziolini sounded vexed. "He's on the Venice-Milan sales trip. Due back now, but he's late." He drew his thick white eyebrows together and slanted a concerned glance at Lucilla, who now sat smoking another brown cigarette, an elbow cupped in one hand, the cigarette to her lips. Her face was expressionless, but a muscle in her jaw twitched. Del Bosco, too, glanced toward Lucilla.

"*Mah!* That always happens when he goes on the Venice-Milan sales trip." He sat down next to Johanna. He smelled of expensive cologne. He scrupulously kept his thigh from touching hers. "Those villas are like a drug to Alessandro—Palladio's and the rest!"

"Villas?" Jeff Thornton said.

Elisabetta turned to Thornton. "Alessandro needn't go on selling trips to the Venice area—he's vice president of *Faziolini e Figlio*, after all! But it's an excuse to visit some of those princely old villas around Treviso, Padua, and Vincenza. They were built in the fifteenth and sixteenth centuries, and they fascinate him!"

"So," Sabina said, "when Alessandro makes the Venice-Milan trip, he takes four or five extra days to explore the villas before going on to Milan. The whole trip is only ten or eleven days. He's been gone just ten days now, so—Vittorio, if you open the red wine now, so it can breathe a little before the lamb is done—yes, Alessandro's *vocazione*—his avocation—is the study of the Veneto villas."

Jeff Thornton said drily, "I remember him as being more interested in *calcio*—soccer—than villas."

At that, they all laughed—all except Lucilla, who sat silent as stone.

"Calcio! Oh, he *is!*" Sabina said, "but you know, it really is comical! He—"

"He always bets on the calcio, the Totocalcio!" Elisabetta broke in. "But he never wins! Never! It's become a family joke."

He never wins. Johanna looked around at the flushed, amused faces in the glow of the candles that Luigi had lit again. Then the unidentified, murdered man with the false name of Botto couldn't possibly have been Alessandro Faziolini. *That* man, "Signor Botto," had implied he often won his Totocalcio bets, even if only small sums. She looked longingly, impatiently toward the house, straining her eyes, head cocked, listening. But there was only the nighttime silence filled with small country sounds: the hum of insects, the tiny crackle of dry grass where field mice played, a soft mooing of a cow from one of the outbuildings, even a clash of pans from the kitchen—that would be Serafina, the cook, old Luigi's wife.

"Those villas," Johanna said suddenly. "Did Alessandro ever go as far as—as to Florence, to visit any of them?"

"Florence?" Vittorio Faziolini looked surprised. "No, not toward Florence. Is there such a villa you know of near Florence?"

Johanna shook her head. "No. I just thought—I Tatti, that beautiful villa near Fiesole outside Florence, the one in which Bernard Berenson lived."

Vittorio said doubtfully, "I Tatti? Unlikely. Alessandro was interested in the area around Vicenza and Treviso to the north, and even further north, to Belluno. At least that's what he talked most of."

"Oh. I just wondered."

❖ 11 ❖

THE GRILLED LAMB RIBS WERE DONE, VITTORIO FAZIOLINI began to serve them. In the glow of the grill, he was startlingly handsome with his high coloring, blue eyes, and mane of white hair. Johanna, remembering Signor Botto—so thin-faced and dark, with the two almost black lines between his brows—felt a surge of hope; Signor Botto bore no resemblance to this Vittorio, father of Alessandro.

"Delicious, *caro*!" Sabina said to her husband at her first bit. "You've outdone yourself! As a chef in Rome, you'd win a—Oh!" Lucilla's lit cigarette flashed past her eyes, arching into the darkness. At the same moment, Lucilla was on her feet, clenched fists yanking down the ends of her shawl. "Damn, *damn* Alessandro!" she cried out furiously. "I'm going in! I—he—" Her voice quavered and broke.

"Yes, darling!" Sabina said quickly, soothingly. "But really you should taste—you haven't eaten a thing! And after, with the Vin Santo, there's a melon, one of Luigi's—''

"I'm going *in*!" Lucilla put a hand to her quivering lips. "Not to care, when—How *can* he? He should be here! Those stupid villas! *They're* more important to him! Damn them! Damn *him*!"

Matteo Del Bosco stood up. *"Calma! Calma!* Don't let yourself get so—if you're going, I'll light you across the field.'' He picked up Elisabetta's flashlight, put an arm around Lucilla's shawl-clad shoulders, and together they disappeared into the dark; the light of the flashlight went bobbing across the field.

"Poor Lucilla!" Sabina Faziolini said softly. She leaned toward Jeff Thornton. "Tomorrow is Lucilla's birthday. The day before her birthday is when she really needs Alessandro, the comfort of his being here. You remember, Jeff—it was the day before her birthday, nine years ago, when she woke at night to go to the baby—''

"But, Mama! Jeff *wouldn't* remember!" Elisabetta broke in, "that was long after he'd gone back to America. Alessandro and Lucilla weren't even married then!"

"Oh, *si,si*!" Sabina was vexed. "I'm mixed up." She looked ruefully at the wine glass in her hand. "It must be the wine, it *can't* be my age!"

Jeff Thornton asked, "What happened the day before Lucilla's birthday nine years ago?"

Sabina and Elisabetta exchanged a look; then Sabina sighed. "The baby. Lucilla and Alessandro's baby, Massimo. Something called a crib death. He was three months old. Lucilla, in the night, went into the nursery to tend him and found him face down, not breathing. She became hysterical. She snatched him up and ran from the house into the garden. She had some desperate, frantic idea that out there in the fresher air, her baby would breathe life-giving air into its little lungs again.'' She was silent. "I thought you knew, Jeff, I didn't mean to bring up such a—such a—''

"That's all right," Thornton said; and he added reflectively, "So Alessandro makes a point of being here at La Serena the day before Lucilla's birthday?"

"Scrupulously," Elisabetta said. "And now—*how* could he have forgotten?"

If he did forget, thought Johanna. *Let it be only that.* She looked across the field, but Lucilla and Matteo Del Bosco were gone; the bobbing circle of light from the flashlight had disappeared. Poor Lucilla Faziolini, still grieving for her baby. For some reason, Johanna's thoughts strayed to the little dressmaking shop on Via Niccolo Nero in Florence, and to a little boy named Francesco; that other child, dark-eyed and so vividly alive. She wondered how old he was, that little Francesco Mantello. Eight? Nine?

"Scrupulously?" Jeff Thornton was saying to Elisabetta. "He'd be here 'scrupulously' the day before Lucilla's birthday? Then he might still arrive tonight."

Elisabetta shook her head. "Absolutely not. If Alessandro doesn't arrive by dinnertime, he doesn't come until the following evening. Funny, that's his habit, his pattern. I suppose because of his business scheduling." She shrugged, sipped wine, and absent-mindedly smiled across at Johanna.

But Johanna could not smile back. The thought of waiting another day for Alessandro's arrival or nonarrival seemed to deplete the blood in her veins. *No*, it was too much! Tonight, while the others slept and she would be undisturbed, she would slip into the salon. She would study the Faziolini family photographs, looking for a face that looked like that of Luciano Botto—and hopefully she would not find it.

❖ 12 ❖

"SIGNORINA MARCH!" VITTORIO FAZIOLINI'S VOICE brought her abruptly back to the darkened field, the faces around her, the candlelight, and the dying embers in the grill.

He handed her a little crystal glass of amber liquid. "*Vin Santo*, 'wine for the saints.' Luckily, it also tastes delicious to those of us who are sinners. How it tastes to saints, who can tell?"

"Thank you." Sipping the nutty tasting liquor, she studied the villa. There on the right, at the southeast corner, those dark windows—that would be the salon. Good. It was close to the bedroom Sabina had given her; she'd find her way easily enough. As she gazed, light suddenly streamed down from an upper-floor casement window next to the loggia. Then a shutter closed, blotting out the light.

"Matteo's room," Elisabetta murmured; she, too, sat facing the villa. She turned to her mother. "I put flowers in his room, Mama, the hyacinths that Luigi was growing in the greenhouse—the first ones to bloom. I put them in the Venetian vase, the cinquecento vase from the dining room, the one that Matteo thinks is so *elegante*."

"*Bene*—good," Sabina said approvingly.

Jeff Thornton said, "Signor Del Bosco is as accurate with his gun as a professional sharp-shooter. Not everyone can shoot out candles at sixty paces." He was addressing no one in particular. His words hung in the air. No one spoke. A heavy silence had descended on the Faziolinis. Luigi, raking coals at the grill, became motionless, a dark statue in work clothes and billed cap. Then Elisabetta sighed. "You're surprised, Jeff, that we allow—you think we're too lenient with Matteo, too tolerant. That—"

"—that I should have reprimanded Del Bosco!" Vittorio said bluntly, turning to Thornton, "Demanded an apology! Yes? But, *ci sono circostanze*—there are circumstances—the Faziolini family is indebted to Matteo Del Bosco. However"—he absent-mindedly stroked his luxuriant white mustache with thumb and forefinger—"that is a private matter."

Into the following silence, Elisabetta said softly, "Indebted. A debt beyond price."

"Yes!" Sabina burst out, "For us, he risked—he took his life in his hands!" In her overflow of emotion her hand shook, and wine spilled and ran over her fingers, but she took no notice. "For us! Our *amico della famiglia* in that awful crisis proved to be—"

"Sabina! It is a private matter!" Vittorio Faziolini said strongly, forbiddingly, from where he stood; he was holding the wine bottle so tightly clenched that in the light of the candles his knuckles shone white. "It is of no interest to our guests. We must not bore them with—"

"But it is Jeff who is asking!" Elisabetta protested. "Jeff Thornton, Alessandro's friend! He isn't just a 'guest.' "

Vittorio Faziolini, biting the inside of his cheek, stared at his daughter from under his fierce white brows; then abruptly he waved the wine bottle in an open gesture of surrender. *"Se tu vuoi, figlia mia.* If you wish, my daughter."

"I wish Papa." And Elisabetta, with the candlelight on her face, and her back to the grill where Luigi, now released from his frozen stillness, was again at work raking the dying coals, related Matteo's part in the rescue of the twins. Her father had refused to reveal the kidnapping to the police for fear of endangering the twins' lives; if he had called them in, the Italian courts would have adopted their new tactics of freezing the family's assets in order to thwart the kidnappers, and then God only knew how the kidnappers might have revenged themselves on the children. Instead, Vittorio Faziolini insisted on dealing with the kidnappers himself. "The kidnappers sent the ransom note to my father as head of the family, everyone knew the Faziolini family acted as one."

The family kept it secret. The crudely written note from the kidnappers told them where to make the drop. "Alessandro wanted to make the drop, he was determined! But we were afraid to let him. He was so enraged by the crime that we dreaded that he would stay hidden nearby after he made the drop and try to trap the kidnappers. It was too risky. They might kill him and the twins both, they would be like all kidnappers lately—cold-blooded, like sharp knives. Shrewd. Merciless. We knew what had happened to the Cinollas' little girl. And others. So Papa put his foot down. Alessandro could not make the drop. We could not risk him losing his head. No, he himself would do it.

"When Papa said he was the only one who could do it,

Mama became hysterical. She couldn't stop crying. She slipped right off the sofa in the Rome apartment and fell on the floor. She couldn't get up. Papa finally lifted her—that's when Matteo volunteered to make the drop."

Matteo, the *amico della famiglia*. Matteo was steadier than Alessandro, less emotional; and of course, less involved. They could count on him to deliver the ransom safely, competently, and the twins would not be endangered.

The drop was arranged through a phone call followed by an obscure ad in *Corrierra della Sera*. Matteo carried the ransom money in two cardboard suit boxes—the kidnappers had specified *cartone*, cardboard. "They wanted nothing of leather or plastic. But cardboard—*that* they could burn up, leaving no trace."

When the ransom was paid and the twins were finally safe in Elisabetta's arms, the Faziolinis called in the Rome police. *Criminalpol*, the Italian antikidnapping squad, was frustrated and furious. Also fatalistic. They had no clues, no leads. Matteo told them what he could, which was little: The kidnappers' call had ordered him to a public telephone booth to wait for another call; from there he was ordered to another telephone outside a bar, then told to sit at an outdoor cafe with the suit boxes for an hour. Then he was sent to the Pincio Gardens, where he was told to wait on an iron bench. Just when it began to drizzle and he feared the cardboard boxes would melt in the rain, a voice from the grass behind the bench ordered him to leave the boxes and not to turn around, but to walk to the right until he reached the corner; then to turn left and keep on walking. Matteo had followed the anonymous orders exactly. He had, however, been able to tell Criminalpol at least one thing: The voice behind him in the Pincio Gardens had been that of a woman.

Above the field, a flat silver moon separated itself from concealing clouds; it cast a slivery sheen on the heads and shoulders. "So you see," Elisabetta said, and her voice was not quite even, "if Matteo Del Bosco cares to shoot out a candle . . ." She inclined her head; it was a queenly gesture of permission.

"Yes," Jeff Thornton said. "I see," and as he spoke,

Johanna realized that he had glanced at her covertly; suddenly she was aware that he had been watching her ever since she and Elisabetta had come walking across the field with the flashlight. And as the bullets from Matteo's rifle had whizzed by, even then had he been watching her? No, of course not. Certainly not. Why would he be?

Vittorio Faziolini gave a little laugh. "Flowers in his room, in a Venetian vase! Matteo is financially successful on the *Borsa*—the Exchange—so it would be ridiculous to try to reward him with a little fortune, remarkable jewelry, or even a boat—he has a mahogany sailing vessel he had made in Portugal. We can, however, bear with his little foibles, make a better effort to understand his, ah—his—"

"Love life, for one thing," Elisabetta said, with a kind of humorous exasperation. "I do wish Papa—especially when he's here at La Serena—last autumn it was one of Renzo's maids"—and to Thornton—"Renzo Grimini, the man you and Alessandro and Matteo hunted with. Anyway, *this* autumn it's already a carpenter's daughter in Treangoli. The girl is hardly seventeen. And Matteo is thirty-three!"

"Thirty-three." Sabina smiled dreamily. She turned to Jeff Thornton. "You know, Alessandro and Matteo were born within an hour of each other. An hour! Can you imagine that? Alessandro at home in our bedroom in Rome, Matteo in a hospital. That night, Vittorio and Ettore, Matteo's father, dined together at the Excelsior to celebrate the births. As for Matteo's mother and me, we lay worn out in our beds, two exhausted mothers of newborn babies!"

"But anyway," Elisabetta said to Thornton, "the Faziolini family paid Matteo a reward in advance, in a way: a reward in love and affection all his childhood after his mother died—he was only ten then. And then later, in the years after his widowed father died."

"Love and affection and *forbearance*," Sabina said. "Such a difficult child! At first, anyway."

"Difficult?" Thornton asked.

"Under the circumstances," said Elisabetta reproachfully to her mother, "how could he *not* be? After what happened to his mother! And then, living in that splendid shambles of a palazzo with his poor father and that ignorant, grasping old witch of a housekeeper.''

"No more, Elisabetta! This time, no more!" exclaimed her father. Vittorio Faziolini had had enough talk of Matteo Del Bosco. "With that moon, and the earth smelling so fresh, why talk of tragedy? We should appreciate that we Faziolinis and our guests are all whole and happy—or at least"—and he smiled suddenly at Johanna, who was resting her arm in the black sling on her lap—"*almost* whole. And certainly not tragic! *Vero?* True, Signora March?"

"True." Johanna smiled back. Yes, she was, despite the black sling, whole enough. As for tragedy, could that be, for the Faziolinis, waiting somewhere in the wings? Tonight, alone in the salon, where the photograph stood, perhaps she would know.

THE TROUBLE WAS, SHE WAS NOT ALONE. SHE DID NOT KNOW it at once, not within the first minutes after she quietly opened the double doors to the salon and closed them behind her. She had waited until long after midnight, sitting by the window in the southwest bedroom, drowsing, resting a cheek on the windowsill. The moon was hidden behind clouds that were edged with silvery brightness, and there was a cool breeze. She loved the coolness, the feel of the wind blowing softly across her forehead.

She wore a delicate, pale yellow silk nightgown that felt like flowing water against her bare skin; over it she had slipped on a wrapper of heavy, dark-gold satin, and she snugged it at her waist with its wide, darker gold sash. She had thought at first that she would not undress. But then she had decided that if she met anyone in one of the halls, it would be easier to say that she had found herself unable to sleep and had risen from bed to get a magazine or book from the salon. She had left the bedroom forgetting the black sling—then with a little shock had remembered. She had turned back, taken the sling from the bedside table, slipped it on, and adjusted it to cradle her bandaged wrist.

And now here she was at last. Someone had neglected to turn off the bracketed wall lights that flanked the floor-to-ceiling bookcase on the left of the fireplace. The lights cast a soft glow on the books and gleamed on the mellow, polished wood. It gave Johanna enough light to guide her to the table with its heavy glass lamp and the silver-framed photographs.

Finally. She switched on the lamp. She was reaching to pick up a photograph when from the corner of her eye she caught a glimpse of movement: Someone was sitting sunk deep into the couch beneath one of the wall-brackets that lit the books. For one frightened heartbeat of time, she thought with total irrationality: *The man from Florence, the man with the beard.*

An instant later, a baritone voice said: "You're a ghost? No, not a ghost. Ghosts don't wear negligees by—?" An amused voice, a familiar voice; her heartbeat slowed, steadied. Jeff Thornton. She let out a breath.

"Dior."

"And gown by?"

"Givenchy."

"Lucky people, aren't we, Johanna? Do you ever wonder what the poor people wear to bed?"

Maybe they wear what I wore to bed a month ago: an old cotton T-shirt and a pair of briefs. She said lightly, "I'm in my let-them-eat-cake mood tonight." She moved casually away from the table and came to stand beside the couch. She looked down at Jeff Thornton. His gray-green eyes met hers steadily, and there was a little quirk at the corner of his mouth. He wore slacks and a white shirt and navy coat sweater, and he sat with one leg crossed horizontally over a knee; he looked comfortably settled for at least a millennium.

She said, "I couldn't sleep. I thought I'd get something to read."

His steady gaze kept her eyes locked with his. "Something with pictures?" His tone was odd, something more than careless curiosity. It made her uneasy: Yesterday afternoon in the salon, had he noticed her interest in the photographs? Or was it something more, something different? Why in the salon had he watched her so closely? And the way he was looking at her now. Yes, with warmth, but with something else, something . . . there was no way he could have guessed about Dr. Rosella and the faked sprain. Unconsciously, she touched the black sling.

"Painful?" Thornton asked at once.

"A little." She felt the heat of a flush mounting to her forehead. She reached blindly to the bookcase and drew out a book. "And you? Couldn't you sleep either?"

"I'm cursed with insomnia. But it has its pleasures: when I can't sleep, I read." His eyelids flicked, but he still held her gaze. "You can learn a lot, Johanna, while others sleep." Now he looked away. He reached out and turned on a reading lamp beside the couch; the light shone downward on a closed book on his lap. He said comfortably, "It's so relaxing here— this salon was made for night reading."

Then why hadn't he turned on the light earlier? Why had he just been sitting there? Waiting for what? For whom? Surely not for . . . *her*? She felt suspended between pleasure and suspicion. *Damn* this man! She eyed the book on his lap. "What are you reading?"

"Ah . . ." he glanced down at the binding. *"La Cucina Italiana del Seicento Secolo."*

"Fascinating!" And with a triumphant feeling that she was getting back at him for something, she said with mocking disbelief, "So you're interested in Italian cooking of the fifteenth century?"

Jeff Thornton said blandly, "I deal in kitchenwares, remember? Who knows what remarkable designs of slotted spoons and soup ladles got lost in the fifteenth century that I could recreate in the twentieth? In aluminum. Or plastic."

She didn't believe it. She only sensed warily that he was

determined to outstay her in the salon. He had waited, sunk in the depths of the big couch, suspecting she would come; waiting and watching for a reason she could not possibly guess. Even now, even though she had discovered him, she felt that any step she took could lead her down a wrong road.

"And your book," Thornton said, "what's *your* selection?"

She looked down at the book in her hand. *Fecondazione Artificiale delle Vache* (Artificial Insemination of Cows). "The Life of Leonardo Da Vinci," she said. She clasped the book in her left hand, concealing the title, and turned away. "Goodnight," she said, and she went slowly, reluctantly, toward the double doors. She was exasperated at herself, because Jeff Thornton, who had unexpectedly become an obstacle, was also a strong reason for wanting to stay.

"Goodnight, Johanna." His voice from behind her was surprisingly serious.

Passing the table with the photographs, she hesitated. How simple, how natural, to pick up a photograph and turn back to Jeff Thornton, saying. "What an attractive family!" or "How charming, these children playing!" Or even, of a family group, "Which one is Alessandro?"

Yet she dared not; an indefinable feeling of danger kept her moving past the table to the door of the salon. It was as though she saw, superimposed on the door, the sodden body of the brutally murdered man the police had lifted from the Arno. Of course it had nothing to do with Jeff Thornton. Yet—yet she walked past the table without a glance at the photographs. She would wait until morning.

❖ 14 ❖

IN THE STABLE THAT SERVED AS THE FAZIOLINI'S GARAGE,
Giorgio awakened just before dawn in the front seat of the
Alfa Romeo. The car smelled of money: perfume and fine
leather and something like cedar wood, a rich smell. He sat
up, blinking, startled. He'd fallen asleep and slept all night
in the Alfa Romeo! His grandmother, Serafina—he hoped
she hadn't worried; sometimes she looked into his room at
night to be sure he was all right, as though evil spirits might
have thrown a blanket over his head and stolen him away.

He yawned. He put an appreciative hand on the suede-
covered steering wheel and looked at the jewel-like dash-
board and the elegant fittings and the gleaming hood. He'd
fallen in love with this car at first sight yesterday afternoon
when the dark-haired American had driven up in it, the pretty
girl beside him. One day he'd earn enough money to have a
convertible like this. He'd take Angela out in it, the top down
as it was now; he could see her long hair streaking back in
the wind, her face glowing. He smiled into the dimness of
the stable. There was a faint dust on the windshield, but that
added something thrilling. It was like the powdery film of
dust on the Madonna's face in the Church of Santa Maria
delle Grazie, in Treangoli, or the chaff from the hay caught
in Angela's hair, the fine hair above her brow; or the sweet
taste of her neck when the perspiration mingled with the dust
of the road, the dust that rose when her bicycle skidded after
it hadn't rained for days.

With both hands on the steering wheel, he stretched back,
yawning, arching his back the way he did in bed when he
woke up. As he relaxed again he saw a movement near the

86

stable door. Someone was coming in, blocking out the light as he entered. As the man advanced, Giorgio saw his muscular outline, the head set on the short, thick neck and the familiar, aggressive swagger. Sandro! Sandro Pavone! For a minute, Giorgio couldn't believe it. That thieving *bastardo*! That he should dare to come back here! He'd better not let Alessandro see him—Alessandro would kill him.

It seemed unbelievable that he, Giorgio, had felt a friendly sympathy for Sandro when he'd shown up at La Serena a year ago. Unbelievable! *Stupido!* Sandro had appeared one Sunday morning at the villa. He had explained that he was from the south, the Mezzogiorno near Naples. His family poor, he had come north by bus "to make his fortune." He knew something of mechanics, and he could do carpentry. Perhaps there was work at the villa? There was. There was a fixing of the tractor, the repairing of a milking machine, even some carpentry and plumbing in the villa itself. So Sandro came several times to La Serena. He also found enough work at Gordini's garage in Treangoli to scrape by, and Gordini let him stay in a room over the garage.

Then, eight months ago, when the Faziolinis were spending the winter in Rome, one night at La Serena while Serafina and old Luigi slept the villa had been looted. Fedele, Alessandro's beloved German shepherd watchdog, had not barked. Next morning, Luigi discovered why—he found Fedele's body bloated with poison near the chicken run. No one knew for a certainty that the dog-killer and thief had been Sandro Pavone. And Sandro was not there to be questioned. During the night he had disappeared from Treangoli.

And now here he was again, in the Faziolini's stable. He was heading for a corner of the stable, but he must have sensed Giorgio's presence. He turned his head on his thick neck and looked toward the gleaming little convertible. Then he came close, very close. He put his hands on his hips and stood grinning at Giorgio. "Hah! *Piccolo* Giorgio! Little Giorgio!" Giorgio saw once more the suggestive ugliness of Sandro's grin. "So, *piccolo* Giorgio, you have become rich and bought yourself an Alfa Romeo to impress the girls? Or—" and Sandro leaned forward suddenly and spat on the windshield—"you like the pretty American girl's car? You would like to marry the rich American girl?" He laughed; it was the remembered, sneering laugh.

In helpless anger, Giorgio looked at the spittle dripping down the windshield. How did Sandro even know that a rich American girl owned the Alfa Romeo? She had arrived at La Serena only yesterday afternoon, so how did he know? How? Sandro was grinning again. He had a dark face with big lips, and one side of his mouth curved upward like a red scar when he smiled. Giorgio thought how pityingly Sabina Faziolini had spoken to Vittorio about Sandro Pavone when he had come up from the dusty road that Sunday. "*Povero!* Poor fellow! Poverty, poverty in the Mezzogiorno! Hunger and rags. They always need help—money from the district, the government. Poverty is in the very bones of the south. And then fate piles on floods and earthquakes besides!"

But here in the stable, Giorgio saw that Sandro no longer suffered from poverty. He wore a black nylon jacket with a little orange fish-squiggle over the pocket. The squiggle meant it was from a Milan designer—Giorgio could not remember the name, but he had seen the jacket advertised in a magazine. "I'm only cleaning the car," Giorgio said. "Why did you come back? What do you want? You'd better be—"

"Want? Only something I left here in the stable!" Sandro still had that grin. "What should I want from the Faziolinis? You see?" Sandro raised both arms, elbows out, and slowly clawed back his reddish-black pompadour. A gold watch with little diamonds glittered on his wrist, and two thick gold rings one with an emerald, studded his hands.

"You see? I am returned from the south with a little *dote*—a dowry from my family. You don't believe it?" Sandro laughed again. He lowered his hands and shoved them into the slit pockets of his jacket. "But what *dote* is ever enough? So I now visit Treangoli to accomplish a little new business, a little golden business! Then I have *gli affari*, businesses, in Milan. A golden road! Once you find that road, *piccolo* Giorgio, you can buy yourself ten Alfa Romeos. Or a hundred!"

On that road, did you poison a dog! Giorgio wanted to

ask. But instead he stared at the spittle on the windshield. He was afraid of Sandro. The southern Italian carried a threat of violence in the very set of his shoulders; it was something Giorgio sensed. Maybe next year, when he himself was bigger, stronger . . . but by then Sandro Pavone would again be gone from Treangoli, far down his golden road. He watched Sandro turn away, still grinning, and climb the ladder to the loft where once or twice the southern Italian had stayed overnight.

Five minutes later he came down. At the bottom of the ladder he turned and looked over at Giorgio in the Alfa Romeo, and the side of his upper lip curved up in the sneering smile. ''They can't prove anything! They can't even touch me while I'm here in Treangoli!'' He walked toward the stable door. Beyond the doorway the gray of dawn was already brightening to pink; Pavone quickened his step.

With Pavone leaving, Giorgio felt bravery surging through his veins like fresh blood. ''You'd better get going before Alessandro gets back! When he buried Fedele—it was only Fedele he cared about! Not the money or the silver. Not even the paintings! Only Fedele!''

Sandro halted in the doorway. He turned, he jerked his head upward, and said contemptuously, ''Fedele! A dog is only a dog! In some countries they roast and eat their dogs! And I can tell you, Giorgio *piccolo*, there should have been more weighing on Alessandro Faziolini's mind than Fedele when he shoveled dirt over that animal! Oh yes, more on that signore's mind!'' And with another laugh Pavone was gone.

❖ 15 ❖

BY SEVEN O'CLOCK, THE COLD GRAY DAWN HAD CHANGED to morning sunlight. As the clock on the landing chimed seven-fifteen, Rosa, bringing Signor Faziolini's usual Saturday morning breakfast tray up the stairs to the salon, saw Signorina March in the upper hall approaching the salon's double doors, walking with hurried, soft steps. The American wore pants and wool jacket against the morning chill; it would be hours before the day's heat pervaded the stone villa.

"*Buon giorno!*" Rosa called out hastily. "*Aspetti! Aspetti!* Wait, Signorina! Do not enter!"

The American girl turned so quickly that Rosa was startled. And such a look on the signorina's face!—a flush like that of little Tomasino's when he was caught and guilty about something, as he so often was!

"*Mi, dispiace*, I'm sorry, Signorina, I didn't mean to startle you." Rosa came up the last few steps carrying the tray. It held on the pot of espresso and the two *biscotti*. "At ten o'clock I will bring up the Signore's *real* breakfast."

On Saturday the Signore always ate the same hearty breakfast: a thick slice of the ham that Luigi cured, and the omelette made with three eggs and parsley; and Serafina's fresh-baked *panini*, the two little rolls wrapped up in a napkin to keep them warm; and the sweet butter and the square of cheese. Signore Faziolini needed that solid breakfast; on Saturdays, he sat at the big desk in the salon, and as he himself said often, in that one morning he accomplished a week's work. There was no telephone in the salon; that was why, as the Signore always said, his work went faster even

90

than the *Coliseum*, the express train that ran between Rome and Florence.

"Every Saturday, at the big desk, Signorina," Rosa said, explaining all this to Johanna. "Is there something I—?" and Rosa looked questioningly at the American signorina.

"No, grazie." The young woman hesitated. "So, he, Signor Faziolini, that is—how efficient! The whole morning? He spends the whole morning working in the salon?"

"Until one o'clock, Signorina. If you would like to take breakfast with the others, it is served in the dining room at half past eight. But if you want breakfast now, Serafina, in the kitchen—"

"Thank you."

"Prego." Rosa balanced the tray on one palm, opened one of the double doors, went into the salon, and closed the door behind her.

Johanna stood a moment, then turned and went downstairs. In the kitchen she found Elisabetta at the table, heavy-eyed, sipping coffee. She wore pants, rough boots, and a worn flannel shirt. There were dark smudges under her eyes and her face had a white, strained look. Serafina was at the stove. "It's Tomasino," Elisabetta said wearily, in response to Johanna's questioning look. "His nightmares! Groaning and crying out. I wake him up, calm him down, and get him back to sleep. An hour later he's groaning and crying out again. The same nightmare! Poor baby!"

"About the kidnapping?" Johanna sat down. She felt as though she had known Elisabetta Faziolini forever, as though they had been, perhaps, close cousins brought up in the same household and had traded confidences since childhood. Elisabetta shook her head; her heavy-eyed, strained face looked puzzled.

"Not the kidnapping—or not exactly. Something *connected* to the kidnapping—I could swear it! But when I question him, he makes his eyes wide and looks around at the furniture, at the walls, at anything but me, as though he has gone deaf. So . . ." Elisabetta put up her hands and rubbed her eyes.

"Panini," Serafina said. She sat down a plate of rolls and poured coffee for Johanna.

"Grazie." Johanna stirred sugar into her coffee. "Alessandro—" she said to Elisabetta. "Has he—have you heard from him since last night?"

"No, nothing. Lucilla probably drowned all night in tears. That Alessandro could neglect . . . and he didn't even telephone! When he shows up tonight, her face will get stiff as a starched collar, she'll look at him with eyes like brown marbles. But inside, she'll be shattered. Lucilla is so easily shattered! She's very sensitive, you know, she's a poet—she has won prizes. But she puts on an iron face. As though we Faziolinis don't know what's inside Lucilla!"

Elisabetta took a final sip of coffee. "When you've finished breakfast, will you come up to the attic? There's something I've got to do there, but we can chat. You go up the back stairs at the end of the loggia—Rosa will show you the way. You'll come?"

"Yes, yes, thanks." Six hours to go; it would be one o'clock before she could get into the salon.

When Elisabetta had gone, Johanna ate the omelette and rolls, wondering if Jeff Thornton had stayed all night in the salon. Or, once he'd driven her away had he gone off to bed? *I am getting a feverish imagination*, she told herself. Jeff Thornton is interested in cooking and kitchenware and sometimes he cannot sleep. That is all.

In the attic she found Elisabetta pulling a mass of ivory, satin, silk, and lace from a trunk. "Our heirloom wedding dress," Elisabetta said over her shoulder. "I have to take it to Treangoli *absolutely* this morning and send it off to Trieste. It has to be refitted, my mother's grandniece will be married in it three weeks from Sunday, just as I was married in it, and Lucilla, and my mother, and *her* mother.

"I was married in Rome, a splendid ball afterward at the palazzo—*magnifico*! But Lucilla! She's so frightfully shy, *pathologically* shy! She shrank from a big wedding in Rome. She and Alessandro were married very simply at La Serena. Later the wedding gown was packed away up here. A country wedding! It was summer, everything blooming, we had the field mowed and a striped tent set up and Luigi smoked three dozen geese and four hams. My mother's family sent *cases* of spumonti . . . Anyway,'' and Elisabetta laughed, ''Lucilla, poor thing, was so in love with Alessandro she would have suffered through a dozen weddings to marry him!''

''Poor thing? Why?''

''Did I say that?'' Elisabetta seemed surprised; she frowned. ''We're distant cousins. Lucilla spent summers at La Serena since she was a little girl. Poor thing? I guess I always thought of her as 'the orphan'—such a pale-faced little girl with brown shadows under her eyes! Not exactly an *ugly* child, just, well, unfortunate-looking.

''But she's talented, too. Here at La Serena she's turned the baby's nursery into a study. She closes herself in and writes poetry. Sometimes one of the little poetry magazines publishes a poem of hers. She already has a small reputation with that coterie; it is something, it helps to make up for— you know, the baby.

''But I *wish* she wouldn't wear those dreary earth-colored clothes! Like muddy roads. So depressing, so—oh, look! Here's a snapshot I took of Lucilla being fitted for the wedding dress. Nine years ago—no, ten. It was downstairs in the dining room. The seamstress, a girl from Treangoli, is pinning up the hem, you see?'' Elisabetta handed Johanna the snapshot. ''But she pinned it all uneven, *yards* of it, it had to be ripped out and done over. Signora Gamba, the seamstress from Treangoli, couldn't come, she was ill, but she'd spoken so well of this young woman's work. Odd, what a botch the girl made of it! Oh, well.''

Johanna gazed down at the photograph. The seamstress was on her knees, pinning the hem; she had turned her head and was looking up and away to the side. Her uplifted face, framed by her dark hair, sent a shiver down Johanna's back. It was a face she had seen only two days ago in Florence. It was the face of Teresa Mantello.

Or was it only a young woman who resembled Teresa Mantello? Johanna gazed searchingly at the snapshot. That delicately shaped face, the way the young woman's dark hair waved against her brow. A resemblance only?

"What's her name—the seamstress?"

Elisabetta said, surprised, "What a funny thing to ask! I don't remember."

"Oh." Johanna handed the snapshot back to Elisabetta. "What's she looking at? She looks so *startled*."

Elisabetta laughed. "You *are* a funny one! You ask questions like a journalist. Or a detective in a *giallo*, a detective story." She gazed at the snapshot, head tipped to one side, lips pursed, thinking back. "I . . . let's see . . . Yes, from that angle she'd be looking toward the door. I remember! Alessandro was just coming in. It must have startled her, she probably didn't know who he was."

"Oh." It seemed to Johanna, and she was never later able to explain it, that she heard a strain of music from somewhere under the eaves of the attic; a sad, thrilling, throbbing of notes. But of course it could only have been in her head, some private response to the words she had just heard.

On the way down from the attic, on Elisabetta's heels, she thought, *Has the murder in Florence distorted my perspective?* Maybe it was only her excited fancy that made this seamstress from Treangoli resemble Teresa Mantello. But if it *wasn't* just a resemblance, what might it mean—not just to her, but to Inspector Grippo in Florence?

It would have to mean something. She was sure of that. What, she could not guess. But she had to find out. *She had to.*

"Elisabetta?" she said, still on the stairs; and when Elisabetta cocked her head she said, "I have to go to Treangoli this morning—I've got to see Dr. Rosella about my wrist. It just doesn't feel right—perhaps an X-ray . . . I'll be glad to drop off the wedding dress at the post office for you."

❖ 16 ❖

AT NINE-THIRTY THAT MORNING, PEPPINO BRACCIA, WHO
had gone upstairs to the bedroom over the trattoria to awaken
Luisa, heard the rattle of Luigi's truck. This was the day that
old Luigi came to Treangoli for sacks of flour for La Serena.
Peppino went to the window. Behind him Luisa was still
snoring; she had returned from Arcidosso wearing green nail
polish like her sister. Luisa had no mind of her own; her
sister ran her. But she had also brought from Arcidosso a
new slicing machine on her sister's advice. The machine
could slice paper-thin prociutto; it would save money for the
trattoria.

Peppino rested his hands on the windowsill and looked
out. Luigi was stopping the truck in front of the post office
across the road; a young woman was climbing down. It was
the signorina from yesterday, the American. Her brown-gold
hair was ruffled. She wore a tan shirt and a brown skirt and
of course the black sling from Dr. Rosella. She had on san-
dals and was barelegged. Luigi handed down a parcel to the
girl and drove off. At the door of the post office, the girl put
down the bundle, turned the handle of the door with her good
hand, and pushed. Then she pushed harder.

Abbandonarlo, quit trying, Peppino thought. The post office wouldn't open until ten o'clock. You'll have a fine wait,
Signorina March. He shook his head, then grinned in sympathy when he saw the American girl kick the door in frustration, then rub her pained sandaled foot on the back of her
calf. But within seconds, the girl headed across the street to
the trattoria. Immediately, Peppino was down the stairs and
unlocking the door. So what if the trattoria didn't open until

one o'clock? He could give a foreigner an espresso at least; such actions promoted good relationships between countries, *vero*?

"I saw you at the post office, it opens at ten o'clock," he told the young woman when she came in. He stood at the bar to drink his coffee, and the American girl sat at the table, the big parcel on the chair across from her. She had barely taken two sips when she announced that she needed a seamstress to mend something. "I'm told there's a very good seamstress here in Treangoli, a Signora Gamba?"

"Signora Gamba, *si*." Peppino was surprised. Who could have told the American girl such a thing? Signora Gamba's good days were over, everyone in the village knew that. Signora Gamba had stopped sewing three, four years ago. Something with her eyes, even with glasses, she—

"Can you tell me where she lives?"

"*Mah! Certo!*" The American's question amused him. Everyone in Treangoli knew everyone else and where they lived, and even their supposed secrets. He himself even knew the names of Signora Gamba's two elderly dogs and how many rabbit hutches she had—eight—and how rusty the chicken wire was across her front gate. He knew that Signora Gamba went to early Mass every morning and how stories poured out of her about the "good" days when she had bright eyes, sharp as her needles.

Perhaps her old eyes were still sharper than he knew, Peppino thought. Perhaps old Signora Gamba could still make a few thousand lire from this young American—this *rich* young American, he amended, looking at the flat, oval-shaped gold watch the girl was wearing and the remarkable way it curved to fit her narrow wrist; it was as though it had been melted to fit, he had never seen one like it even in advertisements, it must have cost . . .

"Then if you could direct me?"

"*Certo.*" He gave her the simple directions. When she had paid and left, he watched her start down the road, her brown skirt swinging against her bare legs—such shapely, tanned legs. A pretty sight. But . . .

"Signorina!" he called after her; and when she turned, "Signorina, the post office is already open. Your package."

"Oh, si." The American girl looked down at the package under her arm as surprised as though she had never seen it before. *"Grazie!"* Even from where he stood Peppino could see the young woman blush. She turned back, crossed the road, and went into the post office.

Peppino leaned against the door jamb and contemplated the sun on the road. A man had to accept that the heads of womenfolk were on upside down. How could the American signorina be so eager to have Signora Gamba mend something for her as to forget to mail that important-looking package? Men were different, *Grazia di Dio*! They did everything one-two-three. That tall American signore, Signor Thornton, for instance.

Yesterday evening, around six o'clock, Thornton had appeared again in Trengoli, this time alone in the Alfa Romeo. He had stopped the car in front of Dr. Rosella's office, which was really Rosella's house. In a half-dozen long strides he was in Rosella's door and in twenty minutes was out again, had jumped into the Alfa Romeo, and—zoom!—nothing but dust behind him. One-two-three, straight as an arrow, no straying from his aim, whatever it was.

Peppino was still gazing at the sunlit road when he became conscious of the *ping, pong, ping* of money dropping into the telephone in the booth across the road, next to the post office. The day had already turned hot and the caller had left the door to the booth open. Peppino squinted across the road. He could see a man in the booth, then the man turned his head and Peppino got a little shock: It was that *porco*, that pig from the Mezzogiorno, Sandro Pavone, the one they said had robbed the Faziolinis! There was no proof that he was the one, at least not yet, but the bastard was taking a risk coming back to Treangoli.

So what had brought him back? Why was he here, to do what? Up to what? "For a thousand lire, he'd cut your throat," Elvio Gordini had said when Pavone had disappeared after the Faziolini robbery. Elvio had regretted hiring Sandro Pavone to work in the garage; there had been the incident of the tourist and the heavy wrench. But Elvio was small and timid, with a nervous stomach. So he was happy when Pavone disappeared. *Ping, pong, ping*. The line must have been busy, or maybe Pavone was calling a second number.

Peppino was still standing in the doorway when the American signorina came out of the post office. She flicked her fingers at him in acknowledgement, nodded, and started off again. He watched her walk past Dr. Rosella's office without a glance and continue down the road until she reached Benucci's on the edge of the woods. Signora Gamba's house was tucked behind Benucci's; Benucci collected feathers and sold them in bulk for pillows. Signora Gamba lived with the smell of the feathers and the smell of the rabbits from her hutches.

Rabbits had become her livelihood: A truck once a week arrived in Treangoli to pick up crates of Signora Gamba's rabbits and take them to three or four restaurants in Bologna where the chefs were known for their exceptionally tasty *pappardelle con la lepre*—spiced hare with broad noodles. It was said that the real reason for the delicious dish was a secret blend of vegetables Signora Gamba fed her rabbits that gave the flesh a sweeter taste.

Ah! The American girl was turning in and starting up the weedy path that led behind Benucci's.

Satisfied, Peppino went back inside; he had wasted enough time. He went through the bar and into the kitchen and began to unpack the slicing machine Luisa had brought from Arcidosso.

❖ 17 ❖

"EH! EH! STAYING AT LA SERENA, ARE YOU, SIGNORINA? A beautiful old villa, but for fifty years a ruin, the walls fallen down, the garden a tumble of stones and pieces of statues— broken arms and legs. And the ivy! I used to play there as a child, the ivy was thick as a man's forearm, it could strangle you. But then the Faziolinis bought the villa, they hired workmen, strong men from Treangoli. They had old drawings of the villa before the Baron's line died out—they did well, the Faziolinis. For already thirty years now, they come to Treangoli. Signor Vittorio Faziolini still loves to hunt. Ah, this beautiful nightgown! *Peccato!* Too bad, the way it is torn. *Squisito, delicato,* like a moth's wing. And it is new! *Peccato!* How did—"

"My own fault! I was hurrying," Johanna said apologetically. "I was late, it caught on the handle of the bathroom door. I yanked it." Johanna sighed philosophically. She felt overwhelmed by the voluble Signora Gamba. She sat in Signora Gamba's living room in an overstuffed chair with a broken spring digging into her thigh. On the wall across the room, a framed picture of Christ in a flowing blue robe gazed down at her with tender, loving sympathy. Signora Gamba's living room had another overstuffed chair, a worn couch, and a veneer sideboard that held a tin teapot and a television set. There were a couple of straight-backed chairs and a round dining room table covered with a yellow oilcloth.

Signora Gamba sat at the table, her fingers caressing the torn Givenchy nightgown that lay on the oilcloth. "You see, Signorina, how the skin of my fingers snags the delicate silk? I have rough hands now, I feed rabbits, I clean hutches. In the old days when I sewed, I put chicken fat on my hands morning and night. They were soft, my nails were oval, the edges were smooth as peeled almonds. *Mi dispiace*, I am sorry, Signorina. And my eyes—it has been years."

Signora Gamba folded the Givenchy gown and pushed it away. "My eyes." She tapped the sides of her face above her cheekbones. She was a thin woman in her eighties, with gray hair up in a knot. Her face was long and shrewd and the whites of her brown eyes were stained yellow. She wore a short-sleeved housedress and her skinny arms had a wiry, outdoor look. A pair of thick-lensed glasses lay on the oil-cloth, one side of the frame tied with a piece of string.

"Oh yes, those years!" Smiling, she fingered the eye-glasses. "Once I made a nightgown for the Duchess of Gonzaga in Orvieto. Sixty miles away! They could have sent to Venezia! Even to Roma, Milano. But no, they sent for me! And once . . ." Fingering her eyeglasses, Signora Gamba slid into the past, reminiscing, recalling one triumph after another. She had the kind of voice, thought Johanna, peculiar to so many Italian women. It had a roughness but with an undertone of something romantic in it; it made Johanna think of a coarse cloth through which ran a gold thread. She listened—nodding, murmuring, exclaiming. A fly buzzed in and out of the room; the clock ticked. Almost eleven o'clock!

"You must have had many trained assistants, Signora Gamba, apprentices—so much to do!"

"*Si! Si!* So much to do! I chose young girls, girls from Treangoli, but only the ones with clever hands. I picked only girls who had the gift, I . . ."

"At the time of the wedding of Alessandro Faziolini to his cousin Lucilla, you were ill, you couldn't come, you sent a young woman instead."

Signora Gamba looked up at the ceiling. The hand finger-ing the eyeglasses on the oilcloth became still. Then she picked up a fly swatter, swatted at a fly, and missed. "So many flies still, this time of year!"

She looked at Johanna. "They spoke of it?" She looked away—at the television set, the blue-robed Christ, the worn couch. "*Si*, the Costa girl. Such hands! She sewed like an angel, each stitch. A romantic young girl, she looked out at the world through a clean window-pane, through the window she saw birds and love and music."

"Costa?" Johanna said. "Her name was Costa?"

Signora Gamba did not seem to hear; she was lost in another time, lost in that April wedding years ago, the gold thread in her rough voice somehow heavier. "That hem, it was not the girl's fault. Did the hem wrong? Yes, she made a *farragine*, a mess of it. That was because she looked through that clean windowpane. And she became all thumbs. She lost her head. I don't know what happened."

I do, Johanna thought. She saw the young seamstress on her knees, head bent, pinning up the bride's hem, saw the door open and the bridegroom-to-be, Alessandro Faziolini, appear; saw the young seamstress look up. And then—the French call it a *coup de foudre*, the Italians call it a *colpo di tuono*: the thunderclap, falling in love at one blow!

She became aware that Signora Gamba was watching her; something alert in the old woman's expression made Johanna think: *She knows*. Or at least suspects what struck the young girl so that she made the hem uneven.

Johanna said: "And this seamstress, this Signorina Costa, did she—"

"*Scusi*, excuse me, Signorina, but she was not a Signorina. She was a *Signora*. She was a very new young widow, nineteen and childless. Her husband had a few weeks before been killed in an accident on a reaping machine. A terrible tragedy! Especially as the young widow was already pregnant."

Signora Gamba cast Johanna a sidewise look. "I had always a tenderness for the Costa girl, I had known her since she was a baby pulling in a cart, then when she was four or five, riding on her father's lap on the Costa's tractor. Frightening to be a widow and pregnant! The whole village was sad for her. She was five months pregnant when she and her mother packed up and went to live in Florence. Her baby was born there. I sent a little jacket that I made myself. Did you know it is more difficult to sew clothes for babies than for grown people? So many little turns because of the tiny

armholes and sleeves and the little collars and buttonholes!
It makes the fingers ache.''

Signora Gamba reached out and caressed the filmy nightgown on the table. ''Such a pretty gown, the color of hyacinths—a blue the French like to claim.'' She ran the flat of
her fingertips gently across the tear; then she tipped her head
and once again, slowly, slowly, slid her fingertips across the
tear. ''*Ahhh!* This kind of rip . . .'' and she looked vaguely
across at Johanna with a half-smile. ''*Peccato* that there is
no seamstress in Treangoli who can mend this properly.''

''Thank you, anyway.''

At the table, Johanna wrapped the filmy nightgown again
in its folds of tissue paper and dropped it into her Fendi bag.
''I'll have it fixed when I return to Florence in a day or so.
Perhaps if the Costa girl is still a seamstress? And in Florence? What is her married name?''

''Teresa's? Signora Mantello.''

❖ **18** ❖

IN THE TRUCK BESIDE LUIGI RETURNING TO LA SERENA, SHE
gazed at the countryside through a veil of bewilderment. At
first, she could not think at all: It was as though Signora
Gamba's confirmation that the seamstress from Treangoli was
Teresa Mantello had frozen her thoughts. Beyond that, she
only felt an unavoidable apprehension. It was as though she
had opened a drawer and caught a glimpse of what was inside
and was now unable to close the drawer.

''*Veda, Signorina—olivéti.* '' Luigi was pointing to the left:
olive groves.

She turned her head. ''*Si.* '' She spoke mechanically, but

hearing her own voice seemed at last to release her frozen mind.

So! Look what she had done! She had come to the Faziolinis' villa, lying to Jeff Thornton, faking a sprained wrist, come with that crazy, stupid need to reassure herself that the murdered Botto was certainly not Jeff Thornton's friend, Alessandro. She had only wanted to see a living, breathing Alessandro; she had only wanted to reassure herself that no one else had a moral claim on her Totocalcio money.

Instead, she had stumbled on a link between Alessandro Faziolini and Luciano Botto; the link of Teresa Mantello. What could it mean? Coincidence? Of course not! She didn't believe in coincidences.

That meant that even if this evening Alessandro Faziolini turned up safe and sound, the mysterious link between him and the murdered Botto would nevertheless still exist. That link, through Teresa Mantello, could be related to the murder of Luciano Botto. Could be? *Had to be!* Why fool herself?

I am wandering down a strange path, Johanna thought. But on that path she might find some crumb to bring to Inspector Grippo in Florence, a crumb that would reveal the murderer of Luciano Botto, whoever Luciano Botto really was. She pictured herself standing confidently in Inspector Grippo's office in the Questura in Florence and turning to a dark figure in a brimmed hat that concealed his face. With an *"Ecco!* Here!'' she imagined herself dramatically snatching off the man's hat to reveal the face of the murderer.

Johanna March, girl heroine.

"Eccola. There it is—La Serena.'' Luigi nodded with satisfaction toward the villa in the distance. *"Una bella villa, si?''*

"Si. '' But she did not look. Instead, she looked at her watch. The first thing she had to settle could be settled in the next few minutes; she didn't even have to wait for Lucilla's birthday dinner. It was five minutes to one.

Vittorio Faziolini would already be getting up from his desk in the salon.

❖ 19 ❖

AT ONE-THIRTY, VITTORIO FAZIOLINI CAME OUT ONTO THE terrace for the buffet lunch, washed and combed and with his white mustache freshly waxed to satisfactory saber-points. Matteo, Jeff Thornton, and the others were all there on the sun-splashed terrace—all, that is, except for the American girl, Miss March.

"Caro!" Sabina called to him, "have you seen Miss March?"

In fact he had. He'd forgotten his favorite pen on the desk in the salon, he'd gone back for it, and there she was, standing at the table with its burden of family photographs. She was holding one of the framed pictures, the one of his parents: his father in a stiff collar, his mother in velvet and a plumed hat. When he came in, she put down the silver-framed picture and said in what under other circumstances he would have considered a despairing voice: "Which of these are of Alessandro? I've been wondering about Jeff's old friend, what he looks like!"

"Alessandro?" Approaching the table, he pointed to one, then another, then another of the photographs. "Those three. They're just snapshots, it's not easy to make out what he is like."

Miss March had looked at the fuzzy, amateurishly-taken pictures of young people playing tennis, sitting on the beach and waving at the camera, even playing croquet. Their faces were indistinct, they could have been anybody. "That's Alessandro, there," Vittorio said. The boy was in the far court, his racquet raised, serving, squinting in the sun, and he'd been about fourteen then. "We're not a picture-taking family," he added apologetically. He genuinely wished there were better photographs; he liked this girl and her sincere interest.

"I see." Her voice was uneven; a touch of—hysteria? Was she still in shock from the accident with her wrist?

"I've been to Treangoli," the young woman said. "I'll just run up and change."

And now here she was, coming out onto the terrace. Vittorio noticed how Matteo and Jeff Thornton lifted their heads and turned from the buffet table. Miss March had changed into loose gray pants and a white cotton shirt; the morning sun had burnished her face with color and turned her heavy eyebrows even more golden. Matteo was instantly at her side to help her at the buffet table—explaining, gesturing. Vittorio could tell that Matteo was attracted to the girl; he had seen enough of Matteo around women to recognize the signs. Now the girl was filling her plate, with her pretty, triangular face tipped down. She was wearing little dangling gold earrings and they swung forward across her cheeks. But if there was one thing Vittorio could recognize, with his years in athletics and the business of sports, it was tension in the back and shoulders. And the girl's white shirt did not conceal it, not from Vittorio Faziolini.

He filled his own plate and went to sit at the glass table beside Sabina. The twins were wandering around the terrace, eating nothing, as usual. They wore blue shorts and jerseys and looked like skinny little poverty-stricken children with their big eyes and chicken-thin necks.

Felicia sometimes trailed after Tomasino, sometimes not. When Miss March sat down beside Jeff Thornton, Felicia came up to her and leaned an elbow on the glass table. Looking up into Miss March's face, she began her story, the kidnapping story. Felicia always told it exactly the same way, speaking in that high, mechanical falsetto that she had brought home in her head after being rescued.

The kidnapping story would just pop out of Felicia at odd moments. It was disconnected, bits about how one morning "the cloth on my eyes slipped . . . I saw a little room and an old woman," and "My head itched," and how "you can't peel an orange with your hands tied, *vero*?" And the part about the radio and the earphones: "Even when you sleep there is the radio and the earphones, that's why your hands are tied."

It was strange and horrifying. Elisabetta, seated across the table, explained about it to Johanna after Felicia had wandered off again, but not before the American girl had suddenly, passionately clasped Felicia to her. "The psychiatrist said it will stop. 'Don't stop her,' he warned us. 'She is saying it like an incantation, to ward off a danger. It's a protection against something. It helps her to tell it and tell it.' " Elisabetta's eyes were full of tears. "He says that later we shall see. But he says, 'Wait. Wait, for now.' "

"And the voice?" asked Thornton from beside Johanna. "That high voice?"

"Yes, the voice of the kidnapper. He had a—as Tomasino described it, 'a high, funny voice.' Really, a falsetto."

"Falsetto." Jeff Thornton repeated. "That's from the Italian word, *falso*, isn't it? Meaning false?"

So it was, Vittorio thought. *Falso*, meaning high, false, artificial. *Falsetto, falso*: The kidnapper's high voice was false.

Vittorio got up and went to get dessert for himself and Sabina: amaretto cookies and ice cream. On the way back, he noticed how anxiously Sabina was looking toward the door to the terrace. Of course! He knew at once, and he looked around. No Lucilla. She had not come down to lunch. She was unhappy that Alessandro had not yet shown up. She was up there in her study, with the door closed, smoking her brown cigarettes and working on her poems, or perhaps reading. Or was she lying on the bed, crying?

Vittorio gave an exclamation of exasperation: If Alessandro was held up a day, he could have at least telephoned! He'd last called about a week ago—yes, Friday around noon, from one of those villas, he'd said. Ah, well. Tonight he'd surely bring Lucilla an especially fine birthday present to make up for everything. And Serafina was baking a birthday cake for Lucilla. Thirty-five candles. Lucilla was two years older than Alessandro.

Vittorio reached his anxious wife and sat down beside her again. Ah, Sabina, his dear Sabina, who always ached for others! She took in stray people the way she took in stray cats and dogs. She had taken in the lonely little Lucilla, and later on the young Matteo. It was because she had always wanted a lot of children, a big family; but after Alessandro's birth, she hadn't been able to have any more.

Minutes later, sipping his espresso, Vittorio noticed that the twins had disappeared.

He hoped they hadn't again gone into the woods. It was strictly forbidden. But yesterday from the loggia, he had seen them skirt the field, staying close to the stone wall, and slip into the trees. Also worrisome was his discovery that the twins took things. Serafina had complained that she'd found her string for rolling the veal missing, then it had reappeared. Then she had caught Tomasino "borrowing" a knife, one of the sharp ones with a serrated edge. "Only to cut some paper upstairs," he had apologized to Serafina. And she had let him borrow it. But you don't use a sharp knife to cut paper. You use a scissors.

❖ 20 ❖

IT WAS FOUR O'CLOCK WHEN JOHANNA ENTERED THE GRImini woods. She had knotted the boy's sweater around her neck and wore Elisabetta's older son's hiking shoes. "I just want some exercise," she had said to Elisabetta, who had answered, "I don't blame you for wanting to be alone. La Serena is sometimes about as serene as a zoo before feeding time."

But it wasn't wanting to be alone. She wanted to breathe a peaceful atmosphere: the green smell of ferns, of woods, the faint scent of pine and wood smoke from somewhere; even the rank smell of bogs left from a rainfall.

She walked among the trees. The late afternoon sunlight was thin, pale gold; it dappled the rocks and ferns. She went deeper into the woods. She drew in grateful breaths of air. She would not even think about Alessandro Faziolini or tonight's birthday dinner for Lucilla. She would not worry that because a young seamstress years before had botched a hem she was faced with a further complication. It was all strange; strange and . . .

Dangerous? Jeff Thornton apparently thought so. Otherwise, why his warning? Why his stopping her on the stairs when she returned from Treangoli? She had been on her way upstairs, he coming down. He had grasped her shoulder. "Johanna!" That hard, firm grip. "Tell me," he said searchingly, "do the police in Florence know you're here?" She had been too surprised to answer, she had merely looked at him. At that, he had impatiently given her a little shake. "Johanna! Damn it!"

"The police? In Florence? I don't think so, I didn't tell . . ."

"All right," Thornton said, but he still gripped her shoulder. It was painful, but she had a feeling he was unaware of how tightly he grasped her. He went on, snapping out the words: "You must have left word at the Pensione Boldini, though. You told them where you were going?"

She only stared at him. What was he getting at? He scrutinized her face, then he gave a half-laughing little sigh. He shook his head, he released her arm.

"What is it?" she asked him then. He didn't answer right away, he just stood looking down at her, gnawing the inside of his cheek.

"A bit of advice for you, Johanna. It can be dangerous to become too involved with—what shall I say?—the underbelly of society. Better to steer clear. The risks are too high. Christ, Johanna!" He was snapping out the words again. "You can get shot. Strangled. *Drowned.* " He looked down at the black sling that held her wrist. He reached out and ran his fingers along the black cotton from elbow to wrist. "Those are the facts, Johanna." Then he shoved his hands into his pockets, turned, and was off down the stairs in his loose-limbed way before she could say, *What? What are you talking about?*

She had not seen him since, except briefly on the terrace at lunch. She had wanted to ask him then, too, what he had meant. *What are you warning me of? Not to meddle?* But what could he know of it? Nothing. Nothing at all. And anyway, she hadn't had a chance—he had disappeared without bothering with dessert. Now she knew she would not ask.

She walked on through the woods. The trees were thicker here, but there were occasional sunny clearings. She walked up brambly little hills and down the other side; she crossed a stone culvert over a stream that trickled among rocks. Her watch showed four-thirty, and it was turning cloudy and damp. She would turn back.

It was then that she heard the music.

She stopped. She was standing among trees on the slope of a small hill. The music was harsh rock music, but played low; it was coming from below. She took a few steps forward and looked down the slope.

The twins.

She could see them through the trees. Felicia sat on the ground. Her hands were tied and rested in her lap. Tomasino was bending over her, he was pulling a blindfold from her eyes. Abruptly, the music gave way to a shampoo commercial. A radio! Tomasino snapped off the radio. He began to untie Felicia's hands.

At that moment, Johanna realized she was not the only watcher. On the slope across, beside a tree and a little below her, was a hunter in a soft-brimmed hunting hat. He was holding his rifle in the crook of his arm. If he were to look across the little decline, he could easily see her in her white shirt; she was not hidden at all. But he was intent on the children. Now he shifted; she fancied he was moving the rifle. What if he were to raise it, what if—

"Renzo!"

The deep-voiced, hearty shout came from behind her. Vittorio! Vittorio Faziolini! She let out a breath. A moment later, Vittorio was beside her; Matteo was with him, both men carrying rifles.

"Renzo!" Vittorio waved again. "Up here!"

The man in the hunter's hat raised his head; in a moment he waved back. "*Saluto!* Hello!" He moved down the slope, and Vittorio and Matteo, with Johanna between them, went down to him. They met only a few feet from where Felicia and Tomasino had been. But the children were not there now. The ferns beside the tree where Felicia had sat were crushed; that was all.

"Renzo Grimini." Vittorio performed the introduction. "Our nearest neighbor."

"And these are his woods," Matteo added, "the Grimini woods that we regularly invade for game!"

"No one could be more welcome," Renzo Grimini said. He had a deep, brooding voice and an unsmiling look to his face. It was a dark and elegant face, with deep-set eyes, an aquiline nose, and a beautifully trimmed, chestnut-colored beard. He was possibly in his forties, lean, and just over medium height. He had noticeably big hands.

"So!" Matteo looked at Renzo Grimini's rifle and raised his brows. "You're hunting again! After all these years!"

Renzo Grimini put one big hand on the rifle that lay in the crook of his arm. "I thought it about time." He paused; then said in his deep voice: "I slay my dragons slowly. But one by one."

"*Bravo*, Renzo!" Vittorio said with hearty sympathy. "You're right to get over it! It was an accident after all. Alessandro himself never held it against you. Only you, *you* held it against yourself!"

"*Forse*—perhaps."

Vittorio, smoothing his white mustache, said how delighted he was to see Renzo Grimini. "I didn't know you were back!" It appeared that Renzo was an art gallery owner in Rome, and he had been in Paris for the last two weeks, bidding on new acquisitions.

"You'll come back to La Serena with us, yes? I have some

early drawings, charcoals, by di Chirico, just arrived, and I'd like your opinion. I bought them this summer since the robbery left the villa walls bare.''

''*Certo.*''

Renzo was looking at the black sling on Johanna's arm; then his gaze flickered to the flattened ferns beside the tree and back to Vittorio. ''And Elisabetta, how is she? She is getting over—?''

''*Mah!* Elisabetta is getting back to herself. You'll see!''

Johanna sank down on the ground, folding her legs under her. ''You go ahead, I want to stay here a while, the woods are so lovely.''

Vittorio looked around at the golden light filtering down through the trees. ''Especially at this hour.''

When the three men had gone she got up. She had glimpsed a spot of white just around the bole of the tree where Felicia had sat. The others couldn't have seen it because they were too far to the left.

In a minute she held it in her hand. But it was nothing, only a man's handkerchief; the handkerchief Tomasino must have used to blindfold Felicia. In their alarm, the twins had fled without it.

She flicked it out and looked at the monogram: *A.F.*

❖ 21 ❖

GIORGIO FELT A BLOODY MESS BY THE TIME HE GOT THE baby lamb free from the barbed wire, the poor little thing bleating in fright. And no sooner had he gotten it safely back in the pen and come into the kitchen and collapsed into a chair at the kitchen table, than Serafina had told him to scrub his fingernails and put on a freshly washed shirt and pants and take a tray with Campari and soda into the little study. Signor Grimini was in there with Signor Faziolini and Matteo.

When he came into the study, Signor Faziolini was closing a leather portfolio and tying it with a string and thanking Renzo Grimini.

"Niente affatto!" Signor Grimini said. A rare smile flashed across his dark and elegant face. He was in hunting clothes and standing in that erect, proud way he had, like a duke or a prince. His chestnut-colored hair was graying, but not his beard. When Giorgio approached him with the tray, it seemed to him that Signor Grimini had an intense, waiting look, and for a moment he seemed to look right through Giorgio. Then with a start, he acknowledged him, gave him a *Buon giorno*, and asked after Angela. Giorgio blushed a little and was pleased. Signor Grimini was a gentleman, no matter how suspiciously they viewed him in Treangoli.

"Strano!" they said, that he refused to have a gardener, so that La Raccòlta was overgrown, weedy, wild. Especially since he was rich! Years before, when La Raccòlta had come into his hands through the death of an elderly relative, it had been in disrepair. Signor Grimini had left it that way. *Strano* too that he spent weeks at a time at La Raccòlta, when he didn't even hunt! And that the only family he visited was the Faziolinis.

Giorgio watched Signor Grimini's elegant hand lift the glass of Campari from the tray. He couldn't help being curious about the man. He'd heard the gossip about how Signor Grimini and his wife in Rome went their separate ways. And in *Oggi* and other picture magazines he'd seen photographs of Renzo Grimini with this or that beautiful woman with whom he was having a love affair; they were pictures usually snapped at glamorous parties or art shows.

Giorgio was cutting up a lemon and Matteo was pouring himself a Campari when Elisabetta came into the study. "Renzo! So you're back!" Elisabetta's voice was an icicle. She stopped just inside the doorway, as though she'd run into a wall.

Vittorio said, "Yes, we see Renzo too seldom. But he's coming to Lucilla's birthday dinner."

"How nice." Elisabetta raised her eyebrows at Signor Grimini. "So! You've had another successful trip? How clever you are, Renzo!" She walked toward him. "So clever! You disappear and consummate one of your mysterious deals and return richer than ever!" Her voice was mocking: "Where are you back from this time? Did you find a priceless Bruegel in the attic of an old Flemish farmhouse? Or maybe an undiscovered Picasso in a Spanish *bodega*?"

Giorgio held the knife suspended over the lemon, looking from Elisabetta to Signor Grimini. He was astonished. He had never before heard Signora Ligouri speak so coldly, so mockingly; it was not like her. Elisabetta was standing and hotly emotional in the air. Elisabetta was standing close to Signor Grimini. She had tilted up her freckled face, as though presenting her jaw for a blow, daring him. Grimini, his deep-set eyes on Elisabetta, looked *furioso*.

"Making a mysterious deal? *Mah!* Certo! But unfortunately nothing I can discuss." Signor Grimini bowed a stiff little bow as though his back were made of wood. Just an inch more, thought Giorgio, and he might have splintered.

Elisabetta stood a moment longer looking at Signor Grimini. Then she turned to her father and said she was looking for Miss March. "If she comes in, will you tell her I'm in my room?"

Before she left, she smiled over at Giorgio, acknowledging him as she always did. Next to Angela, who was seventeen, Giorgio liked Elisabetta Ligouri, who was forty and kind to him. Also, she made him think of the refreshingly cold, clear pebbly brook in the neighboring Grimini woods. Since the kidnapping, there was a different look in Signora Elisabetta Ligouri's eyes; a look that made him want to protect the household.

For that reason, on the way back to the kitchen he again considered telling Vittorio Faziolini about having seen Sandro Pavone at La Serena. And once again he decided no. The southern Italian had only returned for something he had left in the loft; so why trouble the Faziolinis with an unpleasant reminder?

The downstairs telephone on the dining room sideboard was ringing again. Rose hurried in from the kitchen, picked up the receiver, and said, *"Pronto?"* But she only heard a click as the caller hung up. Rose shook a furious fist at the phone. "The devil take you! The devil!"

Enough to drive her crazy! This was at least the tenth time that the phone had rung in the last two days and when the caller heard her voice—*click!* Was the caller expecting another voice, a different voice, not hers? If so, whose? Or was it one of those nuisance calls you read about—a new kind maybe, not one of the dirty ones. In any case—

"The devil pull out your tongue! And cut off the finger you dial with!" She left the study and went back to the kitchen.

COMING INTO ELISABETTA'S BEDROOM, JOHANNA THOUGHT instantly: *This* is a room I'd love to sleep in. Sleep in? Live in! *I'm glad I'm this rich, and soon, soon* . . . Elisabetta's bedroom was square, white, and spacious, with a high ceiling and a frosted-glass chandelier that looked like an enormous opening rose. Soft chairs were drawn up to a tiled fireplace, and three or four table lamps, already lit, shed a soft glow. It was a carelessly personal room: Books and letters were scattered on tables, and hair brushes and combs were stuck upright in water glasses on an antiqued-ivory dressing table. The pictures on the walls were obviously the products of Elisabetta's children, who had crayoned with wild abandon.

"I'm just back from the woods," Johanna said, "your father told me—"

"*Cara!*" Elisabetta turned from looking out the window. "Yes! I guess I'm a little crazy this afternoon—I thought the twins had gone to play near the lambs' pen, but then I couldn't find them. I got so upset. And then I turned around and there they were!"

"I can guess how relieved you were." She didn't know what to say.

"*Anyway,*" Elisabetta said, "it made me forget—I got so mixed up—you gave me the receipt from the post office for the wedding dress, but I don't know what I did with it, did you happen to—"

"You put it in a blue mug on a shelf in the kitchen."

Elisabetta clapped a hand to her mouth. "Of course! *Idiota!* Sometimes I wonder about myself."

"Well, you were worried."

"I'm still shaken," Elisabetta admitted. "What I probably need is a good meal. Nothing soothes me like food. That's what Sabina always says about me when I'm upset. 'Give her pasta, that's all she needs.' It's a wonder I'm not fat."

Johanna was looking at a crayoned drawing, a barnyard of ducks and baby chicks. "What a delight! Why doesn't someone open a gallery of children's art?"

"Because only parents love their children's artwork. *Their* child knows how to draw a cow! Not their neighbor's child. My father mentioned, by the way, that you were looking at our family pictures?"

"Yes."

"But of course most of our family photographs are at home in Rome. We have only a few snapshots at La Serena." Elisabetta nodded toward the far wall. "Over there, next to Felicia's orange elephant, that framed one—that's Alessandro and me standing in the field. Vittorio took it when we were kids."

Politely, incuriously, Johanna approached the far wall: A snapshot of children would tell her nothing.

She looked at the snapshot. She felt little prickles along her arms. Elisabetta had approached and was at her shoulder. "That's me—those braids! How I hated them!"

"And the boy?"

"Didn't I say? Alessandro, of course!"

Alessandro. Only—only the little boy's face, frowning in the sun, with the two dark lines between the brows, was the face of Francesco Mantello.

❖ 23 ❖

BACK IN HER OWN ROOM, JOHANNA COLLAPSED ONTO THE chaise. Francesco Mantello in the snapshot? Of course not! It was his father, whom he so strongly resembled. His father, Alessandro Faziolini.

All along, on some subterranean level, she had suspected that Francesco Mantello was Luciano Botto's child. "Signor Botto" who visited Florence, stayed at the Pensione Boldini, and bought his little son Francesco beautiful art paper at Dordanno's expensive shop, calling himself Signor Cardarelli. And always paying in cash.

Only, of course, not really Signor Luciano Botto, but Alessandro Faziolini.

On Via Niccolo Nero, Teresa Mantello, with her swollen eyelids, had confessed in her heartbroken whisper: "There is no Signor Botto, just as there is no Signor Cardarelli. The false name . . . He had a reason. I loved him."

Johanna thought, *So now I know the reason.*

Now she knew that Alessandro Faziolini never interrupted his Venice-Milano sales trip to visit the villas of Treviso, Padua, Vincenza. No, he visited his lover Teresa and his child Francesco in Florence. Hiding his identity under the false name of Luciano Botto.

And that terrible rainy night in Florence, Luciano Botto had been murdered.

Alessandro Faziolini had been murdered.

On the chaise, elbows on her knees, Johanna sank her chin in her cupped hands and stared before her with an anguished need to deny that awful knowledge. But she could not. The apprehension that had brought her to La Serena had proved, terribly, to be true. She had come here for reassurance and she had found death.

It had not been a mugging with a chance victim. Alessandro had been killed *because he was Alessandro Faziolini.*

That had to be so, there was no way around it; it had to be so because *Luciano Botto did not exist,* he was only the cloak under which Alessandro visited Teresa and Francesco.

Somewhere out there was the murderer.

A chill swept over her so that she lifted her shoulders and rubbed her arms; but it was not the breeze from the partly open window that chilled her. And on the heels of that chill came a sense of fury, of outrage. She felt her jaw go tense with it—the "Johanna's jaw" look. Her father used to call it that, but he had respected it, valued it.

Go to Florence, go to Captain Grippo at once! Tell him—

But . . . She stared at the partly open window, not seeing it, seeing instead the seamstress' little room on the Via Niccolo Nero, seeing Teresa Mantello beside the ironing board, so slender, so defenseless. Her dark, tear-swollen eyes had been wide with fear, as she said: *"The killer does not know that I exist.* Signorina, if you tell the police, the murderer will follow the trail to me!—to Francesco and me! Signorina, I beg of you!" That low, despairing plea; and Johanna's own pitying reply, "Signora, I promise you, I won't tell the police."

So, impossible. She could not go to Captain Grippo. What now?

If only she could ferret out something that would expose the murderer!

Again she saw herself as the heroine.

She looked at the dresser on which lay her expensive perfumes and her Florentine gold bracelet and into whose drawers she had slipped silken underclothes she had not yet worn. The Totocalcio money. If she could find a lead to Alessandro Faziolini's murderer she'd feel entitled to keep the Totocalcio money. Or at least most of it! She put a hand on the watch that was like melted gold around her wrist. What was it her father had once written in an editorial? "If you are rich for even five minutes, you feel the pinch of poverty the moment the money is snatched away."

But what could she do? Even Captain Grippo, if he knew that the murdered man was Alessandro Faziolini, would be weak-handed. He had no cards to play.

Where could she find a card?

Teresa Mantello. Even the tiniest clue! The smallest bit of information! It was the only possibility. She would promise to keep Teresa out of it, she would swear it, she would beg, plead, and—

It wouldn't work. Teresa would be too frightened.

But I will try.

First thing in the morning she'd leave for Florence.

She looked at her watch, this time checking the time. Six o'clock. At eight, aperitifs would be served in the loggia; at eight-thirty, Lucilla's birthday dinner. She wanted to weep. She thought of Sabina and Vittorio, of Alessandro's wife Lucilla, of his sister Elisabetta—all the Faziolinis expecting Alessandro, who would never come.

She went to the dresser and stood gazing steadily into her eyes. This was the way it was; this was the sad, terrible reality. She could only try to do what she could.

Get on with it.

Six o'clock. She must call Dr. Rosella in Treangoli right away, cancel their appointment.

She used the phone on the stairway landing. When Dr. Rosella answered in his fussy manner, she explained that she would not be coming in after all for "a change of bandage," as they had originally agreed. Instead, she was returning to

Florence first thing in the morning. In answer to the doctor's chuckling query about the romance, she answered, "Ah, yes, *Dottore!* I am still in love with Signor Thornton! And now he with me! Our love affair is working out perfectly, thanks to *you, Dottore.*" She added that she would be sending the good doctor another little envelope of lire from Florence, with thanks. She refrained from adding: *To insure your secrecy about the medical diagnosis, Dottore.*

Back again upstairs, showering and changing, she thought of Jeff Thornton's watching her, and of his warning and her uneasy suspicions about him. And she thought, too, about the explanation she'd given Dr. Rosella for her faked sprain: That she was in love with Jeff Thornton, she wanted to be with him at La Serena. Had she really wished it, unconsciously, but so deeply, that the wish had determined her choice of an excuse to Dr. Rosella? She wondered what Freud's disciples would have said.

Dr. Rosella put down the phone. He was in the dining room, which was really his office. He was tickled that he'd be receiving another packet of lire. Such a rich, pretty girl! Now he must finish up with his last patient. Why was it always at the last minute, on Saturday, that the whole village needed him? They poured over him like a bucket of water; they wouldn't do that if he had a real office instead of his dining room. Also, because he was now a widower, they thought he had no other life—which was true, and that was why he was so often in Peppino's trattoria, drinking wine.

Dr. Rosella sighed and trotted into the kitchen, which was his surgery. Peppino was sitting on the tall stool beside the sink, holding his cut finger in the air with the bit of cotton pressed to it. "That's what a wife does for you!" Peppino had grumbled, white in the face when he'd arrived ten minutes earlier. "Brings home a slicing machine so you can slice off a finger!"

Now when Dr. Rosella came trotting back into the kitchen, Peppino said, "So the American girl leaves La Serena tomorrow morning, eh?" For the thousandth time, Dr. Rosella thought with a sigh how the walls of this house were made of paper; you could hear everything, there was no privacy even in the bathroom. Dr. Rosella pulled the cotton from Peppino's finger and answered only with a shrug; but an instant later he could not refrain from a sly little wink. Love, that was what mattered; love like the American signorina's.

When Peppino had left, Dr. Rosella tidied up the office, putting his surgical tools away in the kitchen drawers and straightening papers in the dining room. What a busy last few days! Matteo Del Bosco complaining of a sprained tendon; Renzo Grimini with something in his eye that for the life of him Dr. Rosella could not find; Elvio Gordini who demanded the two-hour examination because he was frightened that his nervous stomach was something dangerous, which it wasn't. And a dozen others. The American, Jeff Thornton, with a sliver in his palm that it took thirty seconds to remove with a tweezers. And some of these patients so curious about the American signorina! Well, such a pretty girl, he could not blame them. And of course when Signor Thornton asked—well, after all, a romance! It would help the romance along, the American signore knowing how the girl felt about him. And how seriously Signor Thornton thanked him! Even adding an excellent amount of lire.

Dr. Rosella locked the front door and went to the kitchen to fix some supper. This evening he would have his end-of-the-week drinks at Peppino's trattoria. From now on, he promised himself, he would be *dignitoso*, dignified. He wouldn't prattle after a few glasses of wine. It wasn't becoming to a doctor and there was the oath. He would also stay far from that southern Italian, that *porco* who was always in Peppino's lately or in the telephone booth next to the post office. *Dignitoso*, yes, that's what he would be. An important, serious *medico. Dottore* Rosella.

❖ 24 ❖

JOHANNA WAS LYING AGAIN.

Jeff Thornton knew it. He stood with a hand resting on the broad railing of the loggia, listening to her tell the Faziolinis that this morning in Treangoli Dr. Rosella had put a stiff little cast on her wrist—"So now I can drive without difficulty. Oh, *awkward*, but not *difficult*!" She was leaving first thing in the morning for Florence. "No sense shopping in Rome with a wrist in a cast, *vero?*" And she laughed and lifted her arm slightly away from her body for emphasis. But of course it was impossible to see the cast or even the black sling, because it was covered with a flowered silk scarf.

He knew she was lying, because there hadn't been anything wrong with her wrist in the first place. He also had noticed that she unconsciously narrowed those very blue eyes when she told lies. And she had told quite a few.

Not a congenital liar. And not an innocent in trouble, either. Johanna wasn't that innocent. Right now, she was acting almost febrile. Her color was too high, and that wasn't rouge, he could swear it. Neither could eye drops have made her eyes that bright and enormous. And although she was talking with Matteo and Lucilla, she wasn't really looking at them, she was looking mostly into the glass of *spumonti* she wasn't drinking.

Johanna March. Right from the start, when she'd bet her Florentine gold bracelet about Alessandro, he'd become alert. He had wondered, *What is she up to?* He had decided to play along. It was not curiosity: He had already known on the road down from the mountain restaurant above Florence when she said "The Italians drive like bandits!" that she was

121

going to ask him to drive her the first part of the way to Rome, and he knew that he would say yes because he wanted this Johanna March close to his side as long as he could keep her there.

And then in Treangoli the faked sprained wrist. Johanna's rushing out of the trattoria and coming back with her arm in a sling—obvious and disturbing. But he had thought *Play the dupe.* He would check later with Dr. Rosella. Well, he had checked.

He frowned. He wished to hell it were true that, as Dr. Rosella had romantically confided, Johanna wanted to stay at La Serena because she was in love with him. But he knew it was a lie. If he were to ask her outright, she might give him a straight look and say "Yes." But her eyes would narrow. Another lie.

Why, then, was she so eager to stay at La Serena?

Thoughtfully he ran a finger along his chin. There were a couple of possibilities, one of which he did not want to think about because it concerned Alessandro. The other, the one he leaned toward—and wasn't it logical, and even obvious?— was that Johanna had gotten herself involved in something crooked; she had found herself in danger, she had faked the sprained wrist in order to stay in the safety of La Serena, away from her—what? *Confreres.* Her *confreres* in Florence who doubtless had connections in Rome.

Yes. Logical, obvious.

He had tried to warn her. She couldn't guess the whole criminal mix; it could turn into a web of drugs, prostitution, kidnapping, slayings.

It was money, of course. An aerobics teacher who had taken the cheap flight to Pisa and the train to Florence—as she had let drop—and then could afford the luxury of an Alfa Romeo, those beautiful new-looking clothes, and expensive perfumes and jewelry! He had seen how sensuously she caressed the honey-colored leather of the Alfa Romeo; caressed it almost wistfully, as though longing for it. *Yet it was already hers.* His guess: she hadn't had plenty of money for long. Her riches were new, a fortune. So where did she get it? Pure greed had led her into danger.

And now for some reason she was going back to Florence. Tempted back by what? He hoped not by the possibility that concerned Alessandro. He looked past Matteo to where Johanna was now listening to Elisabetta, who was presumably telling one of her funny stories and laughing. Johanna was laughing along with her. Then, past Elisabetta's shoulder, Johanna's eyes met his. It was like a small shock, a shock he had never felt before. And he thought grimly: When she goes to Florence in the morning, she will not go alone.

In the kitchen, disaster was already in the air, disaster like a fog drifting even into the corners. Rosa and Franca in their white aprons moved distractedly between the cabinets and table, and Serafina moved the splendid birthday cake from table to counter and back again. "Giorgio! Take it to the dining room! No, leave it! Rosa, finish clearing in there first!"

"I already finished. In that dining room—*Dio!* One minute they're like ghosts and dummies, the next they're all talking at once! Lucilla has spilled water on her dress and she's half dead from smoking cigarettes one after another, her hands shaking! Matteo is drinking wine almost from the bottle and Vittorio looks like a thunder storm!"

Giorgio stood against a cabinet, feet crossed, eating an apple. He was not going to get crazy like the others. Anyway, Sabina Faziolini or Elisabetta would come into the kitchen any minute now and tell them what to do. He looked at his grandfather sharpening knives at the little wheel, pretending nothing was happening; Luigi looked like an old blackbird pecking away at his own affairs.

That was the way to be. Like his grandfather.

After all, it wasn't the end of the world just because Alessandro Faziolini hadn't shown up for his wife's birthday dinner.

✦ 25 ✦

LUCILLA LOOKED AT THE BIRTHDAY CAKE SET BEFORE HER, its candles glowing in the darkened dining room. The candles lighted the faces around the table, and voices called out *"Buon compleano*, Lucilla!"* It was a white cake with a thick, buttery frosting, and it said *Buon Compleano Lucilla* in rose-colored curlicued lettering. Creamy-looking rosebuds edged the cake.

"Buon compleano, cara." Sabina's voice at Lucilla's left merged with the baritone of Vittorio who sat on her right. The other voices seemed far away, though they were only further down the table—Matteo's tenor, Renzo Grimini's deep tones, Elisabetta's, and the voices of the two Americans.

Every voice but Alessandro's. Alessandro's, the only voice she cared about. The bitterness in her mouth was the taste of Alessandro's not caring enough to arrive in time for her birthday. Her eyes ached from scanning the road all day from her bedroom window, going from her poetry on the desk to the window, finally pulling her chair to the window. Alessandro! Alessandro!

"Isn't it pretty, *cara?"* Sabina said, at her left. "American style! But with Italian champagne! You blow out the candles, then Vittorio will pour the champagne."

Lucilla stood up. She looked down at the candlelit confection. *Buon compleano Lucilla.* She clenched her fist and drove it straight down and hard into the cake.

Except for Sabina's gasp, there was silence around the table. Lucilla stood motionless, staring down at where her fist was buried in the cake, her loose, green satin sleeve covering the curlicued *Lucilla*, the green satin among the burning pink candles, the green now slowly edged with an orange glow, a little wisp of smoke rising, a flicker of fire—

And suddenly it was as though a terror-stricken animal were let loose in the dining room.

"No!" Matteo screamed a high, terrible scream. *"No! No! Mamma!"* His chair went over backward and he scrambled onto the long table and wildly clawed his way toward Lucilla, scattering plates, dishes, glasses. *"No! No!"* Sobbing, gasping, he flung himself forward and beat madly at the green satin sleeve. *"Mamma!"* A high, thin wail.

It was Vittorio who finally managed to calm him, but only after Lucilla, with her scorched sleeve and frosting-covered hand, had been taken away by Elisabetta, one arm around Lucilla's waist, murmuring soothing words. Matteo's jacket was a mess of frosting and candle wax and his face was still stained with a look of horror. Vittorio poured cognac and made Matteo drink it. By the time Matteo had drained the glass, his handsome, heavy-jowled face looked more normal, though a little dazed. Then with embarrassed, muttered apologies, he too left, first kissing Sabina goodnight and bowing to Renzo Grimini and Miss March and Jeff Thornton. Directly afterward, Renzo also took his leave.

Vittorio picked up the crystal stopper and put it back on the cognac. Then he went over to Sabina and touched her shoulder. *"Vieni, cara."* He looked at Miss March and Jeff Thornton. "You'll excuse us?"

A moment later, Johanna and Jeff Thornton were left alone. Across the ruined table, their eyes met.

In the study, Vittorio picked up the phone. "Don't worry yourself," he said gently to Sabina, who had sunk down on the sofa and was staring into the fire. She had taken the festive, rhinestone-studded comb from her coronet and was holding it clutched in both hands like something to cling to in a shipwreck. As for himself, he was more exasperated at Alessandro than worried. All that in the dining room could have been avoided if . . . Enough! He would have their business associates in Milan track down Alessandro. The business trip to Venice and then Milan was supposed to have been a week, broken by three or four days visiting those villas that so infatuated him. And here it was eleven days Alessandro had been gone. A week or so ago he had telephoned around noon, saying he was calling from the hotel in Venice, his business there finished.

"Moritori e Figli," the voice on the phone in Milan answered; but it was a mechanical voice, a recording. Saturday èvening, the office was closed. He tried *Bustimanti Figli* next. No answer. The same with *D'abbigliamento Sportivi.* Holding the ringing phone, he looked at Sabina worrying the rhinestone comb. He'd try their personal residences. He made the calls, but he reached only servants. No one was home.

The hotel then! The Principe e Savoia. Alessandro always stayed there. *"Buona sera, Principe e Savoia,"* came the politely inquiring voice. But, "No, Signore, Signor Faziolini has not yet checked in."

Vittorio put down the phone. Sabina was looking at him; he couldn't bear the anxious look in her eyes. He picked up the phone again, called the Grand and then the Palace, only to hear, "Signore Alessandro Faziolini? No, Signore. We have no guest by that name."

"Basta—enough!" he exclaimed—and to Sabina, "I'll call Gianni Moritori or Gino Bustimanti in the morning. It won't matter that it's Sunday, we're old friends, after all!"

But Sabina on the sofa still looked anxious; she had always been a worrier over her cubs. And while he smiled encouragingly at her, in the silence there was a small sound, a *crack*, and he saw that she had broken the rhinestone comb in half.

"So you see," Elisabetta said to Jeff Thornton and Johanna; she dragged the big woolen shawl off the back of the couch in the salon and tucked it around Johanna, saying, *"Brrr!* You'll get chilled—it's cold in here. Jeff, will you fix the fire? So you see, I ought to explain to you. It wasn't Matteo just being crazy."

"As a good psychologist would tell us," Thornton said. He was lighting the fire that had been expertly laid by— Giorgio? Luigi? It required only a match.

"A *tragedia*," Elisabetta said. "Ettore Del Bosco and his wife, Graziella, a beautiful young woman, used to visit us at La Serena with little Matteo. Ettore was my father's best friend—Vittorio admired him enormously. Ettore was a botanist, he was utterly fascinated by flowers. Luckily, he could afford to be! He was rich through inheritance. The Del Boscos lived in an old palazzo in Parioli, in Rome.

"But then Ettore invested enormously in cross-breeding projects. He had some theory, a genetic—he became fanatically—anyway, he lost the entire Del Bosco fortune. Everything!"

In the worn chair, Elisabetta gazed into the fire. She said softly, "Poor Graziella, bewildered by it all! With the financial disaster, the palazzo deteriorated, the servants were dismissed. One old servant was left, Caterina, the faithful old witch, as Ettore called her.

"Graziella was a romantic young woman. I sometimes think of her, how she must have drifted unhappily around that old palazzo making ineffectual stabs at household duties that were foreign to her. As for cooking! She had never so much as cooked an egg or washed a dish!"

Elisabetta suddenly gave a shudder and put her hands to her mouth. After a moment she dropped them and went on evenly. "It was the negligée. Matteo was about ten years old when Graziella awakened early one Sunday morning and went down to the kitchen to make breakfast for her husband and son. She—she must have been bending over the stove, half-asleep, reaching to pick up the coffee pot when the sleeve—they said later it must have been the sleeve of her chiffon negligée—it must have fluttered over the lighted gas and burst into flames."

No sound from the listeners. Thornton was leaning back with his hands thrust into his pockets, gazing at the rug. Johanna, huddled in the woolen scarf, looked stricken. Elisabetta said quietly: "Caterina heard her screams, she rushed in, but it was already too late. 'The Signora was a blazing statue' is how she later described it, breaking down in tears."

They were all quiet.

Johanna said at last, "Matteo. He screamed *'Mamma!'*"

Elisabetta nodded. She told them then what little there was left to tell. *"Culpa mia, culpa mia!*—My fault!" Ettore Del Bosco had wept to Vittorio. "If I had not played the fool with money, my Graziella wouldn't have been leaning over a stove!" Ettore's ten-year-old son, Matteo, was bitterly of the same opinion. He hated and despised his father. He barely spoke to him. But the boy worshipped Vittorio Faziolini. To him, Vittorio was all that his own father should have been: wise, businesslike, rich. Through the kindness of Sabina, he spent his summers at La Serena. But at home in Rome in the deteriorating palazzo, he lived under the reign of the "old witch" until he was eighteen. Caterina learned to cook, but poorly; she also did the shopping and otherwise ran the Del Bosco household.

"And Ettore?" Johanna asked curiously. "Does Matteo still not talk to his father?"

"Ettore died when Matteo was eighteen and at business school. Matteo got a loan—Vittorio vouched for payment. With the money he had the palazzo put into reasonable shape. He rented it to a Swedish diplomat and his family. For himself, he moved into a modern apartment. And *now*! Now Matteo is again 'that rich Del Bosco!' "

The fire made a little rustling sound as a log fell. Elisabetta got up. "I'm going to go back to Lucilla and stay with her for a little bit, if she'll let me. Not that there's anything any of us can *do*."

When Elisabetta had gone, Jeff watched Johanna unwrap herself from the wool shawl. She put on her shoes and stood up, a slender figure in a tan shift and the flowered silk scarf that concealed her black sling and its new "stiff little cast." Her eyes were still bright, but she yawned. Her hair had a tousled look after the long evening, and her lipstick was gone.

"What do you say to me driving you to Florence?" he asked. He was still leaning back, hands in his pockets.

"Drive me to Florence? But you can't! Your business is in the south!"

"That can wait."

"No," she said quickly. "I wouldn't consider, I couldn't

possibly—'' She was folding the shawl, folding it too carefully, patting it; patting it too many times and too nervously,
then laying it across the back of the couch as though it were
her best friend and she hated to part with it. Anything except
to look at him.

''I can do some business in Florence,'' he said. ''And in
the meantime there are a lot of places you probably haven't
seen yet, not to mention the restaurants, and we could—''

''*No!*'' she said. ''It's not possible! Work—I have some
work to do in Florence, some things I should have—I won't
have time! Not now! Later, when you get back from your
business in the south, *then,* yes. Restaurants, whatever—
yes!''

In full retreat, she was almost backing into the couch. She
didn't want him on the scene in Florence. And she was lying
again, her eyes narrowing. He kept his own eyes friendly and
ingenuous.

''Have it your way.'' He yawned and stretched. ''Have a
good trip. We'll do it all later.''

When she had gone he sat up. Why argue over it and spoil
Johanna's sleep?

Tomorrow morning—Sunday—after breakfast when she
came out to get into the Alfa Romeo, she'd find him already
in the car.

❖ **26** ❖

SHE WAS DREAMING OF BLOOD; SHE COULD SEE STREAMS OF
it flowing over the chaise lounge where she had flung the
sling and the flowered scarf, and rivers of blood, ribbons and
ruby bands of it, crossed the . . . ceiling. She lay looking at
it through her lashes, then with her eyes open. It was not

blood, it was lights; ruby-red lights crossing the ceiling, disappearing, then crossing. And now below the window, voices; now a white light was crossing the ceiling mixed with the ruby. The lights seemed familiar; she had been where lights like that—

A police car.

Quickly, she was out of bed and at the window. She looked down at the police car beside the outbuilding and at the milling figures below—a half-dozen people. Light fell on Vittorio Faziolini's white mane, on Luigi, on Matteo's heavy shoulders; she could not distinguish anyone else, but she saw the police, and she saw a light go on in the police car as one of the officers opened the door and reached in. Then the door slammed and the light went out.

There was a confused hum of voices, then abruptly, shockingly, came a single scream, a woman's voice screaming and screaming—*"Dio! Dio!"* and *"Giorgio mio! Giorgio!"* It was Serafina. Now the white blur of faces was looking up at her window. It concerned her, it—

Someone was knocking on her door.

"Momento!" She flung on her robe.

It was Elisabetta. "Now don't get upset, it's your car, but they're all right! They've been taken—"

"Who? What?"

"Giorgio and Angela! Thank God the truck was coming over the hill and they had to swerve, otherwise they'd have been killed altogether! The hospital at Arcidosso, did I say? In the ambulance—I have to sit down."

Elisabetta's face had suddenly paled. She shivered in her flannel robe. She collapsed shakily onto the chaise. "Johanna, you'll have to go down, the police are waiting. The Alfa Romeo, it has already been hoisted from the ditch, Vittorio had it taken to the garage in Treangoli. Oh, Johanna, I'm so sorry! Those poor youngsters! Just for a romantic little ride! They're in love, you see. You see?"

Johanna managed a nod. She slid the flowered scarf and the sling from the chaise and walked toward the dresser, her back to Elisabetta, slipping them on. She was seeing again the long-haired girl on the bicycle, Giorgio pulling her close

and kissing her. In the hospital at Arcidosso! *Damn* that Alfa
Romeo, that it had ever existed to hurt those children! Boys
always thought they knew how to drive, as though they had
been born with legs made of wheels. And now . . .

She sat down beside Elisabetta and put her arm around
her. "Let's go down."

It was one-thirty in the morning, and the wrecked Alfa
Romeo had been brought into Elvio Gordini's garage only
half an hour before. Elvio was sleepy, and he'd charge plenty
for being roused out of bed, besides making plenty on all the
damage to this expensive car. But sleepy or not, Elvio was a
very good mechanic, and he also knew that young Giorgio
was a very good, careful driver who regularly brought in the
Faziolinis' Masarati and Ferrari and Lancia to be checked.

It didn't take Elvio more than that half hour before he
straightened up and wiped his greasy hands on a rag and
turned to the gray-eyed American who had been sitting patiently on the fender of Silvestro's old truck with his arms
folded.

"The brakes," Elvio said. "I never saw brakes do that by
themselves." The American, who Elvio knew was staying
at La Serena, sat still for a minute; then he took out his
wallet. He told Elvio that there was no need to disturb the
Faziolini family with such a possibility—they'd had troubles
enough what with the—

"Kidnapping," Elvio said, and nodded. He was agree-
able. As for the rest of the damage to the car—and Elvio
surveyed the broken windshield, the crushed door, the collapsed hood. He shuddered for Giorgio and Angela.

"A week anyway, with myself and my two men on it. As
for the brakes, I'll take care of that myself." He put a finger
to his lips because the American didn't know that Elvio Gordini had a reputation in Treangoli for knowing when to keep
his mouth shut. And he added reassuringly, *"Nemméno una
parola!* Not a word!"

The promise earned him another folded note from the
American's wallet.

❖ 27 ❖

AT EIGHT-THIRTY IN THE MORNING, JOHANNA GOT INTO THE Ferrari beside Lucilla Faziolini.

There was a snap to the morning air, and a gust of wind almost pulled the car door from her hand. To her amazement, she had eaten breakfast with a ravenous appetite; she wondered if it had been some instinctive defense, as though she had been girding herself with sustenance before seeing the wreck of the Alfa Romeo.

Beside her, Lucilla crushed out a cigarette and jerkily put the car into gear. "I'll drop you at Gordini's garage. I'll pick you up after I mail my—my work, at the post office." Lucilla ran a thin, nervous hand over the envelope of poems at her side. Her face was white, and her corona of wild hair looked wilder than ever.

It was not a joyful journey. Within minutes it turned uncomfortably chilly and blustery, and though they both wore sweaters, Lucilla had to roll up the windows. She kept looking distractedly at the road. She drove fearfully and badly and she knew it.

"I can't do anything mechanical!" she blurted out suddenly. "I can't even use a typewriter! I write with a pencil!" It sounded desperate, like an appeal, and Johanna remembered Elisabetta saying, "Lucilla makes me think of a baby eagle with its beak open waiting to be fed and afraid the mother eagle will not return." Yet Lucilla obviously tried her best: Johanna, getting into the Ferrari, had glimpsed in the back seat, among old magazines and newspapers, a book on auto repair.

Poor baby eagle. And Johanna thought: Alessandro and

Teresa Mantello have a son. Lucilla has not. Is she afraid? Afraid that one night she might go into a baby's nursery and once again. . . ?

She glanced at Lucilla's white face. *I swear, I swear this:* Whatever happens, I will find a way to keep the knowledge of Teresa and Francesco Mantello's existence from Lucilla and from *all* the Faziolinis.

I vow it.

Elvio Gordini was a small balding man with a tick in his left eye. He wore brown overalls over a faded red jersey. *"Mi dispiace!"* he exclaimed sympathetically when he saw the shock in Johanna's face. "Not as bad as it looks, Signorina! The engine, *per esempio*—running like a clock! It is only the—" and he waved at the crushed doors, the collapsed hood, the stained, torn upholstery.

They were in a dank, gasoline-smelling, shedlike corner of the garage; the floor was concrete, the windows dirty. Elvio Gordini said to a mechanic whose legs showed from beneath the car, *"Bascone!* Go finish up with Panicelli's crankshaft!"* and when a fat little man wriggled out from under the car and trotted off wiping his hands, Gordini said softly to Johanna, "And that other little thing. *Nemméno una parola!"*

"Che?" She hardly heard; she had one hand on the car door and was looking at the torn upholstery.

"Nemméno una parola!" He whispered. Something in his voice made her turn. His eye tick was working furiously. Only now she realized it was not an eye tick: Elvio Gordini was winking at her, a click-and-shutter of significance.

She said, "Yes—*Nemméno una parola!"* She felt that something terrible was happening, but she did not know what it was.

"Non si preoccupi, Signora! I promised your American friend, not a word about the brakes, not to anyone. I am, *come si dice*—a tomb!"

She felt colder than death. *"Si, grazie."*

"They should go to prison, whoever did it. The girl Angela, sixteen, and with that long hair—plenty of *ragazzi* are jealous of Giorgio Cartucci. But this is more than a *scherzo*, a joke!''

"Yes. More than a joke.''

Five minutes later when Lucilla drove up, Johanna was waiting on the road. *Peccato*, Lucilla, but it would take her at least an hour longer at Gordini's! "But don't worry about me, Lucilla, Signor Gordini knows someone who can drop me off at La Serena.'' So Lucilla was not to wait. Johanna would certainly be back at the villa in time for lunch. *Ciao*, Lucilla. *Ciao*.

When the Ferrari was out of sight, she walked quickly down the road to the *tobaccaio* and bought some *gettoni*. In the telephone booth across from the post office she dropped in *gettoni*, got the telephone number, and made the call. Her hands were cold and shaking. She heard the phone picked up on the third ring. *"Pronto!"* came Teresa Mantello's voice.

"Signora Mantello? . . . Johanna March.'' She pressed the phone to her ear and said rapidly, "Signora Mantello—Teresa! I'm calling from Treangoli, I've been to La Serena. I can't tell you why, but I know now that Luciano Botto is Alessandro Faziolini. I swear I will never tell anyone about you and Alessandro! I swear it!''

From Teresa, an inarticulate sound—a sob, a groan?

"But please, Teresa, help me! *Someone is trying to kill me*. Who? Why? It must be because of Alessandro, the person who killed—''

"No!" Teresa's voice was full of fear and desperation. "I cannot!''

"But—''

"Run away! Go back to America! I can't help you! And you promised to protect me and Francesco. You *promised*! If I say anything, they'll learn about me—the police, the Faziolinis. *The killer*.''

Sweat was cold on her neck. *If I say anything*, Teresa had said. So Teresa did know something. What? "Teresa! I beg of—''

A dam broke. "If the Faziolinis learned about me, it would destroy Alessandro in their eyes! Knowing that all those years—he suffered enough in his conscience! He had such ideals. And he fell so short of them!''

"Teresa—"

But the flood swept on, a heedless outpouring of anguish: ''Seeing him suffer so, I would have sent him away. But Francesco! Alessandro loved him so much! How could I deprive him of his only child? And with his wife there could never be another one. The doctor said his wife's fear, her anxiety—''

In the background Johanna heard a child's voice, Francesco's; then a door closed and the voice was gone. And Teresa Mantello's requiem continued. ''But it was hopeless, we would never be together, Signorina March! Now I must protect my life and Francesco's!''

In the phone booth, Johanna hung desperately onto the phone. *Someone is trying to kill me.*

"Teresa? Signora! Protect yourself and Francesco? Don't deceive yourself! You'll never be safe while Alessandro's killer is free. He could be anyone! Even a supposed friend or acquaintance. And some day you might let slip the wrong word—''

A silence. Was that awful eventuality sinking in?

"But Teresa! One little clue, the smallest clue! It could catch the killer, then you and Francesco would be safe forever. *Forever!* Never in danger.'' She paused. "Never in the danger I'm in now.'' Rapidly she told about her brakes being tampered with. "Signora, it is only by chance that I am not lying mangled and dead on the road to Florence. Signora, they, or *he*, will try again to kill me!''

Silence. Hesitancy? She could not know. She wanted to weep over the pity and frustration of it all, just as she had wanted to weep when Felicia had come up to her on the terrace and begun her falsetto kidnap tale. *Her kidnap tale!* And with a shivery, eye-widening inspiration out of nowhere, she said into the phone, "The kidnapping. It had to do with the kidnapping!'' It was not a question, it was an affirmation dredged out of some depth of instinct.

What came then was the telephone company signaling for more *gettoni.* She dropped in the tokens. *Ping, pong, ping.*

Then Teresa's voice came, frightened and distracted. "Please! Not now, I need time! Maybe—if you can call me back later—"

"In a half hour?"

"A half hour?" A sigh. "All right." At Teresa's end the phone clicked off.

Johanna hung up. The murder in Florence was connected to the kidnapping! *Teresa Mantello had not denied it!*

An interminable half hour to wait. She would stay close to the phone. She'd go no further than across the road. An espresso, she desperately needed an espresso.

She crossed the road, circumvented a flashy-looking green car, and went into Peppino's.

"Bustimanti?" Vittorio said into the phone in the study. "Gino! *Buon giorno!* . . . I know, on a Sunday morning, so early! . . . Yes, at La Serena, yes, brisk but sunny . . . and in Milan? . . . Rain? . . . *Peccato!* . . . That son of mine, is he still . . . What? But he was due in Milan on Wednesday! Those damned villas, no doubt!" He listened; he even managed a laugh.

When he clicked off the phone he did not put it down but put in a call to the Gritti in Venice. Alessandro always stayed there.

"Si, Signor Faziolini . . . Alessandro Faziolini . . . his usual visit, three days." Signor Faziolini had checked out for a few days of touring the Palladian villas to the north. In a rented car, they believed. "He has not yet returned. However, we certainly expect him, because he left his briefcase as usual with the hotel. He picks it up and takes it on the flight to Milan."

Vittorio hesitated, then said, *"Grazie."* He put down the phone and sank back in the chair. He didn't understand it, not any of it. Alessandro's briefcase. Why did Alessandro leave his briefcase at the Gritti in Venice "as usual"? Would it have been so difficult to take his briefcase along in the rented car on his tour of the villas?

"Babbo? Daddy?" Elisabetta came in. She looked at his face. *"Babbo!* What's the matter?"

He told her.

"I don't understand it either," Elisabetta said. She frowned, thinking. "Unless—unless there's something in the briefcase that's—you know, *valuable*, that would be better off in the Gritti safe than in the trunk of a rented car?"

Vittorio looked at his daughter. "*Possibile*. But what? He had only business papers for Venice and Milan. His shaving things and shirts and so one would be in his traveling bag. Presumably he took the bag with him."

They sat, thinking. Elisabetta said finally, "What are you thinking?"

Vittorio said: "That in the briefcase there might be something to tell us—something to relieve our—"

"Fears," said Elisabetta.

"First the briefcase. I'll go to Venice and see what's in Alessandro's briefcase. Then, if necessary, a visit to the police. Something might have—who knows?"

"But to get to Venice! We're at Treangoli, remember. You'd have to drive hours and hours. Why not—"

For a long minute, father and daughter exchanged a look. Then Vittorio stood up. "I'll leave right away. I'll be there in five hours, maybe less." He sighed. "I'll have to figure out something to tell your mother."

Elisabetta said, "What about the truth?"

❖ 28 ❖

PEPPINO PUT THE ESPRESSO AND THE PAPER NAPKIN DOWN before the American signorina. He did it a little awkwardly because of his bandaged finger. There were only a half-dozen patrons in the trattoria, it wasn't busy, so he hung onto the back of the chair opposite the girl, expressing his regret about the wrecked Alfa Romeo and saying how lucky Giorgio and Angela were.

"If you call that luck, getting yourself half killed!" That was Lucca, the butcher, breaking in where it was none of his business. He sat two tables away, but it was a quiet Sunday afternoon and everyone in the room could hear—Silvestro, the baker, who was reading the paper; even the couple of people drinking espresso at the bar—Giacomo the black-smith, and that southern Italian, Sandro Pavone.

But the American girl paid no attention; she kept glancing at her watch, and though she'd just come in seemed ready to fly out the door. She looked prettier than ever in that sweater with the rolled-over neck; he knew that sweater, the Faziolini *ragazzi* had been wearing it for the last twenty years, but on her it looked special. She wore a red scarf as a sling for her wrist.

"Anyway, I'm sorry." Peppino glared at Lucca. He was turning back to the bar when the American signorina asked him if he knew of anyone from whom she could rent a bi-cycle. She'd driven in to Treangoli with one of the Faziolinis, who'd already gone back to La Serena—a mix-up, as the American girl explained it.

Peppino said immediately, "You don't need to rent a bi-cycle, I have my old one, it works well enough. You can borrow it." He felt good, making the offer. Being generous with the bicycle would help make up for slicing the proscuitto too thin. Not that he hadn't already been paid back for his stinginess: Beneath the bandage on his forefinger, the whole little tip was gone—sliced off! Now he was making the pros-cuitto slices thicker again.

The American girl thanked him, looked again at her watch, and took a sip of espresso. In the next twenty minutes she had another espresso and looked at her watch a dozen times. Then she asked for her bill.

At the bar, Peppino scrawled the bill with his pencil stub. Beside him, someone struck a match and lit a cigarette. Pa-vone. Peppino wished there were two bars in Treangoli so Pavone could frequent the other one.

Paying the bill, the American signorina said, "I just have

to make a phone call across the road, then I'll be back for the bicycle.''

''You can use the telephone here, Signorina.'' Peppino nodded toward the pay telephone against the wall beside the table where Silvestro sat reading the paper. Someday he'd have a booth for the phone.

The American signorina thanked him and said no, she'd rather not, and from beneath her dark-gold brows she gave him a significant little look. Of course! She didn't want this roomful of *contadini* listening to her private affairs.

She left. Through the window he could see her crossing the road to the telephone booth.

''Teresa?''

In reply, a woman's voice—formal, guarded, but certainly Teresa Mantello's—said: ''Ah! Signora Marchetta? About the dress—yes, the shoulders, a little wide, but the padding will take care of that . . . *Mi dispiace*, Signora, but I have another customer here, she must not be late for an appointment, she—''

''Teresa! *When?* When can I—''

''*Si*, Signora Marchetta! Certainly in an hour, if you will call back then? I will surely be through by then.'' The guarded voice was beginning to sound exhausted.

She hung up. An hour. Meanwhile, nothing. An abyss. A dark figure, faceless, trying to kill her. He must have seen her with Alessandro in Florence, perhaps breakfasting at the pensione, perhaps in the stationery shop, perhaps on her balcony. He could at first have assumed she only went to bed with Alessandro; American girls always went immediately to bed with a man, the two sweatered Italians at the pensione had implied.

But then she had come to La Serena.

To the murderer, that must surely have meant she had known that Luciano Botto was Alessandro Faziolini. How much, the killer must have wondered, had Alessandro told her? *How much did she know?* In any case, enough to be dangerous. Otherwise she would not be here—to find out how much more? And for whom? The Questura in Florence? Yes, she was a danger.

And frightened. Her hand at her neck felt the pulse beating in her throat. An *hour*. All right, relax. Wait it out at Peppino's. But now call La Serena, tell Rosa they're not to expect you for lunch due to a delay.

She picked up the phone and dropped in her token. But there was no sound. The line was dead.

Then she almost panicked, but somehow did not. *Hurry!* Hurry across the road; Peppino would report the out-of-order public phone, the telephone company would certainly come at once—but maybe not within the hour! Where then could she call from? Dr. Rosella's! But—Dr. Rosella's inquisitive eyes, his pricked-up ears. No, *no!* So then, *what, where?* What if she raced across the road and got Peppino's bicycle? If she peddled fast, she could be back at La Serena in an hour and phone from there. Yes!

She stepped from the phone booth.

"Signorina?"

The man standing there was a stranger. He had a reddish-black pompadour and wore a new-looking black nylon jacket.

"You need a lift, Signorina? I was in Peppino's, I heard— I am going that way, Signorina, toward La Serena." He waved toward the green car outside of Peppino's. "It would be no trouble, Signorina, not out of my way."

She felt a tightening in her shoulder blades. Was everyone now to be suspect? Even the truly well-meaning? Yes. *Everyone!* It was not just that she disliked this man on sight. "No, *grazie*," she said politely. "I enjoy the bicycle."

The man came closer. He smiled; he had big, ugly lips, very red. "The road is rough—too stony for a signorina on a bicycle. Besides, a signorina with an arm in a sling!" He made a gesture, just not quite taking her by the elbow. "Come, Signorina, get in the car." He bulked like a mountain, muscular and thick-necked; the road was empty.

"*No, grazie!*" She took a step back.

But abruptly his smile was gone and he was not looking

at her but beyond her, an ugly look, and at the same instant she became aware of a car motor; it raced, then died.

"Johanna!"

She turned. Jeff Thornton in the Ferrari.

"Get in!" His voice was curt.

They left the man in the nylon jacket standing in the road. In the Ferrari, Johanna thought, *Danger here, too.* She stared ahead at the wooded countryside.

Jeff Thornton said: "Did that *contadino* offer you a lift? This is not a countryside where you play like children! Two years ago, a mile outside Treangoli, in the pine woods, a woman's body—this is wild country, woods for miles. When Lucilla came back alone . . ." He drove expertly but moodily, muttering under his breath.

She was unable to answer. A woman's body. *Nemméno una parola.* She saw Elvio Gordini's left eye winking at her. During the night Jeff Thornton had come to Gordini's garage. He must have paid Gordini well for the *Nemméno una parola* about the brakes. But Gordini had mistakenly assumed that the secret was hers as well. She slid a glance at Jeff Thornton: A strong, secret face; the bony nose, the mouth that seemed now to her to be only pasted with a semblance of humor, a mask for something else. But with all that, his magnetism remained.

The Ferrari sped on through the countryside, and she sat tensely, waiting, hoping desperately that he would say: *Johanna! There's something important I must tell you. Last night, I was concerned for you, I went to the garage, and I must warn you, Johanna . . .*

And when he did not say it: Ask him, she thought, ask him! *Why did you pay Gordini to keep it secret?* Twice, she opened her lips to speak, but her courage failed her; she dared not ask, suspicion held her back.

So they drove on through the lonely wild country, passing a pine woods; possibly, thought Johanna, the woods where that other woman's body was found. And still he said nothing. *Other* woman? Why had she thought *other* woman?

By the time La Serena was in sight, all he had said about the smash-up was that Serafina and Luigi had gone to Arcidosso to be near Giorgio in the hospital. "Giorgio, Serafina, Luigi—the Faziolini staff has been diminished by three."

Vittorio Faziolini's car was a costly, custom-made little white car, an MG type of convertible with doors cut so low that Vittorio could step in without even opening them. It had cost him a fortune, and it delighted him. *"Piccola mia!"* he called it. "My little one!" He would drive around the neighboring countryside in his *piccola mia*, bareheaded, his white mane flying. He kept the little car at La Serena year-round. He would have been embarrassed to use it in the city. In Rome he had a respectable car, a dark gray *dignitoso* Mercedes.

This morning, gunning the motor of the little car in front of La Serena, he thought: A flighty-looking car for such an anxiety-filled trip! But under the hood was a motor that would get him to Venice in under five hours.

"Vittorio—you'll call from Venice when you—when you—" Sabina's voice faltered. She stood beside the car, her hands on the door.

"Certo!"

Sabina leaned down and kissed his cheek. "Your hair! We'll have to wash it when you get back! All that road dust!" Tears were in her eyes; she always talked about his hair when she was worried. But at least she'd have the comfort of Matteo and Elisabetta while he was gone. And Renzo Grimini. And Miss March, whose wrecked car was in Treangoli.

Driving off, he saw the Ferrari, Lucilla and Alessandro's car, approaching. Jeff Thornton was driving, Miss March was beside him. They must have been in Treangoli to see the smashed Alfa Romeo. A pity. But Miss March would surely at least enjoy this beautiful countryside. And the villa wasn't exactly a cage.

Passing the Ferrari, he waved.

❖ 29 ❖

In the dining room, Rosa vacuumed bits of birthday cake off the terrazzo floor. Last night, she and Franca had cut away and saved the undamaged parts of the cake. No one would want to see that cake again, but she would give the good pieces to the twins for dessert for the next few days. She turned off the vacuum.

"Stop it, Tomasino!" He was walking through the dining room trailed by Felicia, and he was at his fingernails again, gnawing them; they were a sight. The twins were already dirty and they'd be a lot dirtier by bedtime. Last night, bathing Felicia, she'd seen red marks on her little wrists besides— not mosquito bites, but marks as though the skin had been rubbed raw. Felicia's skin was more delicate than Tomasino's.

And there had been an upset while bathing Tomasino. Tomasino had always been "her boy," Rosa's boy. When he was bad, she was the one he came to. But not after the kidnapping. Well, yes, last night. She'd been giving him his bath, and the weather had turned so chilly that she had warmed a big old linen sheet on the radiator, and when he'd jumped out of the tub she'd wrapped it around him and begun to dry him off. Then suddenly he had loosed a damp arm from the sheet and grasped her around the neck. He had buried his face beneath her chin and in a strangled, wretched little voice cried out, "I took something!" And he'd sobbed out that he had been punished for it by being kidnapped, and "It is my fault that Felicia was kidnapped! They took her too because she is my twin!"

Rosa had pulled his arm from around her neck, gasping

143

out, *"Calma! Calma!"* It was frightening. "It's all right!" she soothed him. "It wasn't your fault! What did you take?" But he shook his head and looked at her with such despair that she said comfortingly, "You take lots of things, Tomasino, but you're a *good* boy, you always bring them back. *Calma!"* she repeated, going back to drying his shivering little body. But Tomasino shook his head again and got that strange, haunted look on his face. "No," he said. "No."

In the dining room, Rosa, watching Felicia trail Tomasino out into the kitchen, thought: Would it ever be over? Out of the children's heads?

In the study, Johanna sat twisting the telephone cord. Teresa Mantello's voice came wearily over the phone.

"Yes, Signorina March, Johanna, it is true. The kidnapping. But I can only tell you . . ." And in jerky, awkward sentences, Teresa told it: How when barely two weeks ago Alessandro had arrived at Via Niccolo Nero, he had told her that he had just made a telephone call to Rome and learned the kidnapper of the twins. "His face! Such cold vengeance! It made me shudder. I had never seen Alessandro like that, he is so kind, so tender. But when something happens, to children especially . . ."

What enraged him more was that the kidnapper was known to the Faziolini family. "He is not a stranger! Neither the Red Brigade nor Mafia! And not the organized kidnappers of Sardinia either! That is what Alessandro—" Teresa broke off. Johanna could picture the slender woman shuddering.

"He did not want the police! He was planning a personal revenge, a dreadful—he was in a passion to do violent justice. A punishment deep and terrible! You don't know, there is that about the Faziolinis, a tradition. It is the old Italian way, vengeance, centuries of—so Alessandro . . ." Teresa's voice expired; then in the space of a breath, returned: "Somehow the kidnapper must have found out, so he killed him, killed 'the unidentified Luciano Botto.' Alessandro."

Johanna wet dry lips. "Alessandro had made a telephone call to whom in Rome?"

Teresa said, "I don't know. Alessandro had gotten onto

the kidnapper's trail through Tomasino. He told me Tomasino had come to him in tears and confessed that the day before the kidnapping he had 'borrowed' Alessandro's ruby ring to play king, and that he couldn't give it back because 'the kidnap lady took it.' "

A pause. A sigh.

"Alessandro made Tomasino promise not to tell anyone else about the ruby ring."

Johanna waited; listening, she breathed shallowly, eyes wide. But hearing nothing, she said: "And?"

"That's all I know."

All? With a sinking sensation, Johanna said: "You're sure? Teresa! That's *all?* Wasn't there some little thing, some *hint* even—?"

"Nothing. *Mi dispiace.*"

Nothing. She was barely conscious of the click as Teresa Mantello hung up. She sat motionless, the phone still to her ear. For some reason, the kidnapper had suspected that Alessandro was on his trail. So he had killed him.

And she was next.

She was about to put down the phone when she heard another click. Someone had hung up another phone. Drymouthed, Johanna sat. An extension. *Someone had been listening on an extension.* How many phones were there in the villa? And in what rooms? She didn't know. Who was in the villa? She didn't know that either. She hissed out a breath. Why, in God's name, had she phoned from the villa? She'd been too rattled, too hurried, she should have—what? Anyway, too late!

If the listener on the extension was the murderer, he would immediately try to trace the ruby ring, source of the leak, and silence whoever had supplied Alessandro with the connection, the person Alessandro had called in Rome. And he would finally seal his safety by silencing her, too.

She conquered an impulse to tear off the red silk sling so that she would have two arms and two hands with which to protect herself.

If only she were not so alone!

* * *

In the stable-garage, Elisabetta was checking the battery of Sabina's Lancia, which Sabina never used because, as she said, "I didn't come to La Serena to race around on gasoline!"

Sabina, watching, said, "Such a *pity*! That he has to rush off to Rome! And before lunch, too! Not that it's going to be much of a lunch without Serafina. I don't think we ever really *appreciated* Serafina!"

Elisabetta said, "The battery's fine, we can always depend on Giorgio taking good care of the cars. Really, Mamma, what a waste—not using your car! This is the first time it's been good for anything. I told him he can leave it at our garage in Rome. I gave him the address, and that he's to ask for Aldo."

She got out of the car. "I'm sorry, too, Mama. But as the French say, *Les affaires sont les affairse!* And after all, that's why he's in Italy. Here's Johanna. *Salute, cara!* Isn't it a shame?"

Here indeed was Johanna, but looking uncomprehendingly from Elisabetta to Sabina. "Isn't what a shame?"

"*Cara!*" Sabina said. "Jeff hasn't told you yet? A business appointment, very important, in Rome. He'd simply forgotten. He must leave very soon. And that goes to show how fascinating we Faziolinis are. Distracting visitors with our charm."

"Oh, Mama!" Elisabetta said. And to Johanna, she said, "He was looking for you, to tell you. Jeff, that is. But—"

"But," broke in Sabina, "he's coming back to La Serena the instant—he swears he's not going to miss seeing Alessandro after all this time! And his business plans have changed, he'll be returning to Florence after all and he can drive you back in the Alfa Romeo. Isn't that wonderful?"

"Yes," Johanna said. "Wonderful."

❖ 30 ❖

In Venice, Vittorio Faziolini sat over an aperitif on the terrace of the Gritti Palace. The sun glittered on the Grand Canal, a *motoscafo* sent waves lapping against the stones below.

Vittorio was waiting for the police. There had been a little problem about the hotel turning Alessandro's briefcase over, even to his father. "A matter of discretion, of hotel policy, you understand," the manager had apologized. The manager had looked embarrassed; Vittorio had been a guest at the Gritti off and on for over forty years.

"Non si preoccupi," Vittorio had told him, "don't worry about it." And he'd had the hotel see to it that the police would arrive as quickly as possible, so that in their presence—and so on.

So now he sipped an aperitif, sitting in almost this same spot where, thirty-five years before, he had looked across the terrace and seen a young woman in a blue dress and fair hair seated nearby. He had managed an introduction, and within six months he had married this fair-haired Sabina Veteri from Trieste. He had been helplessly, hopelessly, happily in love with her ever since; in love with her contralto voice, her kindness, her slightly distracted air, her lovely, untidy hair, her ample figure.

He only hoped now that the news he would bring back to her from Venice—

"Signor Faziolini." The waiter was at his elbow, bowing. Two officials from the Questura were at the reception desk with the manager.

147

In the manager's office, the police official, a Captain Zacchera, clicked open the briefcase.

Vittorio Faziolini looked down at the contents. There were the business papers as expected.

But—

Totally mystified, Vittorio stared down at the rest of the contents: Alessandro's monogrammed watch, his credit cards, and his anagraph—the identification card that in Italy is mandatory.

When an hour later Vittorio left the Questura itself, he stood for some minutes in the sunlight, pulling at his white mustache. The officials had asked sympathetic, significant questions. They'd already begun efficiently to make telephone calls to car rental agencies, and to the villas in the north inquiring about tours by bus; by boats, such as *il Burchiello*, that so many tourists took; or by trains. No one had mentioned the canals; neither was the word *suicide* so much as breathed. Nor had the police, so far, questioned the oddness of Alessandro possibly going off somewhere yet leaving his anagraph in his briefcase. In the car, Vittorio, stroking his mustache, clung fiercely to the word *usually*. "Signor Faziolini *usually* left his briefcase to be picked up before his flight to Milan," the clerk at the Gritti had told him when he'd phoned from La Serena. But—had Alessandro also *usually* left his anagraph in the briefcase? Or only this time?

He returned to the Gritti and booked himself a room. Tomorrow morning would again find him at the Questura. As for now—he stopped at the concierge's desk and asked for folders on the centuries-old villas to the north. On the way up in the elevator he tried to think of what to say when in the next few minutes he would call La Serena. And he thought of Alessandro, and he also thought: If Alessandro had intended to do what the police had sympathetically implied, he would have kept his identification on him, so that we would know. *He would not have done it like this.*

❖ 31 ❖

BEHIND ELISABETTA, THE DEEP VOICE WITH THE NEAPOLI-
tan accent said, "You know what will happen to you if you
cry!"

Elisabetta turned quickly and knelt down and pulled
Felicia into her arms, holding her close, thinking: Not
the falsetto, but another voice, threatening; a Neapolitan
accent . . . A man or woman?

"What, *cara*, what?" she begged, smoothing Felicia's
dark curls, but afraid to hear. And as always, whether
Felicia had spoken in the falsetto or that other deep voice,
Felicia only stared back at her with her huge dark eyes,
and her little mouth closed like a bud before an icy blast.

Elisabetta sighed; she kissed Felicia and stood up. They
were in the salon. Elisabetta had been turning on lights. It
was only five o'clock, but the sky had darkened. Rain was
pelting down, whipped around by the wind. Rosa would be
coming in to light a fire; and already here she was.

Elisabetta stood with a caressing hand on Felicia's curls,
but—"I want to find Tomasino! Where's Tomasino?" Felicia
cried out, and she ducked away and dashed out the door.

Rosa said, "Franca is fixing their supper. Tomasino is in
the kitchen making her crazy—he wants to eat the cake first."

Elisabetta felt tension slip from her shoulders. Tomasino's
naughtiness was so reassuringly normal. And the word
kitchen itself somehow eased her mind; it was a homely word
that spelt food, security, warmth.

But at a blast of wind that sent rain rattling against the
windows, she shivered and turned to the basket of kindling
beside the fireplace. "Rosa, find the purple comforter with

the red carnations and bring it up to Miss March's room, it'll be cold tonight. I'll take up some kindling for her fire.''

Alone, she gathered kindling from the basket. Johanna—she must keep a careful eye on Johanna. She would dog her every step, she would watch her with the eyes of Argus, a hundred eyes.

''Johanna is in shock,'' Jeff Thornton had confided, drawing her aside before departing for Rome. ''In shock?'' She was surprised. ''Yes—that Giorgio and Angela were almost killed. And in her car! She feels responsible, she's not herself.'' Jeff had frowned. ''I'd hate to see her injure herself. Accidentally, of course. But guilt—one never knows. So if you'd keep an eye out . . .''

''Of course!'' she'd promised. Jeff Thornton, so attractive in his ugly way; that darkly humorous style, and a certain kind of, well, intelligent *daring*. At least he gave that impression. And so concerned about Johanna. Lucky Johanna!

Elisabetta straightened up, the kindling in her arms; but then she just stood there, listening to the silence in the salon and the pelting of the rain on the windowpanes. She was thinking that at least, thankfully, the two Americans knew nothing of the family's fears for Alessandro.

Lucilla. Sabina. She felt worn out from coping with their emotions. Two hours ago, Vittorio had called from Venice. Except for Matteo, Elisabetta was considered the strong one; she and Matteo had taken it well, at least concealing their fears. And after all, the police in Venice so far had nothing concrete about Alessandro's disappearance. ''Amnesia,'' Elisabetta had suggested to the others, but they had looked at her with blank despair.

She'd had to give Sabina a sedative. Sabina was now sleeping but had said valiantly that she'd be down to dinner. Lucilla had gone woodenly out into the rain without a raincoat or even a scarf over her head; an hour later she'd come back, dripping through the dining room and up the stairs to her room, walking like a robot. Matteo had sat on the couch, elbows on his knees, smacking a clenched fist into his palm, frowning.

"Perhaps I should go to Venice," he had suggested to Elisabetta; but she had shaken her head.

"No. Vittorio would feel better if you were here with us." *Strano.* She would have expected Matteo to know that.

Another scattering of rain like buckshot on the window-panes brought her back to herself. Yes, the kindling. For Johanna.

Sandro Pavone stepped into the phone booth. His feet were wet and the shoulders of his black jacket were sopping. He dropped in a *gettone*. This *maledetto telefono*! A half hour ago, when he'd tried, it hadn't been working; now it was. He listened to the phone ring. He held the paper napkin he'd taken from Peppino's at the ready: This time he would not hang up, he would disguise his voice like in the movies, he—

"*Pronto!*" It was Rosa.

Sandro held the napkin to his mouth and said through it: "I want to speak to Alessandro Faziolini. This is his office." A drop of rain dripped down to the end of his nose: he shook it off. When Alessandro picked up the telephone, he would only say, "*Francesco,*" and wait for Alessandro to shiver and beg. And then he would name his price.

"Signor Alessandro Faziolini? *Non c'è.*"

Through the napkin he said: "When is he . . . How can I . . ."

"*Non c'è,*" that *stupida* repeated. "Signor Faziolini is not presently at La Serena. I don't know when he arrives. Do you have a message?"

"No." He smashed down the phone, furious. Alessandro, that adulterous northern Italian! Where was he? Rolling around in bed with his *inamorata*? Swilling in that other pen? And their little bastard, Francesco!

That summer day at La Serena, doing some carpentry in the hall outside the study, he had heard Alessandro Faziolini's voice on the phone, excited, angry; something like, "No, no! I'll call the hospital myself! For a tonsillectomy I forbid that kind of anesthesia for our son!" and more gently: "*No cara, non ti preoccupare.*"

But, thought Sandro, Alessandro Faziolini had no son; and

his wife, his *cara*, his Lucilla, was upstairs writing poetry. So why shouldn't a poor southern Italian later manage to open Alessandro's private drawer, where the child's thank-you notes for birthday presents were and the drawings signed "Francesco" and the photograph of a dark-haired woman with her arms around a little boy.

A river of gold! He had hidden them in his old vest in the loft, but blackmail was more dangerous than robbery of an empty villa, and he had been dreaming all summer of that robbery when the Faziolinis would be in Rome for the winter. A robbery was a solid thing, you could hold silver and watches and radios in your hands; and on the way up from the Mezzogiorno he had learned of someone in Rome, in Trastevere, who paid well for stolen goods. He'd meant to get the vest that same night, but he'd wanted the things in the villa so badly that he couldn't resist robbing first; and then toward the end the light had gone on in the kitchen—Serafina? He didn't want murder; poisoning the dog was as far—

Someone was banging on the phone booth; a villager in a head scarf glared at him, the wind tearing at her umbrella. He opened the door and got out. But that wasn't good enough for her. "Perhaps you rented this booth, Signore?" she shot at him, and she got in and jerked the door closed.

He stood in the rain. Already he felt the pinch of poverty. He had to get to Alessandro soon. He'd hoped to learn something from the American girl, so he'd offered her a lift. If she couldn't give information, he'd hoped at least to touch her maybe here and there, nothing she could complain about; a *mano morta*, the "dead hand," like in a crowded street, sliding over a breast or down the curve of the girl's behind— "*Scusi, Signorina*, an accident . . ." But that tall American had snatched her away.

Sandro ran a wet hand over his chin. He would have to wait for Alessandro to show up. He looked down at his jacket and cursed. He'd torn the pocket and a sleeve of his jacket on brambles these last couple of days, spying around the Grimini woods. He'd been hoping to find Alessandro hunting or just walking. Twice he had thought he spied him. But both times, it had been Renzo Grimini—Grimini, standing motionless as a tree in the woods, his dark hunting hat pulled low over his bearded face.

In Treangoli, they said that Grimini did not hunt, did not shoot. But yesterday, Sandro, skirting La Raccòlta on the overgrown road in the Grimini woods, had seen Renzo Grimini practicing with his rifle. He'd had a straw-filled target stuck up on the stone wall of that old, unused stable. That's how much those *idioti* in Treangoli knew! They couldn't see more than their *ombelico*, their belly buttons.

JOHANNA COULD HEAR HER FATHER, ANDREW MARCH, saying, "Don't shilly-shally, Johanna—either side of the fence is better than sitting on it."

Run away immediately! That side of the fence looked inviting. The nearest airport was Pisa. Then an international flight to Istanbul, Budapest, Cairo, Nice. Forget the Alfa Romeo, forget her expensive clothes and jewelry and luggage at the Pensione Boldini! Let it all rot. She would escape: bankbooks, checkbooks, tucked into her purse; a rich young woman boarding a plane, first class. She heard the click of her safety belt as she buckled it, she felt the lift as the plane left the runway; she looked from the window at the landscape falling away.

She glanced around the bedroom. Her small traveling bag was on the bench near the chaise lounge; she'd throw everything back into it.

She'd need a car. She'd rent one from Gordini's garage in Treangoli, even buy one if she had to. She'd tell only Elisabetta that she was going; she'd find an excuse, Elisabetta would drive her to the garage in Treangoli. Later she would write a note to Sabina.

"Signorina?" A tap on the door. Rosa. She came in carrying a red and purple comforter; she laid it on the foot of the bed and looked around. "I see that Signora Ligouri brought the kindling. Do you want me to light the fire?"

"No, *grazie*, I'll do it. And Rosa, is there a—" She broke off; she stood staring at the door.

"*Si*, signorina?"

Johanna shook her head. "Nothing, never mind."

Rosa gone, Johanna approached the door. There hadn't been a key in the lock; she'd been about to ask Rosa if there was one, and if so could she please find it. Only now—now there was a key in the lock. Someone within the last few hours had put it there. *Who?*

She turned the key, heard the lock click.

Who was protecting her?—and from whom?

From whom? The question ached in her head and in her very bones. The eavesdropper on the telephone—Jeff Thornton?

Before leaving for Rome, Thornton had knocked on her door: "Zounds! as they say in melodrama. I've got a business dinner at the Hassler in Rome tonight—I'd forgotten it. But I'll be back tomorrow in time to sample Rosa and Franca's lunchtime specialty, whatever it is. I hope you'll miss me." A light tone, but his face looked strained, and his gaze slid past her and made a quick tour of her room.

Tomorrow, lunchtime. At lunchtime tomorrow he'd find her gone. She couldn't take a chance. *I have only one life.* She thought bitterly of how they'd met, she so innocent, so unsuspecting. Jeff Thornton had seen her on the balcony with Alessandro. Later, why had he really come to the pensione? To contrive to meet her and learn how much she really knew? But—a bearded man? Or maybe a man *in a false beard*. Bitter, bitter! And still, foolishly, she felt torn between saving her life and what could be a deadly attraction.

Get off the fence, Johanna.

She folded a shirt and slid it into the traveling bag. She dared not even make a plane reservation from La Serena.

She trusted no one, *no one*; she must leave no trace. Tonight it was storming and already dark, and she didn't know the roads. But in the morning with a map, the road to Pisa—thank God she'd kept her passport with her; she hadn't liked the idea of leaving it at the pensione.

In the bathroom she turned on the water for a bath before dinner. The narrow bathroom window suddenly blew open and a gust of wind tangled the shower curtain before Johanna managed to fasten the window closed. The storm was worse than she'd supposed.

The bath was soothing. She lay there in the long marble tub that was big enough for a giantess. Dinner in less than an hour. Then she'd come back to this bedroom, lock the door, lie on the chaise lounge, and let her mind go twisting down every labyrinthine path, exploring every possible way to find and expose the criminal, whoever he was.

Because, even escaped from La Serena, wherever she might be—Florence, Cairo, Boston, Bombay—somehow she would find a means, a key, a method, that would still conceal Teresa Mantello. And then she would go to Criminalpol.

In the bath, she swished the soap around. It could be costly. But she was not, after all, a woman without resources: She had money, Alessandro Faziolini's *Totocalcio* winnings.

"You look like a flower," Sabina said when Johanna came into the salon.

"Sabina's right," Matteo said. He flashed her an admiring smile; he had probably the whitest teeth she had ever seen.

"Thank you." She wore lavender silk pants and a pink silk shirt with a ruffled neck, and she had sleeked her hair up so that it shone gold in the light from the chandelier. Her traveling bag had held enough clothes for a weekend; it was incredible that she had been at La Serena only two nights: Friday and Saturday. And now, tonight.

Sabina, in a dark red velvet caftan, looking vague and she had spoken slowly, pushing out each word oddly, with an effort: " . . . like . . . a . . . flowerrr." Elisabetta—again medieval-looking by some strange magic, or perhaps it was the shape of her face and her white eyelids—looked at Johanna as alertly as a nurse checking a patient. There was only one dinner guest, Renzo Grimini; he was frowning into a glass of something that he held in one elegant hand and he seemed not to notice Johanna at all.

Only Lucilla was still missing.

Something was terribly wrong. Johanna sensed it at once. It had to be about Alessandro: They knew something. Vittorio suddenly, mysteriously gone away; Elisabetta with vigilant eyes; Sabina strongly sedated. Johanna had taken care of her father long enough to recognize the signs of despair: the vague eyes, the flaccid cheeks, the placid smile that went beyond placidity.

Within the next half hour while they waited for Lucilla, she was positive. Tension seemed almost to vibrate in the room, increasing as the storm outside increased, battering the windows. It slid into voices, gestures, the erratic sipping of drinks; it surfaced in Elisabetta's almost impassioned, insulting remarks to Renzo Grimini—"Renzo gets Sabina to invite him! He's always here," Elisabetta had said angrily to Johanna earlier. "You'd think La Raccòlta had no kitchen, no cook! And I don't suppose it has!"—but Renzo was impervious to Elisabetta's remarks, and that seemed to inflame her more. As for Matteo, he had taken to pacing the room and scratching under his chin. A nervous habit? A rash?

And then suddenly—Lucilla.

Lucilla in the doorway.

She wore old slacks and a black jersey. Her wild aureole of hair was wilder than ever, her face paler, her protruding brown eyes stared.

Instead of coming in, she lurched and put a steadying hand on the doorjamb.

"Drunk! She's drunk!" It was a whisper from Matteo.

Lucilla swayed. "Alessandro! Don't go yet. Please! Don't go!" A piteous voice. "Please! *It is too soon!*"

"Lucilla!" Elisabetta said sharply, "Stop it! *Stop it!*"

For a moment there was only the crackling of the fire: It seemed to Johanna as though the Faziolinis, alas, were waiting for a phone that was not going to ring, the sound of a door opening that they were not going to hear. Then Sabina broke into tears and left, and Rosa half carried Lucilla off to bed.

They ate dinner from the coffee table in the salon, the four of them that were left: Johanna and Elisabetta, Matteo and Renzo.

Afterward, they played cards in the study. Bridge. Renzo played shrewdly; Elisabetta played with boredom. Matteo tried to see his opponents' cards and scratched constantly under his chin. It *was* a rash; Johanna could see the red, inflamed irritation when Matteo tipped back his head to look at the study clock. She'd had a similar rash as a child, she couldn't remember why, but she'd try. She'd been given an ointment for it. Maybe it could help Matteo.

Back again in her room by ten-thirty, she locked her door and went to bed. Her last sight of the shadowy room as her eyes closed was of the long hump of the chaise, on which she seemed to see a shape, a man's figure lying on its side, a bent arm supporting his head; she could even see him watching her, see the glint of Jeff Thornton's eyes. But of course he was not there, she knew that; yet she pulled the blanket more closely up around her shoulders. Not there— not there. But in Rome.

IN A HOTEL ROOM IN ROME, JEFF THORNTON SAID INTO THE phone: "Signora, an emergency! I have an important message for a client of yours—Alessandro Faziolini. It may save a life! Please connect me at once with whomever is handling the case! *Grazie, grazie!*"

He waited, holding the phone. He sat at a little desk that held a thermos of coffee and a telephone book.

"Signore?" came a young woman's voice. "*Mi dispiace*, there must be a mistake, we have no—"

"*Scusi*, Signora! The mistake is mine, the similarity of the agency name. *Scusi, scusi.*"

He hung up. With a pencil he made a tiny check mark in the *Pagine Gialle*, the yellow pages, that lay open to *Agenzie Investigative*. Twenty-three so far. Some hadn't answered, some were recordings. Sunday, after all. About twenty more to go.

He picked up the phone.

Aldo Furia's office on Via Frattina was modest, decent, clean. It was a one-man office, exactly the size Furia liked; it fitted him like a custom-made suit. He was happy with it, he was his own boss, he had an answering service; and the small cases he took on brought in a reasonable living. He'd enjoyed doing the small job for Alessandro Faziolini; it was easier than biting into a peach. Such a simple little case, hardly a case! And Signor Faziolini had paid well, in fact had already paid half.

But at ten o'clock tonight, that alarming telephone call! Furia's answering service had immediately telephoned him at home. And now, an hour later in his office, this American sitting across from him in the straight-backed varnished chair. The American, a Signor Thornton, was dark-haired, in his thirties, with a tanned, long-jawed face. He conveyed an enviable impression of being *padrone di se*, in charge of himself. He was looking back at Furia with assessing gray-green eyes and saying in his resonant voice that he was Alessandro Faziolini's closest friend and that something terrible had happened: "An accident on the Autostrada outside Milan." Signor Faziolini was dead. "Killed on impact."

"*Mah! Orribile!*" Furia sank back in his chair and stared at the American. He felt shocked and confused. "I don't understand! My answering service said, 'An important message for Alessandro Faziolini!' "

"No, no!" the American said, "I told them an important message *about* Alessandro Faziolini." He spread his hands, an apologetic gesture. "My Italian—I do not speak as fluently as I could wish. Perhaps—"

Furia blinked. "And the message was, "It may save a life!' Surely—"

"Scusi! Peccato! Peccato! 'Too late to save his life,' I thought I said. Your answering service is not to blame. The death of my closest friend! You can understand I hardly knew what—the confusion was certainly mine."

"Capisco," Furia said. He felt terrible. And not for his bill, but because he had like Signor Faziolini, little as he had known him.

The American sat silent for a moment, looking grave; then he said that Alessandro had confided something to him about the case. And certainly, as a good friend, he would sign whatever papers were necessary to further carry out the investigation. And of course he, Signor Thornton, would pay the bill. It was the very least he could do for a friend.

"Si. Capisco." But Furia felt something in himself close up. Cold fingers of warning touched him behind his ears. In this business, caution was everything.

"So if you'll just fill me in . . ." the American said.

But Furia instead looked down at the plastic desk set on his desk; the set was made to look like marble, a gift from a satisfied client. *Sicurezza*—reliability, his ad said. And *Massima segretezza*—highest secrecy. He wished he could trust this American. But caution demanded—

"I should mention," the American said, "That Alessandro has already told me about the ring. The ruby ring."

Furia looked up, the weight of the world rolling off his shoulders. *"Mah!* The ruby ring! But that's all there was!" He ran a hand over his jaw; he almost laughed at himself for hesitating. That simple little case! Not really a case for an investigator at all! A job for a clerk.

"That's all there was," he repeated.

The American looked puzzled. "I don't understand."

"That was it," Furia said patiently. "Signor Faziolini wanted me to find the ruby ring. I found it."

"Ah," the American said. He sat back and loosely folded

his hands. "I'm glad—glad for Signor Faziolini's sake that you were able to—" He broke off.

Furia said, "Signor Faziolini had lost the ring, he thought it lost or stolen, it was not valuable, but he had a sentimental—he did not wish to go to the police. He thought someone might have pawned it. He hired me to check out the pawnshops in Rome, even in *la periferia*, the suburbs. Three days it took me! But I found it. In a shop in Centocelle, one of the suburbs. Because I'm an investigator, the pawnshops are cooperative, they may even know my reputation—I have always been—but never mind. The pawnbroker was cooperative."

Furia looked seriously at the American. " 'Lost,' you understand, is different from 'stolen'—it makes things easier."

"I see."

"The ring had been found by an elderly woman of good reputation, a neighborhood resident. The pawnbroker knew her. He had only good words for her. It is a small neighborhood. Over the years she has pawned a few personal things."

"And the ring?"

Furia unlocked the middle desk drawer and took out an envelope. *"Eccolo!"* He handed it across the desk. "Signor Faziolini asked me to keep it until he could come for it."

The American opened the envelope and looked at the ring. It was gold, with a small ruby in the center and a tiny diamond in the lower left side.

Furia said, "Signor Faziolini of course wished me to investigate a bit further."

"Yes. And so?"

"It appears the woman found the ring on the street. And since the ring wasn't valuable, and no one advertised . . ." Furia shrugged.

The American slid the ring back into the envelope and laid it on the desk.

"You went to see her, Signor Furia?"

"Certo! You understand, Signor Thornton, that Alessandro Faziolini was paying me for the facts of the case. I believe I already said that."

"Yes, yes. You did. So?"

So Aldo Furia had neatly, methodically, in his careful handwriting, assembled all that Signor Faziolini might wish to know. The elderly woman, a Signora Scalzo, lived on a narrow, shabby street of small houses.

Furia leafed through a notebook and read aloud carefully to the American: "Living on small income from savings, previously a nurse for well-off invalid who left her a modest sum of money and some bits of family possessions, which she pawns from time to time when she runs short: crocheted doilies yellow with age, an eagle-headed cane, an old tray that is not plate but real silver, a lady's enamel pin shaped like a peacock, a half-dozen dishes of good quality. That is all. At one time or another, all these possessions have landed in the pawnshop. But Signora Scalzo always redeems them. They are her 'treasures,' according to the pawnbroker."

When Furia finished reading the notebook, the American asked him to please read it again. Furia obliged; he enjoyed his neat handwriting and the sound of his voice in his neat office.

At the end, the American said abruptly: "And you told all this to Alessandro Faziolini?"

"No. I read it to him."

"When?"

"*Mah!* Eleven, twelve days ago! He telephoned, long distance it sounded like, and I read it out loud. He said I had done an excellent job. He said that was all he wished done. He thanked me. He said he would send me a check. But—" Furia blushed; the money part was always the most difficult to handle. "But then I did not hear from him."

The American said: "Did you tell him anything else on the phone? Any other—names of anyone?"

Furia looked at the American, mystified. He shook his head. "Nothing."

For a moment, the American just sat; his gray-green eyes were thoughtful; Furia noted for the first time that the man's eyelids were a little reddened as though he'd been without sleep. Then the American took out his pen and a checkbook. "I have an account at the Banco Nazionale. If you will give me Signor Faziolini's bill . . ."

When he left, he had the envelope with the ruby ring in his pocket. But because Aldo Furia was neatly methodical, he wrote out a receipt and dated it; and after the American had signed it and left, he put it in the clean, almost empty file marked "Alessandro Faziolini."

❖ 34 ❖

IN THE EARLY MORNING DARKNESS, HE DROVE. HE HAD taken the Autostrada north out of Rome; at Orvieto he would turn left onto the regional highway and from there take the little roads that stumbled through hilly villages with stone houses, where dogs would raise their heads at the sound of the car, their eyes glowing in the headlights.

His own eyes felt grainy. He'd had no sleep since he had eavesdropped on Johanna's telephone conversation with the unknown woman and then quietly put down the phone. Then Rome and the neat little office of Aldo Furia with his clean-cut, decent face. And the envelope with the ruby ring. Thornton's right hand left the wheel and strayed to his pocket. Then he ran his hand over his face, blinked, and pressed down on the accelerator—unconsciously he had been slowing down. Now he overtook a car ahead and once past resolutely kept up his speed. The Autostrada was wet from a rainstorm and a mist covered the windshield; the windshield wiper clicked back and forth, as dangerously lulling as a lullaby.

So far he had driven two hours through the wet dawn on the road that was treacherous after the rain, while he probed at his tired brain, forcing it. In Rome, he had almost found what he was looking for, but not quite. He had hoped that with his knowledge of Alessandro, he could have guessed. But no. Back again at the hotel after leaving Furia, he had lain on the bed for hours, hands behind his head, prying at the mystery, but it was like a tin can for which he had no opener. At five in the morning, he had stripped, showered, dressed again and driven out of Rome.

An elderly woman of good reputation. No, not that. Wearily he went through it again: *A nurse for a well-off invalid.* What else? *Crocheted doilies, an old silver tray, a lady's enamel pin shaped like a peacock, an eagle-headed cane.* No good. Nothing came to him.

He drove on, shoulders aching, jaw tense. He should stop for hot coffee before he fell asleep. The Autostrada was drying up. Sunlight suddenly fell dazzlingly across the wet windshield. His watch, surprisingly, said eight o'clock. He turned off the windshield wiper. He'd been driving for three hours. Two more before he reached Treangoli.

Treasures. "Her treasures," Aldo Furia had said.

With a sudden intake of breath, Thornton snapped upright.

It was eight-thirty by the time he saw a gas station ahead. At the phone he called La Serena. The line was busy. At five minute intervals he tried again, pacing back and forth between calls, frustrated, impatient, flicking a thumbnail and ready to instantly pick up the phone again if anyone else showed up to use it. But no one did. Six times he tried, the line always busy. Then, in desperation, "Enough!" he said aloud. In twenty minutes, speeding, he could reach the turn-off at Orvieto. He would call from there, and then get back onto the highway, and at Orano turn left onto the narrow dirt road toward Treangoli.

Outside, he jumped into the car. Nine-thirty. The sun had disappeared; it was clouding up again, darkening. Wind whirled, raindrops spattered the road.

Her treasures.

At Orvieto, frustration again. He pulled at his nose, cursed, and splashed back to the car. Orano, a village the size of a haystack. But then he tried once more, and—

"*Pronto!*" came Rosa's voice on the phone from La Serena.

"Rosa! This is Signor Thornton. Let me speak to Signor Faziolini!"

"*Non c'è*. Signor Faziolini is still in Venezia."

"Then Signora Ligouri, *per favore*!"

"*Mi dispiace*, I am looking for her myself. I can't find her, not even in the attic, I—"

"Signora Sabina Faziolini! Get me—"

"*Mi dispiace*. Signora Faziolini sleeps, they gave her pills, I cannot—"

"Then get me Signora Lucilla Faziolini!"

Silence. Then: "The Signora has locked herself in her room, she does not wish—"

Thornton gripped the phone. He said urgently, "Rosa! How long have you worked at La Serena?"

"*Mah!* From the time the Faziolinis first—"

"*How long?*"

"Signore, thirty years. Franca, too, we came the same—"

"Rosa! I'm going to say something. Listen carefully! *D'accordo?*"

A hesitant "*Si*, Signore."

He went over it then, trying not to rush, saying each word carefully, silently cursing his poor Italian. When he had finished, he said, "What does this mean to you?"

"*Scusi*, Signore. *Significa qualcosa*, but I don't know what. I remember—no, I don't remember. *Mi dispiace.*"

He was beginning to hate the words *Mi dispiace*.

"Rosa! Where's Franca?"

"Changing the linen, Signore. It is Monday, we always—"

"*Find her!* I want to speak to her right away!"

"*Si*, Signore."

In minutes, he heard Franca's voice on the phone, anxious, worried: "*Si*, Signor Thornton?"

He went over it again, carefully. Then he waited seconds that were eons.

Franca remembered. "*Si*, Signore! *Ricordo!*"

When she had told him, he took an enormous breath. Then quickly he said, "Signor Grimini—is he there? And Matteo Del Bosco?"

Neither one, Franca told him. Signor Grimini might come for lunch, that was all. Signor Del Bosco was somewhere, maybe in the salon or in his room. "Impossible to hunt today, Signore, it is still too wet, we've had a nasty rain, such terrible—"

"Miss March! I must speak to her!"

"*Non c'è*, Signore."

"Where is she?" He almost shouted it. *"Where is Miss March?"*

His tone must have frightened the woman. He heard a hurried spate of whispers, then not Franca but Rosa came back on the line. "Signore? *Si*, Signorina March—she can't be far. A minute ago she went out on the terrace, I saw her through the window. Then Tomasino—yes, Tomasino came running up to her, he came from the woods, he was crying, I could see that, his little face gets so—Miss March knelt down, she pulled him to her. But then the phone rang, I came to answer, it was you, Signore." Then worriedly she added, "I hope they have not gone into the woods! The storm passed over, the rain stopped an hour ago, but now there is lightning and thunder again. Trees attract lightning, *vero*, Signore? So—"

He slammed down the phone, swore, called the operator, verified a number, made a call that lasted less than a minute, and thirty seconds later was driving like a Le Mans racer, hanging fiercely onto the wheel, his reddened eyes fierce, a pulse beating in his temple.

❖ 35 ❖

ONLY THE SCENT OF HER PERFUME REMAINED IN THE BED-
room; she stood near the door beside her packed weekend bag
and swept the room with a final glance. It was nine o'clock in
the morning. The windows were open to the rain-freshened
air, the fireplace held ash, the bed was as yet unmade, the
cushions of the chaise lounge still bore yesterday's imprint of
her body. On her left wrist she wore, for some rebellious,
strange, unhappy reason, the Florentine gold bracelet.

She had dressed in the yellow dress and high heels in which
she had arrived. Her tan coat was already downstairs, lying
across a chair near the front entrance. Now she slung the big
Fendi pouch from her shoulder, picked up her traveling bag,
and went downstairs.

She stood in the front hall. "Elisabetta?"

No answer. Where was she? Early this morning, at no
more than seven o'clock, Elisabetta had knocked on her door,
saying, "Johanna?" And when she'd unlocked the door,
Elisabetta had looked relieved and said something vague
about having heard a crash as she'd been passing in the hall;
she'd thought something might have fallen.

"No, nothing," Johanna had told her. But she had seized
the chance to fumble out a lie about having to rush back to
Florence right away; she'd awakened in the night remembering that she was to sign some important legal papers at the
Banco Americana, a date deadline.

"*Peccato!*" Elisabetta had said. "I'll miss you, Johanna." But, *certo*!—she would drive Johanna to Treangoli
where she might rent a car at Gordini's.

The only thing was, explained Elisabetta, that at nine-thirty

166

she had to give Sabina some sedatives. "Sabina is a little disturbed, a family situation—she was on the phone with Vittorio for an hour this morning! He's in Venice." Elisabetta's light gray eyes did not quite meet Johanna's, her reddish hair was drawn back more carelessly than usual, and her face looked tired. "I don't trust Sabina to take the pills correctly, she forgets how many she's taken, even while she's taking them."

So it was settled. They would leave right after nine-thirty.

Only here it was, nine thirty-five; no, nine-forty already. Johanna's traveling bag was at her feet in the front hall, the tan coat over her arm.

But where was Elisabetta?

Johanna walked out of the great curved doors and stood in the gravel drive that was still wet with rain. "Elisabetta?"

Back inside, she called, "Elisabetta?" No sound. Upstairs, she found Franca at the linen closet in the hall. *Si*, Franca had seen Signora Ligouri just minutes ago; she had been coming from Signora Faziolini's room, and she had stopped and chatted with Matteo Del Bosco, then gone downstairs, "to the kitchen, *penso*, I think."

In the kitchen she called, "Elisabetta?" But there was only Rosa in the kitchen. "*Si*, Signora Ligouri was here in the kitchen, she was looking in a drawer—*Scusi*, Signorina March, the telephone is ringing, Franca is upstairs—"

Alone in the kitchen, she stood a moment. The wall clock ticked. She could hear Rosa on the phone in the dining room; outside, thunder rumbled. Were they in for another storm?

She went out onto the terrace. It was rain-swept and deserted. The sky was bulbous with dark clouds, and beyond the field the Grimini woods looked greenish-black.

And there in the long grass of the field was a little figure running toward the terrace, running toward her; the little figure reached the terrace, stumbling and crying.

"Tomasino!" She knelt down, drew him to her, and looked into his contorted face. "Tomasino! What's the matter?"

"Felicia! She's so frightened, and I can't—!" His sobbing was near-hysterical. "I can't untie her! The rope is too wet! She's in the woods, I tied her up, and now—she's so afraid

of lightning, even in bed she gets stiff all over and screams!''
He was dirty, wet, and trembling; his face was scratched.

''Where is she? Come on!''

He ran ahead of her, crying, skinny little arms flying. In the
woods, the trees were thicker than she remembered, the rocks
were blackened by the rain. Bushes soaked her, brambles tore
at her, her feet were quickly soaked and gritty with dirt.
Branches whipped across her face, but she was never more
than a foot or so behind Tomasino as he ran on, down a ravine,
up the other side, onto an old road so overgrown that it was
hardly a road, and then across the stone culvert over the trick-
ling stream. Only now it was not a trickle, it was a rushing,
tumbling stream; she heard it before she saw it.

''Felicia, I'm here!'' Tomasino cried out. ''I brought
somebody!'' He ran in among the trees at the top of the
slope, flung himself down on his knees, and turned his anguished face up to Johanna. ''You see! You see!''

Felicia was on the ground, she sat propped up against a tree,
her hands and feet tied. A handkerchief that must have been a
blindfold had slipped down and hung around her neck. Her
sturggles to get free had twisted her navy jersey around her
body and torn her shorts. Her big eyes were dazed with fright.

''My heavens!'' Johanna said in a light voice, ''look at
you!'' And she knelt quickly and smiled at the little girl as
she began to untie the ropes around her wrists. ''A fine thing!
But in two minutes I'll have you free, and we'll run back to
the house and Rosa will make you all dry and clean again!
And then we'll all have some hot cocoa in the kitchen. Maybe
even some of that leftover cake.'' She was trying to untie the
ropes, but they weren't really ropes; they were strips of torn
cloth, and she was hampered by her arm in its sling. She
yanked off the sling and plucked with her narrow but strong
fingers at the stubborn binding, loosening the knots.

It was a slow business, but finally Felicia's wrists were
free. The bindings around her ankles were more difficult;
meanwhile the sky had darkened. At a flash of lightning,
Felicia cried out in fear.

In the lightning flash, something in Johanna's range of vision
gleamed; something behind a tree. Her heart went cold.

With one last pull at Felicia's binding, "There!" she said, and she pulled it off. She stood Felicia up and laughed and gave the child's hips a little wiggle. "See? It wasn't even tight or anything! So you can run off home now. Go on!"

They ran, Tomasino first grabbing up the radio from beside the tree. Johanna looked after them. The children first. No harm must come to them. Whatever was happening, she had brought it on herself. She watched them out of sight.

Then she dropped the strip of torn cloth still held and was careful not to look toward the rifle barrel whose gleam she had glimpsed in the flash of lightning. Yet she was agonizingly aware if it; aware of exactly where it jutted from behind a tree barely a dozen feet away—a tree with low, leafy branches.

Now, only now, could she move.

But where? How? She could make a run for it, but already she saw her soaked shoes sliding, twisting; saw herself falling, felt the bullet strike her body, saw herself lying huddled, wet blood seeping. She drew in an enormous, trembling breath and slowly let it out. Words were weapons; with words she might have a chance. So—so now she would begin to stroll toward the villa, as casually as though—

The falsetto spoke from behind the tree: "What did Felicia and Tomasino think they would remember, with that radio to help them? They would remember nothing, *nothing*—not with the soup that drugged them a little every day so they wouldn't remember!" From behind the tree came a laugh in that falsetto. Beneath the false voice was the timbre of a voice familiar to Johanna. *Whose* voice?

"You and your lover, Alessandro!" The falsetto was shrill. "I never suspected Alessandro—lovers! In Florence, in bed, whispering in each other's hair, he told you secrets! And then you saw too much: the mugging, the drowning."

"No! He didn't! We weren't lovers! I only saw—"

"But after, in Florence," the voice shrilled on, unheeding, "when I saw that you went about your own frivolous business, shopping, dining, I was relaxed, I didn't—I was a fool not to suspect!"

Among the lower branches, close against the tree trunk, she saw something; it was a leg in a dark-brown hunting boot.

She tried to summon a protest, to plead innocence; at the same time, in some strange way, glimpsing that finite leg somehow gave her a rebellious courage, a will. She lowered her eyes; under their lids she frantically searched the ground. A weapon, something, if only—"No," she meantime cried out, "I never—"

"—not to suspect," the falsetto repeated. "But then *you came to La Serena*. That was a shock. Faking a sprained wrist. Clever! On the trail! Four million dollars in American money. Did you expect to squeeze out a share for yourself?" The falsetto mocked her.

No weapon anywhere; among the leaves and grass she saw no stick to throw or stone to fling and startle him—nothing. *Nothing* with which to defend herself. Only—only there to the left of that tree that hid the killer, there at the left in those thick bushes, those bushes with red berries—why was there a faint rustle in those bushes? Why were they trembling? A bird feeding on the red berries? Or had someone come, and hearing the strange falsetto . . .

She looked away from the bushes and toward the tree. Now she saw not only the killer's hunting boot, but a khaki-clad elbow below the rifle. She cried out: "You killed him! You killed Alessandro! You drowned him!"

Silence. Then, "Ah, yes, Alessandro," came the falsetto. "And now, *peccato*, there will be a second drowning. An accident. The American girl, walking in the woods, slips and falls over the culvert and strikes her head on a rock in the stream below. Unconscious in the stream, she drowns. I am holding in my hand the rock on which the poor girl unfortunately—"

From the trembling bushes with their red berries, a figure burst forth with an inarticulate cry. It was Elisabetta, wild-eyed, with a face of shock and horror.

"Murderer!" she cried out, *"Murderer!"* She launched herself toward the concealed killer, arms out-stretched, hands like claws—and the muzzle of the gun swung to cover her. He halted, her arms fell to her sides.

"Murderer," she whispered, in a hesitant voice. "Murderer."

Then, lazily, Matteo stepped from behind the tree. He

dropped the rock from his hand. "Elisabetta, *cara*, you change my plans." The falsetto voice was gone. Matteo's heavy, handsome face was calm; it was as calm as a mask made of ice. He glanced from Elisabetta to Johanna. Johanna gazed back at him in disbelief. He gave a laugh and turned again to Elisabetta.

"Why aren't you performing your household duties? Like taking care of the broken bottles in the wine cellar?"

Elisabetta whispered incredulously, staring at Matteo with his rifle. "Matteo . . . *You* . . ."—then with growing horror—"*Monstro!* Monster!"

The frozen calm of Matteo's face abruptly shattered. "*Dio!* I didn't want to do it! Not any of it! Not Alessandro. I never meant—"

"*Meant?*" Elisabetta took a stumbling step toward Matteo. "*Dio! Dio!* You never *meant!*" She pulled her faded red hair about her ears, as though to shut out the world. Johanna impulsively moved toward her. Immediately, Matteo lifted the rifle. He cursed.

He cried out angrily at Elisabetta: "I only meant to borrow the twins for a couple of weeks! I needed the money, I was in trouble! I could have gone to prison!"

A wind swept through the trees; the word *prison* swelled around the three of them. Johanna thought, Matteo will do any madness now. *He will kill us both.* She tensed her muscles to spring. If she could leap at him, grab his gun, and scream to Elisabetta to run, then maybe . . . She measured the distance to him: twelve feet at least. Hopeless.

"Alessandro," Elisabetta said woodenly, fingers tangled in her hair. "But—"

"Alessandro was on my trail because of Caterina Scalzo, that stupid old witch! He had an investigator, I saw him! I made her confess. I knew that when Alessandro would hear the name Caterina Scalzo, he would know. But he'd already left for Venice. I followed him there, then on the train to a pensione in Florence."

Elisabetta, fingers twisting and twisting in her straggling hair, stood staring at Matteo. "You followed him," she said numbly, "and you . . ."

"He would have been merciless!" Matteo cried out

fiercely. His forehead was gleaming with sweat. He thrust out his head suddenly toward Johanna.

"Do you know why? Or do only the Faziolinis and their *amico della famiglia* share that secret!" And he turned back to Elisabetta and said with bared teeth: *"Because he had nothing to lose."*

Elisabetta gazed at Matteo as though he were too loathsome to fathom. *"Dio!"* she whispered. "We treasured each day of Alessandro's life. His life was running out like sand. Perhaps only another few months—and you took that from him!"

"Alessandro was dying! I could not let him destroy me first! His months, or maybe even a year or two, against *my whole life*!"

With a cry of rage, Elisabetta launched herself at Matteo; he stepped back and brought up a meaty fist that exploded on the side of Elisabetta's head. She went down and lay still, her face in leaves and dirt.

"Damn you!" Matteo turned his fury on Johanna. "You did it all! Coming here! They would never have known. Now it's all broken open! You! *You!*" He picked up the rock he had earlier dropped; he was out of control. He strode to where she stood beside the stone culvert. He gripped her arm; his fingers were iron, his face was terrible. A grimace of hate. He raised the rock.

A rifle shot. The rock flew from his hand.

They stood like statues in a child's game; Matteo with one empty hand raised, the other gripping Johanna's arm. Johanna simply stood, helpless in that grip.

"Let her go," a voice said, a man's voice. "Step away from her."

Matteo, dazed, released Johanna. He stepped away.

"Johanna, pick up the rifle." Johanna obeyed. The rifle was heavy, unfamiliar; she hated the touch of it.

Then, out of the bushes across the culvert stepped Renzo Grimini.

"Renzo!" Elisabetta's voice. She was sitting up, one hand at the side of her face, brushing away wet dirt and leaves. She looked dazed, her reddish hair straggled across her forehead.

Renzo gave her a quick glance, but he kept his rifle unswervingly on Matteo. "We are going to have a procession." His deep voice was courteous. "A little parade to La Serena. There we will make a telephone call to the police. The order of the parade will be thus—Matteo Del Bosco in the lead, followed by Renzo Grimini with the rifle aimed at Del Bosco's head. Bringing up the rear will be Elisabetta Ligouri and Johanna March. *Capite?*"

Now Renzo cast a smile at Johanna and Elisabetta. Except for the rifle, he was oddly dressed for hunting. He wore an exquisitely tailored suit, as though he were going for a stroll on Rome's Via Veneto and to lunch at an expensive restaurant. His French cuffs gleamed and his silky dark beard was carefully combed.

He waited until Elisabetta was on her feet, pushing back her hair with shaky hands.

"You're all right?" At Elisabetta's nod, he started across the culvert, rifle trained on Matteo.

Johanna, moving to Elisabetta's side, awkwardly clutching the unfamiliar weapon, was thinking confusedly but thankfully. *We're alive, we're safe! Matteo, the murderer, is trapped! How—*

"No!" Elisabetta screamed as one of Renzo Grimini's feet sank into the ground and he pitched forward on his face. But still he gripped the rifle, gripped it tenaciously; and twisting around, he aimed and fired desperately and uselessly at Matteo who disappeared into the woods.

"*Maledizione!*" Renzo pushed himself to a sitting position. With one hand, he brushed aside some branches and looked down at the crude little trap the twins had made: a hole that had at the bottom a handful of upright little stakes made from pine branches. Not enought to trap a mouse, much less to damage an expensive city shoe. But, unfortunately, enough to let the murderer escape. And he himself had even seen the twins at their pathetic labors. "*Maledizione!*"

Johanna, dazed, looked at the green depths of the forest, where Matteo had disappeared toward La Serena. His bullet-shaped car was in the stable-garage; in minutes he would be gone. She looked down at the rifle she still held. Matteo's rifle. Matteo. It had been Matteo. She was bewildered. She could not understand it. Jeff Thornton, where did he fit in? An accomplice? Yes, surely, since he had gone to Rome.

She drew a trembling breath. She wished she could be happy; after all, she was alive. But she felt miserable. She said soberly to Renzo, who was now standing and brushing dirt and twigs from his fashionable suit: "Thank you. You saved my life. *Fortunato* that you arrived just in time!"

Renzo smiled. "*Fortunato?* My dear Miss March! Do you suppose that 'luck' arranges such fortuitous circumstances? Do you think perhaps that I go strolling in the Grimini woods dressed for Rome?"

"Then . . ." She frowned, puzzled.

"Jeff Thornton. You can thank him. He reached me at *La Raccòlta*, he was phoning from Orano. He told me a fifteen-second horror tale. He had learned that Matteo Del Bosco—you were in the woods. I was to take my rifle."

❖ 36 ❖

THE TWO MEN FROM CRIMINALPOL WERE EFFICIENT, CON-cise, angry, and forbearingly sympathetic. The balding one kept leaving the salon and calling Rome from the phone in the study. They had arrived a bare five hours after a dirty, bruised Elisabetta had telephoned Criminalpol. They had already been here an hour. They snapped out questions, made notes, and drank coffee that a bewildered and frightened Rosa brought in on a tray.

Jeff Thornton thought: *For now, lie low. Wait. Listen.*

He glanced to his left at Vittorio Faziolini, impressive as a lion, a dust-stained lion, sitting stiffly upright in a hard-backed Florentine chair. Vittorio had arrived from Venice twenty minutes ago, and had been greeted with the awful revelation. His melancholy eyes with their secret sorrows were fixed hypnotically on the figures in the faded carpet.

So now, Jeff thought, one of Vittorio Faziolini's secret sorrows had surfaced: Alessandro's fated early death, that congenital heart disease in his only son.

But the means! The means! The brutal killing, and the perfidy it exposed. Sabina had collapsed with the shock of it. Dr. Rosella had arrived, given her an injection, and departed. Now she slept.

Lucilla, though. Across from Jeff, Lucilla sat, her protruding brown eyes staring down at her hands that she was twisting and twisting in her lap. "I knew!" she had cried out, when Elisabetta had told her as gently as possible. "I *knew* Alessandro was dead. *Dead!* I knew it, finally. Or he'd have come for my birthday! Dead, dead, dead! But it was too soon! Too soon!" Lucilla seemed indifferent that Matteo had been the instrument of death; she seemed equally indifferent that he had been the kidnapper of Elisabetta's children.

As for the other three people in the salon, Johanna, Elisabetta, and Renzo Grimini, they were no longer the wet, disheveled, wildly-waving figures who had come running toward him as he brought the Lancia screeching to a stop in the drive. They had had time to wash and change into dry clothes. Johanna was sitting at his right, so close that he was aware of her light breathing, and, peripherally, of the curve of her cheek. But he did not even look her way: He was wondering what lies she was planning to tell. He also wondered if, when he lied, his own eyes narrowed as hers did.

". . . broken bottles in the wine cellar, Matteo told me. He must have knocked them off a rack himself," Elisabetta was explaining to the men from Criminalpol. "I was the only one here to take care of it. The door latch is defective, he knew he could make the door lock 'by accident' and lock me in, while he—" She looked at Johanna, then back at the man from Criminalpol. "I don't know what! Throw her down the stairs? But there are a few things about La Serena that even the *amico della famiglia* didn't know, such as the old abandoned exit from the time the wine cellar was truly a cave. I had only to move the . . ." Elisabetta's voice died.

"So then?" prompted the taller of the Criminalpol agents, the one named Tostelli.

"I was going to drive Miss March to Treangoli but I couldn't find her. Tomasino said she was in the woods. I thought she might have gotten lost. I went to find her, and—and I heard a voice, a falsetto voice." Elisabetta made a gesture, an opening out of her arms, her hands empty; something they had held was lost forever. She shuddered.

The bald man from Criminalpol, Ponroni his name was, came back into the salon. He was caressing his head and looking at his notebook. "Del Bosco's blue Lamborghini has been found. He abandoned it at Civetavecchia, between Route One and A-Twelve. If he had lire, he could have got a fisherman to get him a cap, sweater, and sneakers and drop him anywhere along the coast." He smoothed a wisp of hair. "Further, in the Del Bosco apartment in Rome, we found mirrored sunglasses. Also a receipt for a rented doorman's uniform, dark gray, with visored cap—"

Elisabetta gave a cry: "Dark gray! That's like the school guard's uniform! Or like enough to have fooled frightened children."

"Si, Signora Ligouri." Ponroni glanced again at his notebook. "Also found, a false beard. We have it from a Captain Grippo in Florence that the assailant in Florence, glimpsed by Miss March"—and here Ponroni bowed to Johanna—"was a bearded man."

Ponroni turned his attention to Vittorio. "In light of Signor Del Bosco's mention of 'trouble' and 'prison' we are in touch with his firm. They are investigating his customers' accounts for dates of funds withdrawn and replaced."

Again, Ponroni consulted his notebook. "Signor Faziolini, at the Banco Nazionale, in a safety deposit box rented six weeks ago by Matteo Del Bosco, Criminalpol has found forty million, five hundred thousand lire. Three-quarters of the amount of ransom paid."

Vittorio smoothed his magnificent white handlebar mustache. His look was sharp, his voice wry. "*Mah!* Likely the amount he didn't need to replace in a client's account. But to have asked 'those rich Faziolinis' for a ransom of only thirteen million, five hundred thousand lire would have been suspicious.''

"*Precisamente*, Signor Faziolini." And Ponroni gave a short bow. Then at a signal from Tostelli, he closed his notebook.

Tostelli turned to Johanna and said politely, "And now, Signorina March. If you would tell us why Matteo Del Bosco wished to kill you?''

"I don't know.''

The agents from Criminalpol did not look at each other. Tostelli smiled down at Johanna, who sat in a soft chair; she wore oatmeal-colored slacks and a brown sweater and her arm was in the red silk sling. She looked straight back at the *agente*, in her very blue eyes a grave and honest look. So honest, thought Jeff, except that those very blue eyes narrowed a bit.

"A supposition, then, Signorina," Tostelli said politely. He pulled a hassock close, almost to Johanna's knees, and sat down. "If you were to form, let us say, a hypothesis?''

On Johanna's face, a tentative little frown; she hesitated. "Well, I imagine when a person feels guilty, and certainly Matteo Del Bosco must have felt guilty, he could get quite paranoid. Suspicious, without any real—" She paused. She said earnestly, "He could have gotten some crazy idea that I knew something about Alessandro Faziolini's death; I had witnessed the actual mugging. Could that be it? Just because of my innocent meeting with him. At the pensione, in Florence.''

"*Sì*, Signorina." Again, Tostelli smiled. "And then your coming to La Serena.''

"I suppose.''

"And why *did* you come to La Serena, Signorina March?''

Johanna blushed; it was a pretty stain, right up to the brown-gold tendrils on her hairline. And then while Jeff Thornton listened, rubbing his jaw, Johanna confessed with narrowed eyes that she had faked—"Yes, faked!"—a sprained wrist in Treangoli because, well, because of Jeff Thornton, because *he* was going to La Serena. And here she gave an embarrassed flutter of eyelashes at Jeff and then cast a shamed glance of appeal at Elisabetta and Vittorio Faziolini. Dr. Rosella? Yes, the *Dottore* corroborated—"It is only because he too has a romantic heart!" Then she ducked her head and pulled off the red silk sling and stretched out her arm; and in a flexible bandage she flexed her wrist.

"*Cara!*" Elisabetta said. "Johanna *cara*! And you ran into such danger!"

"*Mah!*" said Vittorio, and he looked at Johanna March and shook his head and pulled at his mustache and raised his eyebrows at Jeff Thornton.

"*Per amore!*" cried out Renzo Grimini, feelingly.

Jeff said nothing. He wanted to laugh. He was also feeling little prickles of expectation. He sensed that the *agente* was getting ready for him.

Tostelli did not keep him waiting long; the *agente* rose from the hassock and paced back and forth, as far as to the bust of Augustus in the embrasure and back. Two trips and he stopped in front of Jeff.

"Signor Thornton, you saved the life of Signorina March. Perhaps also the life of Signora Ligouri. Now if you would please explain how you discovered that Matteo Del Bosco was the kidnapper of the Ligouri twins."

Jeff nodded. "Yes, gladly." He was aware of Johanna's sudden tension. She couldn't *know* he had eavesdropped, but she was watching him, fear in her eyes. In an instant, he could destroy her plausible tale of lovesickness. And he still didn't know why she had come to La Serena. What if he were to tell the truth? What if he were to reveal that he'd overheard Johanna March speaking to a woman on the telephone . . . a woman named Teresa? He looked at the dust of the road on Vittorio's white mane and he looked at Lucilla's tear-swollen eyes. And he looked finally back at Johanna, meeting for an instant her widened gaze.

"It was like this . . ." he said, and he waited until the bald one, Ponroni, who had broken the point off his pencil, had taken out a pen. Then he carefully explained that a month ago in New York he had happened to pick up a weeks-old news magazine and had read about the kidnapping. He had immediately written to Alessandro.

"We'd quarreled years before, we were out of touch. However, under the tragic circumstances . . ." Alessandro, moved by Jeff's sympathy, had responded. "By then, I was again in Europe, his letter was forwarded to me, it reached me at the Excelsior in Florence. He said that the twins had been ransomed. He confided that he'd stumbled across a clue, his ruby ring. The kidnappers had it. He said he was going to follow it up himself, secretly. And he wrote, 'Remember how at school we used to say, Into deepest danger?' "

A sob. Lucilla said in a strangled voice: "He used to say that to me too! When we were children! *Into deepest danger.*"

For a moment, he could not go on. That part about *Into deepest danger* had been true when they were students. Alessandro, with his passionate, iron-hard, medieval ideas. Vengeance without law. As though it were his obligation as a man.

"*Si?*" prompted Tostelli.

"Yes. So when Alessandro didn't show up on Saturday for his wife's birthday and then not on Sunday either, I became uneasy. I began to think that he'd followed the ruby ring 'into deepest danger.' So I went to Rome."

He glanced at Johanna and decided that she still looked pretty, even with her mouth hanging open like that.

He told quickly about Aldo Furia, private investigator, about the pawnshop, the elderly woman, the pawned ruby ring, the other pawned objects.

"It meant nothing to me, none of it. I was puzzled. But on the road, driving back here from Rome, I realized it could mean something to someone in this household. As it turned out, it was Franca."

"*Scusi*—Franca?"

"One of the maids. She's been with the Faziolinis for thirty years." He stopped. He was thinking of the many years when the Del Bosco family used to visit the Faziolinis at La Serena; all those years until in the old palazzo in Rome, Graziella Del Bosco's negligée—

"*Continui, per favore.*"

"It was the peacock pin. Also the eagle-headed cane. The peacock pin belonged to Graziella Del Bosco, Matteo's mother. It was her 'signature,' she wore it always on her breast. It was gold, with turquoise enamel and a diamond eye. The eagle-headed cane was Ettore Del Bosco's, Matteo's father's. He was never without it."

"So that was when you—"

"Telephoned Signor Grimini."

Now, like Vittorio Faziolini, the two agents also studied the carpet. Jeff whistled under his breath. Let them learn the rug pattern by heart. Even if they didn't believe a word he said, there was no way they could refute it.

The bald one, Ponroni, said, "May I ask, Signor Thornton—when you realized that Del Bosco was the kidnapper of the Ligouri twins, and possibly a murderer, precisely why did you hurry to telephone Signor Grimini? Although, in the end, *Grazia di Dio*, you managed to save—" He paused and waited.

"It isn't obvious? I could not risk *not* hurrying! Del Bosco seemed to me off the rails—*come si dice*, a madman, *pazzo*. Capable at any moment of doing away with the entire family that trusted him. The women at La Serena were here alone. Alessandro's wife, his mother, his sister, in danger! Even, perhaps, the guest, Miss March! And, as it proved, this was only too true."

An hour later, after having eaten a warming minestrone and a dish of lean veal with tonnato sauce; and after making four more telephone calls to Rome and receiving three, the two men from Criminalpol departed.

They left behind them the information gleaned from Rome, slight as it was: The "respectable woman," Caterina Scalzo, who was sixty-eight years old and had a Neapolitan accent, was not an invalid's ex-nurse, but the Del Boscos' former housekeeper. She had collapsed with fear and confessed to hiding the twins.

"Matteo, that poor little Matteo, he was only ten when his mother was burned up! I never could resist anything he wanted! He brought the twins in a car, at night. He had kept them covered with a blanket. He said if he didn't get the ransom money, he would go to prison. *For life*." The words, quoted aloud by Ponroni from his notebook, sounded sad and yet strangely comical. Lucilla sat with a hand to her throat; Elisabetta kept her lips pinned in against the curl of anguish.

As for Del Bosco: "He is a fox," Tostelli said, "but we are wolves." He smiled, but his teeth, as he raised his head, looked like a shark's teeth.

When the sound of the Criminalpol car had dwindled, they still sat at the dining room table. A marvelous evasion of eyes, thought Jeff, no one quite meeting the glance of anyone else. Were they all gnawing at the same question: Why hadn't the *agenti* asked why Alessandro was staying in an obscure little pensione in Florence under a false name? Why, as Jeff had learned from Elisabetta only an hour ago, had he left his true anagraph in a briefcase at the Gritti in Venice?

He picked up a breadstick from the basket on the table and broke off a piece. "Funny. When we were at the university, Alessandro used to love to escape for a week or so from his own identity. He'd play at being someone else, not a rich, noble Faziolini, but someone who lived in a modest pensione, had a totally private life. He was a romantic in that way. He said it gave him a different perspective on society. 'An odd kind of hobby,' he said about it. It embarrassed him. He didn't even like to talk about it. You know how he used to love quotations?"

"Yes," Elisabetta said. They were all looking at him, waiting.

"Well, he quoted an American philosopher who said, 'By becoming someone else, you open another window from which to view society.' "

He bit off a piece of breadstick and chewed it. Not a marvelous quotation, but the best he could create on short notice. And chewing, he wondered about a woman named Teresa. He was thinking too of logistics: that if Alessandro wanted to keep a trip to Florence secret—say, an assignation with a woman—he would leave his true anagraph at the Gritti in Venice and later return for it before flying to Milan because—because, well, the company bills for his trip, his expenses, would have to include a Venice-Milan flight. The bills would be verified by the Faziolini company accountant. Or they might even cross Vittorio Faziolini's desk.

He looked up from the breadstick and met Vittorio's gaze: tragic, aware. They were all silent: Elisabetta beside Renzo Grimini; Lucilla, frowning, pushing back her thicket of frizzy hair as though it got in the way of her thoughts. Johanna seemed deeply involved with the tablecloth.

Vittorio said: "In Venice, I feared he might have dropped in the street, and without his anagraph—" He stopped. Then with a sigh, he said: "He had a congenital heart disease for which there is no treatment. And lately it was apparent that he . . . we Faziolinis had made our peace with Alessandro's illness. But *he* had not. How could he? A young man, knowing that before long . . . And in Venice, I also thought, Did he do away with himself? Far from us, to spare us that awfulness? He had left no note. Still, I feared that. I thought perhaps he could not wait, perhaps it was too much of a torture. Because it *was* a torture to him. A parent can look at a child's face and know such things.

"But Matteo! Matteo! That murderer!"

He rose suddenly, flung down his napkin, and left the room.

"*Damn* Matteo!" Johanna said abruptly, fiercely. She had been biting a cuticle and listening, trancelike, to Vittorio. "Damn him! We've got to—I've got to—" She stopped, frustrated; she went back to biting the cuticle, head tipped down with a concentrated stare at nothing.

"There's nothing *we* can do," Elisabetta said. "It's up to Criminalpol to find him."

"But how can they?" Johanna said unhappily. "They've no lead. There's got to be *something*. Something Matteo said. Or did. Or—wore? A—a trick of speech? If we could only pin down something, *something important* about Matteo. But what?"

"He's a murderer," Lucilla said bitterly. "That's important."

"He cheats at cards," Elisabetta said.

"If only," Johanna began, "if only I could—oh!" A startled look flickered across her face. Then she said more softly, "Oh." And her face was bright and alive.

What now, thought Jeff, looking at Johanna. *Now*, what?

❖ 37 ❖

IN THE WIDE MAHOGANY BED, ELISABETTA RAISED HER HEAD from Renzo Grimini's naked shoulder and sneezed. She looked at the dusty draperies of Renzo's bedroom. "This villa is a hovel!" She sneezed again.

Renzo slid a hand up to Elisabetta's nape, under the long reddish hair that hung down around her face and across her breasts. "I'd give all the medieval paintings in the gallery for one that looked like you. A hovel? Yes. I didn't want *her* coming here. But now . . ."

Elisabetta said, "I'd have sworn you'd never do it! I didn't think you loved me enough. It made me so miserable, so bitter—and so hateful to you." She looked over at the white envelope on the table under the window. The document, with its special postage, had been delivered to Renzo when he had returned from the woods to change from his dirtied, fashionable city clothes and go to La Serena to await the agents from Criminalpol.

"You drew blood like a Borgia torturer," Renzo said, smiling. "I'm surprised I have any left! But I swore not to tell you I was trying. With my history with women, I knew you'd think, 'Renzo Grimini's cheap trickery to get me into his bed.' " He drew Elisabetta's head down to rest against his bearded cheek. "Besides, my application had a terrible prognosis." He gave a snort of a laugh. "Nepotism in reverse! It wasn't easy, being related to a bishop, and with a grandfather who was a cousin to a pope. That was the worst. Lorenza's greed didn't bother me. I'm not rich any more, Elisabetta."

"I am," Elisabetta said comfortably. "We can fix up this *hovel*." She wanted to cry, though, to cry for all the biting, scornful things she had forced herself to say to Renzo, while loving him so deeply. But she hadn't been able to bear the thought of becoming just one of the women with whom he had affairs. It had made her furious to think that he assumed she'd accept his marital situation, as other women had. Furious, humiliated, and heartbroken. She wormed a warm arm under his neck and rested her head on his naked chest. "Oh, Renzo! All along, you were *trying*! And you didn't fail."

Later, downstairs, they poked around the big, dreary kitchen and ate stale cheese and old crackers and got grease spots on the legal document. They talked finally about the twins.

"I watched over them in the woods," Renzo said. "I thought they might harm themselves—they had knives and ropes. Sometimes they cut branches and made sharp stakes and built traps. Like the one at the culvert."

"The traps," Elisabetta said, "Tomasino told me about. That old bitch, Caterina! She threatened the twins that the kidnapper would come for them again if they cried. So they were terrified, because Felicia cried. 'We didn't know if the kidnapper would come for *just* Felicia, or for me too!' Tomasino told me, crying. 'We would rather he took *both* of us!' They were like little animals in the woods, protecting themselves against being stolen again."

"*Dio!* Here." Renzo buttered a stale cracker and held it out; food was always a comfort. "And the radio?"

"The radio, yes. At Caterina's once the radio went dead. Tomasino was sleeping, but Felicia *heard things*. Only she couldn't remember. Tomasino was trying to get her to remember before 'he' came for them in the mirrored eyeglasses, maybe coming along the old road that nobody uses, the overgrown road, and across the stone culvert. Oh, Renzo!"

"*È finito*, it's over."

"I've made the others swear never to tell them it was Matteo. Or about Alessandro, that Matteo—that would be too—what's the word—traumatic. Will they catch him?"

"Criminalpol? *Certo!* The taller one, Tostelli, said that in a few days they'd have enough background to begin working out the possible areas. They'll do it with computers."

"I can hardly wait!" Elisabetta said. She sniffed and brushed tears from her eyes, smearing them across her cheekbones.

Renzo looked down at the grease-spotted document, then across at Elisabetta—his beloved, medieval-looking Elisabetta, who was biting into a stale cracker. And he thought: *At last I have slain my dragon.*

❖ 38 ❖

"WHY DIDN'T YOU TELL ME ABOUT SOMEONE TAMPERING with my brakes?" Johanna said meanly to Jeff Thornton. She'd found him in the stable-garage; he was in his shirt-sleeves, washing Sabina's little Lancia.

"Please, Miss March! You're talking to the man who saved your life."

"Oh, *that*. I already thanked you."

"And the same man who put a key in your bedroom lock."

"Oh. Was that you? You're also the same man who left me in danger here while you went off to Rome to play detective."

"But only on Elisabetta's promise to guard you and see that you'd be safely locked in your room overnight. I was coming back in the morning, no matter what. I was sure Renzo wouldn't have a chance—"

"Renzo? Renzo Grimini?"

"I thought it might be Renzo."

"Really? Anyway, about the brakes. You must have crossed that garage man's palm with silver to keep him quiet about it."

"I didn't want to frighten you. I thought I'd do a little investigating on my own." He squeezed water from the sponge into the pail. He'd been expecting this attack from

Johanna. It was bound to happen, just as soon as she'd gotten over the miracle of finding herself alive.

"So?"

He smiled at her. She had brushed her hair to the side above her forehead. She looked glossy as a palomino. She frowned at him.

"I almost thought you were—involved."

He shook his head. "It was that simple, Johanna."

But it hadn't been. The brakes: That had turned him around. The threat to Johanna was not from Florence, it was at La Serena. It was strange enough to make him begin to suspect that the man he'd seen on her balcony had indeed been Alessandro. It had turned him into an amateur detective. He had eavesdropped.

And the can of worms had turned into a nest of snakes.

"Well, thanks," Johanna said. She stretched out her arms and flexed them pleasurably; she did that a lot, now that she no longer wore the bandage and sling. "But you frightened me! I thought *you* were the—the murderer. And kidnapper."

He dripped water down the windshield. "I'm just a ped-dler of housewares."

"Well," Johanna said, "you'd had a terrible quarrel with Alessandro."

"Yes. You want to hear? It isn't pretty." He sat down on the fender of the car and told it: how his sixteen-year-old sister, visiting Rome from the United States, had gone out with his friend, Alessandro, then eighteen. She had returned crying. Alessandro had given her drinks, then seduced her. Jeff contemplated the sponge in his hand. "I went out of my head. I'd trusted him." Then a month ago in California, his sister had confessed that it was a lie.

"*She'd* done the seducing. Then she became panic-stricken—what if she'd become pregnant? Our father was the kind of man who'd make Cotton Mather look lenient. She lost her head."

"And Alessandro?"

". . . was too honorable to tell me the truth about my sister."

"Damn! I'll *never* understand this Italian culture! An Italian man's idea of honor, that on the one hand—" She broke off.

"Yes?"

"Nothing." But then she said with a sigh: "A Roman tale of Claudius' time. A legend. Or myth. That's what it's like. Lucilla and the dead baby. Alessandro and Matteo. Vittorio." She hesitated. "Vittorio, perhaps the most tragic of all."

"Vittorio? Why?"

"I don't know."

"And where do you, Johanna March, fit into this mythological equation?"

She gave him that bright-faced smile. "I'm not exactly sure. Not yet."

❖ **39** ❖

IT WAS WEDNESDAY MORNING, TWO DAYS AFTER MATTEO Del Bosco's escape.

In Rome, at his desk at Criminalpol, Tostelli slammed down the phone and swore, exasperated. Those blunderers in Florence! *Dannazione!* The police in Florence had had that *rapitóre*, that kidnapper, right in their hands; he had been the visitor to the Medico-Legal Institute to view the body, saying the unidentified man, Luciano Botto, might be his missing cousin. *Dannazione!* He'd wanted to make sure he hadn't drowned the wrong man!

"But the visitor was clean-shaven!" that *idiota* at the Questura in Florence had protested on the telephone, "and the American signorina had said a bearded—"

"A beard, a beard! You have never heard of a false beard? *Forse, no?*"

Now, shaking his head, Tostelli pushed away the phone and picked up the computer printout marked *Del Bosco*. His blood quickened. This was the kind of thing he liked; he sometimes thought the blood of a bloodhound ran in his veins. The printout listed nine areas likely to attract Del Bosco as a hiding place. But Tostelli's attention centered on one. He eyed it, pinching his chin, thinking.

The printout listed the area between Sorrento and Vetri Sul Mari, along the coast. Del Bosco had no relatives; he would have to stay with a friend or lover or somebody with sticky fingers, no one else. Not a hotel or pensione—Del Bosco couldn't use his anagraph. A bus driver from Rome to Sorrento had said he'd picked up a fisherman who slept all the way. The local bus winding from Sorrento along the cliffs over the Amalfitan coast would then be most likely. Del Bosco could drop off at any point, go down to the outskirts of one of the little fishing villages along the shore, or climb up into the craggy wilderness above. Del Bosco was a hunter, he'd hunted in those wildernesses. That's where he'd go.

And be hidden forever.

On the other hand, maybe not forever.

Tostelli sat back and thought about the telephone call he'd received from the American girl, Miss March. She had called two nights ago, after Del Bosco's escape. His first impulse, recalling how pretty she was, with those dark-gold eyebrows and amazing blue eyes, was to assume she was wasting his time. But five minutes after he'd hung up, he'd found himself stroking his jaw and thinking: *Perchè no?* Why not? A sliver of possibility.

So he had given the order.

"Tostelli?"

He looked up. Ponroni had come in and was standing beside the desk, holding one of the tissue-thin interoffice memos. He wore what Tostelli thought of as his investigative look, his nostrils fairly twitching as though at a scent.

"The Del Bosco affair. A little scum has already risen to the top of the soup."

"*Davèrro?* Really, Ponroni? You have something?"

"*Si.* A coincidence only that it occurred on the Amalfitan coast, where the 'fisherman' might have headed. It could just as well have happened in the Bergamo region, or Valle d'Aosta, or plenty of other places. But it at least indicates something.

Yesterday afternoon, there was a religious pageant at the Duomo, Sant'Andrea, in Amalfi. Sixteen children took part—an extravagant affair, new costumes, top to toe. One of the children, a boy, was affected. The child became frantic."

Tostelli's eyebrows rose. Then he nodded, pleased. "Sometimes, the thinnest thread can turn into a rope, *vero*, Ponroni? That American girl is no fool. We'll see what develops. There is certainly a possibility . . ."

❖ 40 ❖

IT WAS AN EXQUISITE, SMALL SUMMER *palazzo* that sparkled with white marble on a promontory high over the Tyrrhenian Sea; when the setting sun touched the marble it turned the palazzo to gold. Seen from the fishing boats returning to their villages with the day's catch, it was like a gold coin up there in the wilderness.

Elena Castellanta adored it. She had bought it six years before. She enjoyed the sometimes angry faces of her guests whose cars got stuck on the steep roads that were hardly more than paths. Their exasperation gave her an imperious feeling, as though they were peasants or vassals who had to come at her bidding. They came, of course, for the champagne, the pâtés, all the marvels of her table; and to mingle with the few movie celebrities who, during the season, also cursed their way up to Elena Castellanta's parties. The celebrities came because Elena was said to be related to a famous movie director whose yacht was anchored down there in the Positano harbor. And, who knew? To accidentally meet him at Elena's . . .

But now the season was over.

Elena Castellanta was forty, looked thirty, and felt herself to be twenty-five. "We are the age we choose," she had once said to Matteo Del Bosco.

Now, with the season ended, Elena had expected to be alone, so alone that she might even relax and allow herself to be thirty. She had expected to torture her brains with how she could wring more money from her miserly aunt, so that she would not have to sell this exquisite little *palazzo*. She would promise that she would be more careful with money. Certainly she had been wasteful, but now she had changed. She was a different woman. She would have a week alone, writing to that aunt who was made of solid platinum, before returning to her apartment in nerve-wracking Milan.

But then, on the second day of letter-writing, she had glanced idly down from her bedroom terrace and seen the fisherman. He was laboring up the twisting, stony road. He was still a hundred yards away when he looked up, and she recognized Matteo Del Bosco.

Since Elena enjoyed television and listened to the news, she immediately felt miserable. It was not just that she hated trouble. It was that she had a peculiar sense of delicacy. It would be embarrassing to greet Matteo Del Bosco. She had no idea how to ask him if he had really kidnapped those Ligouri twins. And she certainly couldn't tactfully ask if he had murdered Alessandro Faziolini.

It was not a matter of etiquette: It was a matter of feeling. She could never again face Matteo Del Bosco if she rushed to the phone and called the police. And what if the charges against him later proved to be untrue? She'd look a traitor and an *idiota*. Her friends would laugh her to death. And then, she reminded herself, frowning, Matteo knew an unpleasant thing or two about her. Was that why he had chosen this particular wilderness?

Moreover, she had dismissed the servants, and she was alone. When you are alone in a cage with an animal of unknown propensities, it is hardly wise to impose on his territory. She left the terrace, walked through the house, and stood in the sun-drenched drive with a fixed smile.

"Elena! *Cara!*"

"Matteo!"

By nightfall, how relieved she was! After dinner, they sat before the crackling fire and talked more about it. And she thought how handsome Matteo was, despite his heavy jaw, and even how glad she was that he was there. She felt indignant about the whole business.

Matteo had explained the truth, the sick truth that the rich Faziolinis' money concealed about Alessandro: How Alessandro was an *alcolizzato*, an alcoholic; drunk on too much wine, he had fallen into the Arno and struck his head on a rock and drowned. How the Faziolinis had managed to involve Matteo as a scapegoat to conceal the truth, Matteo himself could not say. But it had disillusioned him in humanity.

"The worst," Matteo said, "is that I can't come forward and explain, because of the kidnapping."

The kidnapping. "Ah, Elena! How silly, how stupid we can sometimes be!" And at the significant look he gave her, she felt a tiny chill at what he knew about her paltry bits of *ricatto*, blackmail.

"So stupid!" he repeated. Why, he had only "borrowed" the Ligouri twins for a couple of weeks; it was hardly more than a prank.

"You know, Elena, like borrowing on margin, in the stock market, to get even richer. I had a chance for immense riches on the *Borsa*. I wanted the money to make a fortune, a great fortune in the market. And I made it—the money is now in a Swiss account. But you know, sometimes we're tempted to take such ridiculous risks."

"I know!" Elena said feelingly. She had drunk too much wine, and she was not sure exactly what she did know. She knew, though, that Matteo was rich and that since a minute ago he had said she could count on it being worthwhile if she were to remain his friend, she would not have to go begging to her miserly aunt. Maybe never again.

She was already aware that she was not going to turn on the television news or listen to the radio, because she did not want to see or hear anything that would make her doubt Matteo's story about Alessandro Faziolini. Because then she might think she'd have to do something.

As it was, she was happy. Besides everything else, the whole thing excited her sexually.

In bed that night, Elena was awakened several times by Matteo beside her; he was having nightmares, crying out in his sleep to someone named Vittorio.

Sometimes he called Vittorio *Babbo*, Daddy, and wept bitterly. But Elena was sure Matteo's father had been named Ettore.

❖ 41 ❖

"*VI SONO NOVITÁ? ANY NEWS?*"

It was what they asked each other, meeting on the stairs, in the salon, in the kitchen. Whenever the phone rang, they caught their breaths and hung suspended in space. *Vi sono novitá?* Had Criminalpol caught Matteo? But no; nothing. Not yet.

Luigi and Serafina had returned yesterday from Arcidosso. Giorgio was still in the hospital, but hobbling around on crutches. Angela was home in Treangoli with a mark "like a vampire's kiss" on her neck, as Serafina put it; but it was actually a scar left by a piece of shattered window glass from the car.

It was all odd and sad. Sabina wept on Serafina's shoulder as well as Vittorio's, and Serafina too wept and comforted her. Luigi did his work with a glowering face; he had always disliked Matteo, and now his dislike was full-blown hatred.

Lucilla in her room cut off her hair, wrote pages of poetry, and sat at the window. She had, Tuesday night, taken a razor to her wrist, then become frightened and had called Franca, who had bandaged up the wound. Minutes later she had had hysterics, waking the whole household.

"How long will they keep the kidnapper in prison?" Tomasino kept anxiously asking Elisabetta.

"Forever," she answered him. She had told the twins that the kidnapper had been caught and was locked up. But they had to be reassured again and again. She and Renzo Grimini took them to Treangoli for ice cream.

Signor Thornton, in shirtsleeves, lived on the telephone, pencil in hand, working out development problems his designer in Milan had run into, and rearranging his upset business appointments in the south. It was believed that after those commitments, he would be returning to Florence.

Signorina March had inspected and tried out the repaired Alfa Romeo and agreed with Elvio Gordini that the car was now in *ottima condizione*; she was leaving for Florence on Friday morning.

Vittorio Faziolini, who as "The Faziolini," was news himself, had restricted media interviews to a single morning session at his offices in Rome. Reporters from *Corriera della Sera* and other newspapers, and from news magazines and radio and television stations, had arrived like hungry birds swooping down. They had all been courteously received. And had learned little.

Now it was Thursday. Vittorio, just back from a half hour with Criminalpol in Rome, pulled off his driving gloves. No one was about, for which he thanked God.

He was shaken.

He went into the study. He sank into a chair. In a stifling little room at Criminalpol, he had viewed a box of Matteo's personal possessions. They'd said, "Perhaps something will strike a chord, Signor Faziolini, provide a clue, a lead." Ten minutes later, he had pushed the box away and stood up, his legs trembling. *"No, niente. Mi dispiace."*

Now, in the study, in memory he again looked into that box. Again he saw the scissored pictures, the other people in the photos cut away, leaving a truncated arm or foot, so there were only the two of them standing together: Vittorio and Matteo. Somehow, Matteo had managed always to stand or sit beside Vittorio. *"Babbo e Io."* Vittorio read on the backs of the pictures. *"Daddy and I."* Then finally another picture of himself standing in the field, a hand on Matteo's shoulder, Matteo aged twelve, when he had gotten his first rifle. Vittorio had taught him to shoot. He had turned the picture over and read scrawled on the back, "When Alessandro dies, I will be Vittorio's son."

He went and stood by the study window, looking out. He could see a corner of the field, and beyond it, the woods. Even then, back then in his childhood years, Matteo must have known about Alessandro's defective heart.

"Vi sono novitá?"

Lucilla's voice.

"No," he said, without turning, "not yet."

❖ 42 ❖

FOR THREE NIGHTS NOW, MATTEO HAD BEEN IN HER BED.

During the day, Elena thought constantly about the money in the Swiss bank account. She and Matteo drank wine on the railed terrace of her bedroom high over the cliffs, making endless plans for his escape from Italy.

Or rather, she planned and he listened. The truth was, Elena knew someone who, she explained, had amazing "connections." But it would involve her making a trip to a small apartment in Anzio.

Meanwhile, "You'll be safe here," she told Matteo, "safe as in a cradle. There's plenty of food and wine, too. And you can see the road for *chilometri*. If you see anyone coming, you can be in the forests an hour before they arrive. Anyway, no one will come."

But Matteo made her nervous. He roamed the terrace like a caged beast and was exasperated that she had no rifle. He wanted to hunt, but she had only her small pistol. It was too bad that on the one trip they'd made down to the coast to see a dermatologist about his rash, giving the *medico* a false name, he couldn't have bought a rifle himself. But he had been too shrewd for that. "At a time like this, a stranger out of nowhere wanting a rifle!" he'd said, when she'd suggested it, and he'd castigated her for being a fool. *"Non essere idiota!"*

Now, at noon, with the remains of breakfast on the glass table on the terrace, she took a final sip of coffee. She would drive down the wicked roads and in one of the fishing villages along the coast, perhaps Minori or Mairo, she would buy Matteo a rifle. From here, eleven hundred feet above the Tyrrhenian Sea, she could look down across the valleys and along the coast and pick out the tiny curves of beach.

"I'll get you a rifle." She stood up. It was chilly; she would take a coat. "But I haven't the least notion about guns. Tell me what kind."

For answer, Matteo made an inarticulate sound in his throat. Startled, she looked at him. He was standing at the railing. He was staring down at the serpentine twists of road.

"Che c'è?" She was at his side.

She too looked down. *"Dio!"* she whispered. The two cars were chocolate-colored; even from this distance, and dusty as they were, she could tell. They were winding slowly up the serpentine road. She knew, because of the color, what they were, even though it was too far to see the little red lights that were not, at the moment, revolving. But they were—*Grazia di Dio!*—several *chilometri* away.

She whirled. "The forest! The pistol! In the bedroom, the drawer in the side table!"

But Matteo was already gone.

The pistol. He held it in his hand. It was warm, small, oily; a toy, but a lethal one—at least lethal for rabbits and pheasant. He caught his breath. Not that he'd even have to use it! For a minute there, he'd panicked. *Ridicolo!* He could hide safely in the forest until they left. Deep enough in the forest. But then, how would he know. . . ?

He stood still for a moment, frowning. Then he went quickly back to the terrace. Elena was still at the railing. She was clutching it with white-knuckled fingers and gazing down at the road.

"Elena! Stop it! Don't be a fool! It certainly is nothing, an innocent—police collecting donations, maybe for the church, maybe for—*Chi sa!* Who knows!" He gripped her arm; she winced. "But I'll be gone anyway. Be an actress, act astonished if it's—if they—"

"Yes! I know, I know how!" For the money in that Swiss bank account, she could be a Sophia Loren.

"When they've gone, tie your scarf—" and he yanked off her orange scarf "—to the railing. Not over the cliff here, but back! Back toward the forest—over there, on the north side, over here—" And when she just looked at him in bewilderment, he gave an exclamation of impatience and dragged her with him, as though she were a stupid child. "Do you understand? As a signal! Here, against the wall, where the trees—" His voice died.

The trees, the forest; he was looking at the forest. There it stretched, a green and craggy wilderness, green and brown and black; but there was no wind, and yet there were white things, small as birds' breasts, moving waveringly among the green leaves. He had sharp eyes, and he saw as they moved closer that they were bands of white on visored caps. For a long moment, he stood watching as they came nearer; but he knew they would stop soon and wait for the arrival of the chocolate-colored cars.

Then he wasn't seeing them any more. He was seeing himself led manacled into a gray-walled room, and there was his true father, Vittorio Faziolini; Vittorio, whom he had betrayed. And Vittorio raised his eyes and looked at him. Vittorio, who had once looked at him with the eyes of kindness and love.

Someone was shaking his arm. "Matteo?" A woman's voice. Elena.

He dropped the scarf and walked into the bedroom.

Elena, alone on the terrace, gave a sudden shudder at what she had seen in his face. "Matteo . . ." she whispered.

Then she squeezed her eyes tight shut and put her fingers in her ears.

But even so, she heard the shot.

❖ 43 ❖

SHE DROVE FAST ON THE AUTOSTRADA, THE ALFA ROMEO singing a song of luxury. The wind tossed her hair, the sun warmed her forehead, but the stream of air cooled it like deliciously cold water. It was a joy to use her two arms again, one of which was faintly tanned and the other pale ivory. The car radio was on; music trailed behind the car like wispy scarves blown away. She'd stop soon at an Autogrill for a roll with prosciutto. Even with that, in two hours she'd be back in Florence.

Ahead, she saw the sign: *Rallentare*. Slow down. Another five minutes to the turn-off. At that moment, the music broke off.

"Un'Annuncia!" It was followed by a confusion of voices, then the newscaster's announcement, terse and sketchy:

Matteo Del Bosco was a suicide. Del Bosco, traced by Criminalpol to a *palazzo* north of Positano, had shot himself as the police closed in. Del Bosco's woman friend, who had inhabited the palazzo alone, was unaware of her visitor's sensational crimes. She never listened to the news. "It is always too dreadful—children in Naples taking drugs, bombings, airplanes falling out of the sky . . ."

Johanna left the car in the *parcheggio*. In the chrome-and-glass cafeteria, she found the phones.

"Teresa?"

"*Si*. Johanna? Johanna March?"

"Yes. You heard the news report?"

"News report?"

Johanna told her.

A silence. Then Teresa's voice: "Did I help?"

"Did you *help*? Of course! Without you, without what you told me about the ring . . ."

Teresa said, low, "Thank God. Thank God."

"*Mamma*? Who was that on the telephone?" Francesco had just come in, sweaty, happy, and hungry for lunch. "Was it Mr. Cardarelli?"

"No. Why do you ask that?"

Francesco frowned, and the two dark vertical lines appeared between his brows. "I don't know. Your voice."

"No," his mother said again. "But it was *about* Mr. Cardarelli. He's had to go away. But he hasn't forgotten about us."

In the kitchen, she made Francesco a sandwich, her heart aching, thinking about Alessandro always putting money in the Banco Americana for her and Francesco. He didn't care that the Faziolinis laughed at him, that he was such an expert on *calcio* and always bet but never won. But he *did* win! He won often, though never any great amount.

And always he deposited the winnings in her name in the Banco Americana—"In case anything happens to me," he had told her. And she had answered, smiling, smoothing his hair, "But what do you expect can happen to you?" After all, he was only thirty-three.

In Rome, the news of Matteo Del Bosco's suicide rippled through the *Borsa*, and in many a brokerage house a custom-tailored broker pulled at his tie, shivered, and erased from his mind alluring thoughts of "borrowing" from a client's account in hopes of making a killing. Such "mistakes" a broker made with customers' money had sometimes resulted in the guilty broker's suicide, but never before had a theft mushroomed into a kidnapping and murder. By nightfall, virtue ran high.

At Criminalpol, Tostelli complimented himself and immediately put through a call to Miss Johanna March at the

Pensione Boldini in Florence. He was informed she was expected but had not yet arrived.

Ponroni, on television, furnished the media with the information that all of the Ligouri ransom had been recovered except for the thirteen million, five hundred thousand lire that Matteo Del Bosco had replaced in his customer's account; once suspicion was aroused, an automatic computering system had brought the withdrawal and replacement of funds to light.

In Treangoli, Peppino's trattoria did an especially good business. Peppino sweated and stuffed the cash register with lire and got a headache from the noise. Everyone, even Lucca the butcher, claimed he knew Matteo Del Bosco better than he really did and disliked him more than he really had. Silvestro, the baker, squeezed in with an anecdote, and so did Elvio Gordini. But the real celebrity was Dr. Rosella. Two glasses of wine, and Rosella was a cornucopia of eye-widening tales. The only one who was silent was the southern Italian, Sandro Pavone.

In the middle of one of Dr. Rosella's tales, Pavone got up and went out. He crossed the road to the shiny new post office trash basket. He took from his pocket the photograph of the woman with the little boy and the child's colored drawings. He held them for a minute, looking down at them in bitterness and frustration. *A river of gold.* Then he tore them in half and threw them into the trash.

At La Serena the news of Matteo's suicide seemed to have struck the Faziolinis with sleeping sickness. Sabina slept for the first time without sedatives; Vittorio fell asleep on the couch in the salon; Lucilla put aside her poetry and curled up on the bed under a blanket, her shorn head on the pillow, and slept. Elisabetta, having just finished telling Luigi that a broken shelf in the wine cellar needed fixing, drowsily put her head down on the kitchen table and a minute later was asleep. *Ci sono novitá?* no longer echoed through the rooms of the villa. The Faziolinis slept.

❖ 44 ❖

On Sunday morning, the sun shone on the domes of Florence, glittered on the Arno, and made the two sweatered Italians optimistic enough to stop the American signorina in the lobby of the Pensione Boldini and propose a trip to Fiesole. *Peccato!* She already had an obligation.

Regretfully they watched the flutter of her silk skirt around her knees as she walked toward the little elevator. Five days the American signorina had been back at the pensione, and had not even taken a glass of Campari with them!

Upstairs in her room, she looked at the watch on her left wrist. In twenty minutes she'd see him. Five days. He'd been five days in the south: Frosinone, Campobasso, Benevento, Avellino, and who knew where else? Or cared? Now he was here.

At the bureau, she put on fresh lipstick. She met her gaze in the mirror. *You're rich; you're more than half a million dollars rich.* She smiled into her eyes. I don't give a damn whom the money legally belongs to, I'm keeping it. Because of me, the Faziolinis have recovered most of the ransom. As for you, Lucilla, you have Alessandro's estate. And though you look like an orphan, you're the heiress to the Sagoni coffee fortune; Elisabetta happened to mention it. All that coffee and the Totocalcio money besides? Not on your life, Lucilla!

She put down her lipstick. Besides, four days ago at the Banco Americana, with the little notary scrupulously at her elbow, she had signed the proper documents creating the Cardarelli trust in the name of Teresa Mantello. The designated date for the funds to become Teresa's was today. For an instant she saw Francesco's dark eyes in his narrow face and heard his eager treble.

Twenty minutes later, she drew the Alfa Romeo up to the curb at the Excelsior. Jeff Thornton got in. Then for a moment, as their eyes met, it was as though she were mindless, only sensory. She smelled the gasoline mixed with her perfume, she saw the odd little dark rays in Jeff's gray-green eyes; she saw as through a magnifying glass the texture of his tanned skin, and felt encompassed. And breathless. She said, "Did you sell a lot of—of spatulas?"

His mouth had a humorous quirk. He looked at the tiny diamonds in her ears and at the soft Missoni coat she wore. He said, "Enough to support an indigent girl like you. Go across the Santa Trinità Bridge, Johanna, then up to the Strettoio—I want to see how well you really drive."

The bridge was three minutes away, but before they even reached it—

"Johanna?"

"Yes?"

"I stopped in Rome. I was at Criminalpol. I saw Tostelli."

"Oh?" Tostelli. On the bureau in her room at the Pensione Boldini was a vase of carnations and ferns with a little card that said *Complimenti*, and then the two names, Enzo Tostelli and Ernesto Ponroni. It had startled her. Did Criminalpol have a budget for flowers?

"He said the police trapped Matteo because of you. What you told them."

"Oh? Yes."

"The rash."

Involuntarily, Johanna raised a hand to beneath her chin. The rash. She felt again in memory that intolerable itching. She went spinning back to being eight years old; she was one of the Three Wise Men in the Christmas pageant, she wore a false beard.

She said aloud: "It could have been the kind of glue. Or the netting. Or maybe something in the beard hair itself. Angora? Goat? Maybe *some* animal. Maybe even human. Something I was allergic to? We never knew. But without the ointment the dermatologist prescribed, I would have gone mad. I was frantic." How gently her father, tipping up her tear-stained face, had applied the ointment to those odd-looking, star-shaped red inflammations under her chin!

She went on: "We were playing cards, Matteo, Elisabetta, Renzo Grimini, and I. Matteo tipped up his head. I recognized the rash, but vaguely. I didn't at first—I knew I'd had it as a child, but I couldn't remember why. Then, later . . ." Her voice trailed away. She kept her eyes on the road.

Jeff said, "Tostelli said the woman, Elena Castellanta, drove Matteo down to Amalfi, to a dermatologist. The doctor sent his son outside to take down Signora Castellanta's license number. That's how they found him."

Johanna nodded. "It probably wasn't only along that Amalfitan stretch that Criminalpol put out the alert. They must have alerted other parts of Italy too. Places they suspected he might have gone."

She added, absent-mindedly, "Did you know they have socialized medicine in Italy?" She slowed down for a dog trotting across the road. "Anyway, in Matteo's bathroom at La Serena, they found an ointment from a dermatologist in Rome. Or an allergist, I don't know. I wish I could feel sorry for him."

"Don't make it a high priority."

She felt the sun deliciously on her hair; under her hand on the steering wheel, the car sped on, the world held beauty and grace.

But she also sensed dark shadows like prowling animals around the edges of the morning. They came closer when Jeff rested his arm along the back of the seat, and turned toward her. Any moment now, he would confront her with those mysteries: *What really brought you to La Serena, Johanna, faking a sprained wrist?* And: *Who is Teresa?*

She kept her eyes on the road. She suspected she'd be spending a long time with Jeff Thornton; maybe months, even years. She thought of all the lies she would have to tell him about what had happened, and she suppressed a sigh. But he'd never know they were not the truth.

"Johanna?" He was toying with a curl just behind her ear with its tiny diamond. "Why did you really come to La Serena?"

She slowed the car. She wet her lips; she would make her voice earnest, she would manage a plausible story. She had prepared herself. So now she would sound as honest as a piece of bread.

She glanced at him, smiling, her eyes narrowing. He smiled back.

"Well . . ." she began.

ABOUT THE AUTHOR

Harriet La Barre has published two mysteries, STRANGERS IN VIENNA and THE FLORENTINE WIN. Most of her other published work has been in the field of travel writing. She divides her time between New York City and Key West, Florida.